DARK ROOM

Steve Mosby

An Orion Paperback

First published in Great Britain in 2012
by Orion
This paperback edition published in 2013
by Orion Books Ltd,
Orion House, 5 Upper St Martin's Lane
London WC2H 9EA

An Hachette UK company

1 3 5 7 9 10 8 6 4 2

A CIP catalogue record for this book
is available from the British Library.

ISBN 978-1-4091-3760-3

Typeset at the Spartan Press Ltd,
Lymington, Hants
Printed and bound by CPI Group (UK) Ltd,
Croydon, CRO 4YY

The Orion Publishing Group's policy is to use papers that
are natural, renewable and recyclable products and
made from wood grown in sustainable forests. The logging
and manufacturing processes are expected to conform to
the environmental regulations of the country of origin.

www.orionbooks.co.uk

Steve Mosby is the author of six previous novels, including *Black Flowers* and *Still Bleeding* which were longlisted for the Theakstons Old Peculier Crime Novel of the Year Award. He lives and works in Leeds. To find out more follow Steve on Twitter or visit his website at www.theleftroom.co.uk

By Steve Mosby

The Third Person
The Cutting Crew
The 50/50 Killer
Cry for Help
Still Bleeding
Black Flowers
Dark Room

For Lynn and Zack

Acknowledgements

Thanks to my agent, Carolyn Whitaker, and to all the people at Orion who have helped with this book and the others, including Genevieve Pegg, Laura Gerrard and Angela McMahon. As usual, without the advice and help of others, this would be a very different book.

Thanks also to my friends and family. Special mentions this time go to Luca Veste and Caitlin Sagan, for comments on an early draft and much additional support, all of it greatly appreciated, and to The Packhorse in Leeds city centre for being so accommodating.

Finally, thanks to Lynn and Zack for putting up with me and being wonderful. This book is – as always – dedicated to you both, with much love.

Part One

Part One

'We just want to know what happened,' the policeman says.

The little boy in front of him does not reply. He just stares down at his hands as he fidgets with them, thumbs flicking against one another.

He is eight years old but, seated alone in the middle of the large red settee, looks much younger.

They all do in here, the children. This is the comfort suite: a large room designed to look more like a lounge than a formal interview room. There are boxes of stuffed toys against one wall, and tattered paper comics in a pile on the table. The boy has shown no interest in any of them.

He is dressed in faded blue pyjamas, and his limbs are thin as sticks. His hair hasn't been cut in a long time: an embarrassing pauper's fringe and upward curls at the back where it rests on his shoulders. From what the constable can see of his face, it is entirely blank, as though the events of the night have slapped the emotion from him. His silence, his impassivity, they hang in the air like bruises.

He has been through a lot, this boy.

'Can you tell us what happened?'

More silence.

He glances at the child protection officer, who is the only other person in the room. She is prim and efficient, dressed in a neat grey suit; her hair is tied back in a bun and she wears glasses. She cannot help him.

The boy speaks suddenly, without looking up.

'Where's John?'

The policeman leans forward.

'Your brother? He's here too.'

'I want to see him.'

'That's not possible right now.'

The boy doesn't look up, but the policeman can see the grimace. The paternal part of him wants to help, but there is no way he can let him see his brother. The other boy – older by two years – is in a room downstairs. They have already spoken to him, and they will have to speak to him a lot more over the coming days.

The policeman shifts slightly.

'We need you to tell us your version of what happened,' he says. But that sounds overly official – too formal for this child in front of him – and he remembers what the child protection officer told him before they began the interview. He says, 'You can tell it as a story if you want. Tell us it as though it's not really happening.'

The boy's shoulders slump a little. He is malnourished, the policeman realises. Uncared for. But then he has seen the state of the house the boy came from, and he knows that whatever the boy has experienced did not really begin tonight. It must have started a long time ago.

After a long moment – gathering himself – the boy finally looks up and meets the policeman's eye.

And . . . there is something there, isn't there?

His expression isn't entirely blank at all. For a brief moment, the policeman imagines he is looking at someone or something a little bit older.

And as the boy starts to speak—

'It was late. After midnight, I think.'

—he can't entirely shake the sentiment. As the boy begins to tell the story of what happened, the policeman touches the cross that hangs around his neck and reminds himself that this little boy has seen so much horror tonight.

And yet the doubt persists.
Yes, he thinks.
This boy has been through so much.
Perhaps.

DAY ONE

One

It started in the grids.

That's what we call the spread of interlocking estates on the northern bank of the Kell, the river that curls through the heart of our city, and the closest we have to a ghetto. The roads here criss-cross each other at right angles, and all of them are lined with identical concrete blocks of flats. At ground level, most are tagged with eastern European graffiti; up above, balconies trail patchwork washing in the breeze like strange flags. Each six-storey block has a small lawn surrounding it, but these token nods to greenery can't hide the blocky anonymity of the buildings behind.

From above, flying into the city by plane, it looks as though someone has laid out odd stone hieroglyphs in endless rows and columns – or perhaps as though the river is pulling back its top lip: baring strange grey teeth at the sky.

I had the sat nav on and the pulsing blue arrow told me I was nearly there, but it would have been obvious enough anyway. If not from the police cordon strung across the road up ahead, then from the woman's screams. I could hear those from the end of the road.

It was half past ten on a Friday morning: a warm day, so I had the car window rolled down and my arm resting casually on the sill, sleeves rolled up, the sun gentle and pleasant on my forearm.

Beyond the cordon, I could see three meat vans and four police cars parked up, the blue light on top of the nearest winking meekly in the sunlight. Grunt-pool uniforms were stationed on both sides of the road, keeping rubbernecking residents from nearby blocks separated and stopping whatever stories they might have to tell us from becoming confused or exaggerated.

I pulled up by the cordon.

The car door echoed as I slammed it. The screams pierced the neighbourhood: an awful noise, drifting down from two floors above. It was the sound of a broken soul: the victim's mother, I presumed. In the warm, butter-coloured sunlight, the cries seemed even more incongruous. It's stupid, but there's always something a little more shocking when bad things happen in the daytime rather than at night.

'Detective Hicks.' I showed my badge to the officer manning the cordon at this end of the street; he nodded once and lifted it for me. I said, 'You doing all right?'

'Yes, sir. Detective Fellowes is over there.'

'Thanks.'

Detective Fellowes – Laura, my partner – was standing outside Block 8 up ahead. She was talking to a handful of the pool officers and pointing here and there, directing them to the hundred different tasks that attend a murder scene.

Under normal circumstances, we'd have arrived on site together, but I'd had the morning off for Rachel's appointment with the midwife. Laura had paged me while we were in the suite upstairs, nearly done: Rachel had been manoeuvring herself awkwardly off the bed while wiping the ultrasound gel off her stomach with bunched tissue paper, and that was when I'd felt the vibration against my hip.

I'd known immediately it had to be something serious for Laura to bother me off-time. But then I was predisposed to feel that way at the moment, especially in those circumstances. Any pregnancy-related activity tended to generate a frisson of dread. Whenever I thought about the baby, the world immediately became fragile and vulnerable, and it felt very much as though something could go wrong at any time. It seemed pretty reasonable to think that bad things might happen in a pregnancy, and not so much weirder to extrapolate that out to the world in general.

I reached Laura just as the other officers moved away to perform whatever tasks had been allocated to them.

'Mor-ning,' I said casually.

'Hicks.'

Laura was dressed in a dark trouser suit, her light brown hair cut to shoulder length. She ran a hand through it now, harried and stressed on the surface, but the hair fell neatly back in place. It took her a certain amount of time every morning to arrange it in such a way that the inevitable grabbing and clenching wouldn't do the amount of damage you'd usually expect.

We had the same colour hair, and the same speckling of freckles across our nose and cheeks, and since we were both in our mid thirties but looked younger, people often mistook us for brother and sister. That annoyed her a great deal. She knew me too well.

'Sorry to call you out today.'

'No worries. Good excuse to get away.'

That earned me a disapproving look. In the eight months of Rachel's pregnancy, Laura had spent an inordinate amount of time trying to convince me that my becoming a father would be a good thing for anyone. She'd never succeeded, but I'd learned to placate her.

She said, 'You don't mean that.'

'No.'

'How is everything?'

'Everything is fine. Everything is normal.'

'Good.'

I nodded up at the building, from which the woman's screams were still drifting down. 'I take it there's a doctor with her?'

'Yes. Shit, yes. I hope the meds are going to kick in soon.

It's doing everyone's head in. Plus she's very elderly and very distressed. It's understandable, I guess, finding her daughter like that.'

'Could end up with two for the price of one,' I said.

Another disapproving look. 'This is a bad one, Hicks.'

Sometimes Laura was at least tolerant of my flippancy, if never quite a willing participant, but today was clearly not one of those times.

'Sorry,' I said. 'What have we got?'

'Victim is – or appears to be – a thirty-two-year-old woman named Vicki Gibson.'

She pointed down the road to the front of the block. A hedge ran along the pavement, dividing it off from a small lawn and the block of flats beyond. The SOCOs had erected their white tent between the hedge and the building.

'Appears to be?' I said.

'No formal ID as yet. The mother – Carla Gibson – she recognised the clothes her daughter was wearing, but beyond that it's a little difficult to say.'

A bad one.

'Right. That's Carla Gibson I can hear?'

'Uh-huh. They share the flat on the third floor. Just the two of them. Carla tends to go to bed early, get up early. Wakes with the birds – four every morning. So she notices her daughter hasn't come home, looks out from the patio up there, more by chance than anything else, and sees the body.'

I glanced up at the third floor, to the concrete balcony where the screaming was now falling silent. It was pretty rough: the balcony would have offered Carla Gibson a clear view down to where her daughter had been lying – was still lying, in fact.

Had the body been left there deliberately?

'Where had she been?'

Laura led me down the street, talking it through as she went.

'Vicki Gibson worked two jobs, as and when she could. Last night she was doing a shift at Butler's launderette. It's a few blocks over yonder.' She gestured vaguely behind us. 'The shift finished at two in the morning, so she was killed sometime between two and four, probably closer to two.'

'CCTV?' I said. 'The launderette, I mean.'

'You're joking, right? But there was another girl on shift, and she says Gibson did the full rota. She might be lying, but it fits. Gibson couldn't afford a car – she walked home every night. And it looks like the attacker got her here.'

We stopped on the pavement, level with the tent. The hedge was about five feet tall, and there was a clear break in it where the foliage had been damaged.

I said, 'So he grabs her here on the pavement, and forces her through. Or else he's waiting behind the hedge and pulls her.'

'Either. Too early to tell.'

Laura emphasised the latter, knowing I was a little too fond of jumping to conclusions – relying on statistics and probabilities and forming judgements on the basis of them. She considered it one of my greater failings, but we both knew it wasn't much of one really, considering I generally ended up being right.

And I couldn't help myself. As we walked down the street to the main footpath, I was thinking it over: putting together what I already knew; preparing a few ideas subconsciously.

The grids are a concentration of poverty. At their heart – in the bullseye – it's mostly immigrants, many of them illegal. The streets there are a hotchpotch of languages and cultures: insular communities; smaller cities beneath the skin of the main. You look up and can't tell how many people might be clustered inside the blocks. The graffiti is mostly second-generation kids daubing flags and staking territory, manufacturing meaning from the environment. A lot of the people who live there never leave even their own grid, never mind the estate as a whole.

But we weren't in the heart now. The builds might look the same, but here at the edge, close to the river, they cost a bit more. It isn't uncommon to find students living here, as the accommodation is rougher but considerably cheaper than they'd find south of the river, closer to campus. And someone like Vicki Gibson, working two jobs in order to keep herself and her mother indoors and alive – in grids terms, she was practically a respectable professional.

Why would someone want to kill her? Robbery was a possibility. A sexual motive? Slightly less likely, given the probability of being seen, but not impossible.

Too early to tell . . .

Across the small lawn, the grass still felt spongy with dew, glistening slightly in the mid-morning sun. It was surprisingly well tended: trimmed down neat, so you could imagine spreading out a picnic in front of a tent very different to the one we were approaching now.

I lifted the flap on the side in time to see the flash of a camera: a SOCO was bent double inside, photographing the victim where she was lying in the shade.

I hesitated. Just slightly.

Vicki Gibson was lying on her back, one leg bent so that the right foot rested under the other knee. Both her red heels had come off and were stuck twisted in the grass; she was still wearing a red skirt and a black blouse, and a fluffy brown coat the gloom rendered as rust. Both arms were splayed out to her sides. Her hair was long: swirling black tendrils in the grass, like she was lying in an inch of water.

She had no face left to speak of.

A bad one.

'Well,' I told Laura. 'You were right.'

I was still noting the details, though – a discarded red handbag rested beside her, the cord lying curled in the grass. Not robbery, then. And the clothes didn't appear to have been disturbed. That left one obvious possibility.

'Andy.' Simon Duncan, the forensic liaison for our department, was standing by the body. He nodded at me. 'Glad you could make it.'

'Wouldn't miss it for the world.'

Simon was tall and mostly bald, with a climber's build.

Beside him, the pathologist, Chris Dale, who looked short and serious at the best of times, appeared even more so now, squatting down by his victim. He glanced up to acknowledge my presence, but only briefly.

'I know it's early days,' I said, 'but do we have anything concrete yet?'

Simon arched an eyebrow.

'You've not got it figured out yet? You surprise me, Andrew. I thought that might explain the delay in your arrival – that you were already off arresting the perpetrator.'

'I do have an idea,' I said. 'Why don't you see if you can throw me off course, eh?'

Simon moved to one side, to allow the SOCO with the camera around to the head end of the body. In doing so, he gave us a better view as well. It couldn't really be called the 'head end' any more.

'There's one very obvious injury,' Simon said, just as the camera flashed across it. 'Or rather, numerous injuries to one specific part of the victim. As far as we can tell, there are no other serious injuries. I think we can probably run with the damage to the head being the cause of death rather than post-mortem.'

I nodded.

Whoever had attacked Vicki Gibson had beaten her about the head and face so severely that it was impossible to recognise her. Even dental records would be unlikely, I thought, trying to examine the injuries professionally. The front of her skull had been caved in. There was her neck, pristine and unblemished, and that hair swirled above, but everything in between was gone.

'No defensive injuries?'

Simon shook his head. 'Looks like the first blow was enough to incapacitate her. He either dragged her through the hedge or else the blow knocked her that way.'

'Too early to tell,' I said.

'Yes. Regardless, he hit her many times, and continued to do so long after her death. As you can see, the entire front of her skull has been seriously damaged.'

Yes, I could see that all too clearly.

I squatted down and peered at the hands.

'No sexual assault?'

'Nothing obvious at this stage.'

'And no robbery.'

'Her credit cards and money are still in the handbag.' He arched his eyebrow again.' I'm not throwing you so far, am I?'

'I'm not telling you yet. Weapon?'

Simon shook his head. 'Impossible to say for sure right now, or possibly at all. But since we've not found it, I imagine it would be something small and hard: a hammer or a pipe. A rock perhaps. Something hand-held anyway.'

I nodded. The weapon would need to be hard enough to inflict this level of damage, but light enough for the killer to be able to carry it away with him afterwards: something that could deliver the force of a boulder but not the weight. That was an awful thought, of course. A heavy boulder might cause this level of damage with only one or two blows. With something like a hammer, it would have taken much more time and effort; many, many more blows.

But it also meant this probably wasn't a spur-of-the-moment crime. The attacker had most likely brought the weapon with him and taken it away again. And that degree of ferocity tended to indicate a personal motive. Not always, but usually.

'Come on then, Sherlock Hicks. Let's have it.'

I stood up.

'Ex-husband.' Then I corrected myself: 'Well, ex-partner. She used to wear a ring, but doesn't any more. It might have been an engagement ring.'

'Never married.' Laura inclined her head. 'The IT guys are pulling her files now, though, so if there's any previous complaints or restraining orders there, we'll know shortly.'

'There will be,' I said.

Bizarre as it sounds, I felt a little brighter. As bad as this murder was – and it was bad – I knew it would also be explicable. Because, ultimately, they all are. I'm not saying the explanation is ever satisfactory or reasonable – I'm not saying it's ever *enough* – but the reason is always there, and it always makes sense to the person who did it.

The fact is, most crimes conform to mundane statistical patterns. The vast majority of female murder victims, for example, are killed by somebody they know, and it's usually a partner or recent partner. Countrywide, two women die every week at the hands of men who are supposed to love them, or once claimed to, or imagine in their heads they did. So – especially having ruled out robbery and sexual assault – an ex-partner was the obvious guess. Most DV murders happen indoors, but this was close enough: someone had known where and when to find her. And now that I thought about it, the fact that Vicki Gibson, at the age of thirty-two, lived with her mother also indicated an ex rather than current partner.

I was sure that the IT guys – if not Carla Gibson herself – would very shortly give us a man's name. At some point in the past, either Vicki or her mother was likely to have called the police before, because these things rarely just explode out of nowhere. Gibson's ex-boyfriend would have a string of reports against his name, and probably some charges. At some point, she would have dared to leave him. And because of the type of man he was, the resentment and hurt everyone feels in such circumstances would have been much blacker and more aggressive than most.

From some of the other domestic homicides I'd dealt with, I could almost picture the pathetic bastard. When we picked him up, he'd probably still be blaming Vicki Gibson for what had happened – even now. Still convinced she'd pushed his buttons, and that it was somehow her fault.

'We'll see,' Laura said.

'We will.'

I was confident. This was a textbook bedroom crime, in my

own personal architecture of murder. Hideous and awful, but comprehensible and quickly tied shut.

It had to be that.

What else could it be?

TWO

'She wasn't here when I got up,' Carla Gibson said.

'No,' Laura said gently. 'I know.'

The flat shared by two generations of the Gibson family – until this morning, anyway – was so small that it seemed cramped even with just the three of us inside.

We were in the front room, which doubled as the kitchen – built in down one side, but only in the sense that the room's threadbare carpet stopped, leaving a stretch of blackened floorboards along the base of the counter. I was leaning against the wall, next to a rusted wall-mounted boiler and exposed pipes that ran out of the ceiling and disappeared down dirty holes in the floorboards.

Laura was sitting opposite Carla at a rickety wooden table. Like most of the furniture in here, it was ramshackle and cheap: just flimsy wood, held together by little more than four metal bolts and a prayer. Laura was sitting carefully, as though worried the chair would break beneath her.

'I crept through to make tea. I always creep through. She works so hard, you see, all the time, and I wanted to let her sleep. But she wasn't here.'

'We know, Mrs Gibson. I'm so sorry.'

The old lady seemed calm on the surface now that the mild sedative the nurse had given her had taken effect, but was still obviously in pieces – frail and shivering. Her eyes rarely met ours; she kept staring off into the middle distance instead, focused on something out of sight beyond the drab walls. Of course, the drug didn't repair the damage, just dampened its effects. It remained obvious that she had been crying long and hard, and that all she was doing right now was avoiding facing the horror of her loss head on.

Aside from this living space, there was a bathroom and a single bedroom, where Carla slept. Vicki Gibson had slept in here, on the settee. It was sunken almost to the floor, but still made up carefully for the night's sleep Vicki had never reached. Blankets and pillows had been laid neatly over it, topped by a patchwork quilt that I suspected had been hand-sewn by Carla herself.

It hurt to see it – a visual reminder that although they lived in abject poverty, they were making the most of it. Vicki worked late and often early too: cleaning at an office block as and when; shifts at the launderette in the evenings. Every night, Carla made up her daughter's bed on that settee; every morning, she folded those blankets away and a makeshift second bedroom was transformed back into a makeshift front room again.

Every morning except this one.

And all the rest now.

'And then I looked out,' Carla said, '. . . and she was there instead.'

Laura said, 'We don't need to talk about all that again, Mrs Gibson.'

'No. No.'

'Let's move on to something else.'

'Yes.'

As much as anything else, I knew Laura was trying to distract the woman from the fact that her daughter still *was* out there. We wouldn't be moving the body for a few more hours yet, which was a logistical nightmare in terms of handling residents of this and the neighbouring blocks.

When we were done talking to her, I planned to have a sympathetic officer stay here with Carla Gibson and gently persuade her away from the balcony at the far end of this room. The sight of the tent down there, while far less horrific than the scene that greeted her this morning, would really be just as awful. The fact was, we were taking care of her daughter as best we could right now. To relatives, though, that doesn't always necessarily appear to be the case.

'That's good,' Laura said. 'Shall we talk about Tom Gregory instead?'

'Tom . . . ?'

Carla stared back at her for a moment.

'Vicki's ex-partner.'

'I know the name, but what does he have to do with this?'

'Well,' Laura said, 'I understand that their relationship was quite volatile.'

'I didn't know about that.'

I folded my arms, still saying nothing, because volatile was an understatement. In the time since viewing the body, we'd had the relevant files through from IT support, and my hunch outside hadn't been *too* wide of the mark. The violence between the couple wasn't as extensive as I'd imagined – but all that really meant was that it hadn't been extensively reported to the police. Given the power dynamics and threats that go along with domestic violence, the two are obviously entirely different things. For every reported peak of violence, there's most likely a bunch of others that are only marginally smaller.

What we knew for certain, though, was that Vicki Gibson had called the police about Tom Gregory in connection with three incidents. Two of those were when they'd been together; the third occasion, six months ago, had been after they separated. Gregory had turned up at the launderette, drunk out of his mind, and a couple of the other customers had needed to physically restrain him.

For various reasons, all three cases had disintegrated at some point before charges were filed. Cases of domestic violence, like rape, carry a huge amount of what we call slippage. Sometimes it's our fault; more often, these days, it isn't. But it's fair to say there have been many, many cases where I wish I could have done more. Wish more than I could say, in fact.

Laura said, 'Vicki never mentioned it?'

'No, no.' Carla frowned. 'And I don't think Vicki would have stood for that. She's such a strong person, you know. So protective: always looking after me. It's very hard for her, I know, but she's such a good girl to me.'

'I understand.' If Laura noticed Carla's use of the present tense, she chose not to acknowledge it. Wisely. 'Did you ever meet him? Mr Gregory?'

'No. I know they were very close for a time, but that was before she moved back home.'

Home.

I looked around again. Peter Gibson – Vicki's father – had died the previous year. Her parents had lived here for a very long time, and this was where Vicki had grown up. I imagined her crawling around on this floor as an infant, the sounds of neighbours' televisions barely muffled by the thin panels on the walls. A bad place, maybe, but a good family. Sometimes that's enough; usually it isn't. Vicki had struck out on her own, tried her best, and eventually been pulled back to where she'd started by the inescapable social elastic of our city. It's a cliché, but it's true: so much of where people end up depends on where they start.

'When they broke up, I told her not to worry,' Carla said. 'These things happen, don't they? It's sad but we have to move on.'

'And you were glad to have her back, weren't you?'

'Yes.' Carla's face brightened a little. 'Yes, I was. She's a good girl.'

'She never mentioned why they'd broken up?'

'No. But I'm sure it wouldn't have been her fault. That's what I told her. She's a catch. Are you married, Detective?'

The last was directed, somewhat hopefully, at me. I felt awkward and sad for her.

'Yes.'

'That's a shame. She's a lovely girl.'

I leaned away from the wall and, for the first time, involved myself directly in the interview.

'Did Mr Gregory ever come round here after they broke up?'

'No, no.'

'Would you have any contact details for him?'

'Oh. Well, perhaps – yes.' She stood up, wobbling slightly. 'They lived together before she moved back home. I need to find my address book.'

'That's okay.' I held out a hand to stop her. We had that address already, and officers had established he wasn't home right now. 'I was more wondering if there was anywhere else you knew of? Places he went, or friends or family he might stay with?'

'In that case, no, I'm sorry.' She sat back down again. The chair seemed barely to register her. 'I didn't know him like that. I didn't really know him at all.'

'That's all right.'

It had been a long shot anyway. Whether out of pride or embarrassment, Vicki Gibson had kept the abusive element of her relationship a secret from her elderly mother. Again, that wasn't remotely surprising. The situation she found herself in did not make her weak, but when you're in that situation you're made to feel that way, and are often reluctant to compound the feeling by admitting to it. People who really need and deserve help are usually at the point when it's hardest to admit it.

There was no real consolation in it, but one thing we could guarantee now was that Tom Gregory wouldn't get away with what he'd done. Not this time. If he was proving elusive for the moment, he wouldn't be for ever.

I was already thinking ahead when I realised Carla Gibson was looking at me, a distressed expression on her face, as though my thoughts had been a little too obvious – already out of the door, in fact. I was about to apologise when she said:

'Vicki was so strong.'

It took me a second to realise she was talking about Gregory

– regressing to the point of the conversation where Laura had described their relationship as volatile. She didn't want to believe her little girl had endured something like that silently. And I understood it wasn't about me being distracted but about Carla Gibson, despite the drugs, being suddenly present again.

'She *was* strong,' I said, looking right back at her. Even though it's not about strength, because that can seem like a judgement on those who don't leave, I said it again. 'She was very strong indeed.'

And I thought:

We're going to catch you, Mr Gregory.

Three

On our way back downstairs, Laura and I talked it over.

'You're convinced?' she said.

'I'm more convinced than ever. You mean you're not?'

To me, it looked clear-cut. People aren't killed for no reason; there's always cause and effect, and the facts here spoke for themselves. It wasn't an aggravated robbery and there had been no sexual assault. All that was left, realistically, was that Vicki had been murdered out of revenge – out of passion, or at least its curdled, ugly flip side. Tom Gregory had form. If it wasn't him, then who was it? The odds, already good, were only getting shorter.

Laura sighed.

'It looks nailed on, I admit. And that's obviously what we move forward with for now.'

'That's what we *move forward* with. Yes. *Blue-sky thinking* there, Laura.'

'Shut up, Hicks.'

'Look. He's got motive. He's got opportunity. He's got form. And he's missing.' I threaded my fingers together, then drew them apart. 'We'll have this sewn up by the end of the day.'

'I'm sure.'

'I sense a but.'

'But . . . something in me doesn't feel it's right. Don't say it: I know you hate it when I use the word feel, but it's true. Don't you feel . . . something?'

'I'm not a monster,' I said.

'Oh God, Hicks, I know you're not.'

'I feel sorry for Vicki Gibson. Don't let my flippancy kid you otherwise. And I feel *intense* fucking dislike for Tom Gregory. And believe me, I'll feel a lot better when he's locked up paying dear fucking money for what he's done.'

'That's not what I meant.'

I didn't say anything. No, I knew that wasn't what she'd meant – we'd worked together long enough for her to take the things I'd said as given. Still, I didn't say anything else. I'd been intending to add something like *I don't feel anything weird* – and yet for some reason I didn't. As far as I could tell, I was totally in the right, and I was still sure we had our man, but a part of me knew what she meant. Not that I was going to admit it.

'I just find it hard to imagine,' Laura said. 'That someone could *hate* someone that much. Don't you?'

I shrugged.

'To a point. I find it hard to imagine me or you hating someone like that. But we don't know anything about this guy. He could have taken it as an affront to his manhood, her leaving him. Maybe he didn't like being confronted with the fact that he didn't own her the way he thought. You know what some men are like.'

'Yeah. Unfortunately so.'

'*Some* of them.'

'Defensive much?'

'Defensive always.'

We pushed our way out into the midday sun. After the interior of the stairwell, it was too harsh and too bright; I shielded my eyes.

'What?' Laura said.

I lowered my hand to see an officer standing in front of us: the same one who'd met me at the cordon. He looked panicked, excited, a bit lost.

He said, 'We've got another body.'

*

26

As Laura and I took my car south through two intersections of the grids, all we knew was that the second body found belonged to a male, but because I tended to go with probabilities, I was expecting it to be Tom Gregory.

Again, we'd both seen it happen before. Most likely he'd been incoherent during the murder itself, with alcohol or anger or both, and the effects, the armour of that, wear off in time. It's fairly common in these circumstances for the perpetrator to take his own life after it hits home exactly what he's done – destroyed not only someone else's future, but his own as well. Plus, it would explain why we hadn't been able to find Gregory so far.

A minute later, we drove out of the end of Lily Street, into a rough parking area on the northern bank of the river. The water stretched out in front, fifty metres wide, and silver in the sunlight. The water was moving along at quite a lick: rippling and shredding. On the far bank, the rich old town clustered, gathering itself gradually upwards into the distant skyscrapers of the business district that glinted and beamed in the sun. On the river itself, a tourist ferry was purring along in the middle. As we parked up, I could see people on the deck, staring in our direction.

As we got out of the car, the wind hit. Whatever the temperature, there always seems to be a cold breeze close to the Kell, as though it's made of ice.

There were already two police cars in the parking area, but only one officer in sight – standing at the far end by a break in the moss-green stone wall, guarding the steps that led down to the old promenade.

'Hicks.' I showed him my badge. 'And Fellowes. Where are we going – down there?'

'Yes, sir.'

The steps were ancient and weathered: blocks of stone from a different world. Our city is several centuries old, and this is roughly the spot it spread out from, the initial colonies clustering along the length of the river. For a long time, the northern bank itself was considered too marshy to develop, and it was only fifty years ago that the grids were constructed on its upper lip, fitted in between the water and the industrial and agricultural areas further north. But you feel the heart of the city here. The rocks and flagstones always remind me of gravestones in an abandoned churchyard.

'Christ.' Laura winced. 'I wish I'd brought my coat.'

'It's a bit more sheltered down here.'

It was often used as a shelter too. The steps led down to a secluded stretch of stone walkway, walled off at either end. They were scattered along this bank, a row of old benches to each, the wood as gnarled and dry as dead trees. These places collected litter. Some of it blew in and couldn't escape; the rest was discarded around the benches – dirty bags of cans and bottles, left by the vagrants you could often find curled on the benches, sleeping, somehow, in the cold. But then, as freezing as it could be here, it was still preferable to other central locations: the parks they'd likely be moved on from; the two derelict underground stations where so many homeless gathering together created a pretty volatile atmosphere.

The second body was lying on the furthest of the three benches here. It was surrounded by four officers, one of them talking into his radio. They looked up hopefully as we approached. We were the first detectives on site.

'Gentlemen.' I showed my badge again. 'Let's give the man some air, shall we?'

They moved to one side to let us see what we had.

'Shit,' I said.

'Language, Hicks,' Laura said.

'Sorry. But shit.'

It wasn't Tom Gregory – I could tell that from the victim's age. It was a man, though, and most likely a homeless one. He was lying on his back, wrapped in layers of paint-stained coats, jumpers and pants: bundled up in the clothes like a mole in a burrow. One arm lolled down, the hand resting on the stone ground. It was the skin there that gave the age away – that and the thin, emaciated wrist, the weathered yellow fingernails. An old man. But it was impossible to tell much more than that, because, like Vicki Gibson, somebody had beaten him relentlessly until his face had been smashed into non-existence. You couldn't tell what had been his forehead and what had been his chin.

I crouched down, slightly reluctantly. Beneath the bench, the discarded plastic bags and food cartons were covered with blood and fragments of his skull that had fallen through the slats in the bench.

'What do you think?' Laura said quietly.

'I think he's dead.'

'You know what I mean.'

I shook my head to indicate that I didn't know what I really thought. She was asking me if this was the same killer – whether Tom Gregory had done this as well. And I didn't know, because at first glance, it didn't fit at all. Obviously it looked like the same killer, but I was sure Gregory was our man for Vicki Gibson and I couldn't imagine what might have led him to do this too. It didn't make any sense.

Come on then, Sherlock.

'I don't know.'

I stood up.

'I really don't know.'

Four

We picked up Tom Gregory in the middle of the afternoon.

As is the way of these things, it wasn't down to any impressive detective work on the part of Laura, me or the officers looking for him, but simply because that was when he ambled back up to his front door, without a care in the world. Until he was arrested with his keys half out of his pocket.

And I say it's the way of these things, because it's usually the way it works. In the movies, there'll be some sharp flash of insight that leads the detective to the culprit, but real life tends to be more mundane – and reassuringly so. The killer is often the first person you think did it, and he did it for the first reason you thought of. In the vast majority of other cases, you catch people through a shitload of hard work: processing the data and winnowing down the options. Flow-chart stuff, really. When it isn't either of those things, it's always down to luck. The right person tells you the right thing. You walk into the right place at the right time. Or else – as in this case – the muppet you want to talk to wanders up to his front door, hands practically outstretched, exclaiming *arrest me*.

That was my experience. By the time Tom Gregory was in a transport back to the station, Laura and I were seated in an office on the fifth floor of the building, holding an unofficial debrief with our boss, DCI Shaun Young, discussing the connection between the cases.

One crime scene of the magnitude of Vicki Gibson was more

than enough to occupy days of activity, and now we had two. Under normal circumstances, we'd have palmed off the second. Given the possible connection, though, we were keeping them linked – cautiously – for the moment.

But, but, but.

'I'm sensing doubt,' Young said.

That was directed at me. I was leaning back a little, one heel trailing back and forth on the plush carpet.

'That's because I'm doubtful, sir. I'm wearing my heart on my sleeve in my usual manner. My guard is down.'

'Apparently so. Stop slumping, by the way.'

'Yes, sir.'

I made a token effort in that direction, but Young was used to me by now. Close to retirement age, he kept a trim, muscular build and a grim face topped with dyed black hair. His manner was generally feared. But while he gave every appearance of being gruff and unforgiving, some strange part of him had always seemed to enjoy my acts of minor insubordination.

'I remain unconvinced that the two murders are linked.' Beside me, sitting more neatly, Laura shook her head. I added, 'Despite my colleague's evident disapproval.'

'They're obviously connected. I don't understand how you can possibly think they aren't.'

'I didn't say that. I said I was unconvinced.'

'Oh God – you're exasperating sometimes. You always go by statistics and likelihoods, and I don't understand why you're abandoning that now. What is the probability of two blunt-force murders occurring in the same vicinity on the same night?'

'Right now, the probability is one. Because it happened. Overall, I don't—'

'And having *two different perpetrators.*'

'Look.' I'd had time to think about this. 'So far, all the evidence in the Gibson case points to Tom Gregory being responsible. Without the second, as yet unidentified victim, we'd still be one hundred per cent convinced of that. Yes?'

'Yes, but—'

'Good. Since it seems far less likely that Gregory killed the second victim, that's my basis for not linking the crimes.'

'Because in your head, you've solved the first murder. And you can't possibly be wrong about that.'

'No, I could be wrong. But it doesn't make any sense that Tom Gregory did both. What – he had a little residual anger left over and took it out on a homeless man? Or he warmed up for the main event beforehand?'

'You're assuming it's Gregory.'

'Actually, no: I'm assuming it's *anyone*. For "Gregory", read "anyone". It doesn't make sense.'

Laura sighed. 'It doesn't always make sense, Hicks.'

'Yes, it does.' I sat up properly this time. 'It really does.'

Because this *mattered*. It *always* made sense on some level. Not in a satisfying way, perhaps, but always in *some* way. And the fact is that people don't go on random killing sprees with blunt-force instruments. If they want to do that, they use guns. And while it was theoretically *possible*, spree killers also don't just stop: they keep going until we take them down, or until they get taken down.

Yes, Laura was right. It would be a hell of a coincidence for two victims to die in very similar ways in such a short period of time. But the alternative – that Gregory, or anyone, had murdered both – seemed even more unlikely. On the basis of probabilities, I was going with my head over my gut on this one for now.

Which isn't to say it wasn't close.

Young had been sitting very still – really only his gaze moving, back and forth between Laura and me, following the tennis match – but now he leaned forward, rested his elbows on the desk and steepled his fingers beneath his chin. Ready to add his input and verdict.

'What about if Tom Gregory had a reason to dislike this gentleman as well? Could there be a connection between the two victims?'

'Possible, sir,' I said. 'But I can't see it. It's the same geographical area, but even given the general poverty, both victims are from massively different social circles.'

Young nodded.

'But we need an ID before we can rule anything out.'

'Yes, sir.'

'And it's possible the culprit went down to the river to dispose of the murder weapon. Encountered victim two and decided to get rid of him too.'

'We're dredging the river now, sir.'

'You take my point, though.'

'Yes, sir. Although if that's the case, why the need for such extreme injuries? And it looks to me like the victim was asleep when he was attacked, so why not just back out and choose a different spot?'

'Well. These are all questions that need answering, aren't they? But in the meantime, we proceed as though they're connected.' He sighed; checked his watch. 'Gregory should be here soon. Let's see what he has to say, eh?'

'Yes, sir.'

I looked at Laura. She looked back, then shook her head.

'Yes, sir.'

What Tom Gregory had to say was, 'You've got to be fucking kidding me. Fuck off. Both of you. Both of you can just fuck off.'

I said, 'Tom, we really can't fuck off.'

We were in one of the upstairs interview suites: a bare, functional room, containing just a steel table, chairs, Laura and me, and the current man of the hour. Gregory was in his early forties, six feet tall, wide at the middle, and had a certain meaty heft to him. The kind of guy who'd never done a day's actual exercise in his life but would still be dangerous in a brawl. He'd shaved away his receding hair, and was wearing cheap blue jeans and a dirty red lumberjack shirt. The overall impression was that a dilapidated lorry was parked up in a truck stop somewhere waiting for its owner to come home.

'You've got to be kidding me,' he said again.

'I can assure you that I'm not.'

He remained incredulous. It was an emotion that sat transparently on his stubbly face, in much the same way I imagined most emotions did. He was not a man of any obvious subtlety, and seemed to wear whatever he was feeling on his features without much concern as to what other people might think. For men like him, I guess, the fact they're feeling it is usually enough to justify its immediate and forceful expression regardless of anything else.

He stared at me for a moment, then leaned back in his chair, which creaked beneath the bulk of him, and folded one beefy arm over the other. It was clear he thought the situation was stupid. To be fair, that was how I felt about him right now too.

'You've got to be,' he repeated.

'You're being a bit slow here, Tom. It's surprising, really. You look like you'd be so much sharper.'

'What's that meant to mean?'

'It's not *meant* to mean anything. It *means* you're acting pretty dumb. Dumber than you look, in fact. Somehow, you are achieving that. Your ex-partner is dead and you have a history of violence against her, so you're going to have to do better than telling me I'm making it up. Because I know I'm not.'

'I didn't kill her.'

'You don't look too broken up about the situation.'

'Why should I be? We were long over with. I'd put her out of my mind altogether – that's the truth. I wish I'd never met her in the first place.'

'Wish she was dead?'

'No.' But then he shrugged. 'I don't fucking care, though, if that's what you're asking. Why should I? You tell me why I should care. You can't. She was a dirty, lying bitch. Something was always going to happen to her eventually.'

'*Something was always going to happen to her,*' I said. 'This is good stuff, Tom. You remember this is all admissible in court,

34

don't you? Keep it up, we can dispense with the trial. I'll just pull my gun out and shoot you now.'

'What I *meant* is living where she did.' He looked slightly more contrite now, probably only because he'd realised what he'd just said. 'That horrible place. All those fucking scumbags and junkies hanging around. Telling lies about people too. That was what she did. It was only a matter of time before she ended up in trouble.'

'Like she used to get in trouble with you?'

'I never did anything.' He tapped the table. 'See any convictions in my file?'

'No.'

'So it never happened.'

Beside me, Laura took a deep breath. I sensed she was losing her patience, which didn't happen very often. But I sympathised. Gregory was sitting there with a smug look on his face now. *It never happened.* At heart, men like Tom Gregory are still children. Their response to being told off is to be indignant, to not understand, to say *I didn't do it.* It's always someone else's fault to people like him. If it happens out of sight, if they can't prove it, you're all right.

I decided to needle him a bit.

'Great logic, Tom. But you know what? We have the call logs and witness statements. Not to mention all the other actual convictions you have. Short temper, haven't we?'

He glared at me. 'Sometimes.'

'Sometimes.'

While none of the charges relating to Vicki Gibson had stuck, others had. He had three convictions for assault and two for violent disorder. The usual drunken bar fights. One count of criminal damage too. Suspended sentence and fine for each offence.

'Lose it when you've had a few, yeah?'

'Sometimes.'

'Anger-management issues.' I shook my head. 'You're funny, aren't you? People like you.'

'Funny?'

'Yeah. You always say you have trouble controlling your-selves. The red mist descends and you can't help it. All that bullshit. But I don't see you losing it with me. Controlling ourselves, are we?'

'Maybe I'm counting to ten.'

'Maybe you can. No, I don't think so. The truth is that people like you are cowards. Right? For some reason, you only lose control when you can get away with it. Funny that, isn't it? It makes me laugh.'

Tom Gregory just looked at me. I stared back, letting the silence pan out. Rattling his cage was more enjoyable than it probably should have been, but I was angry. Partly it was what he'd done in the past – the kind of man he was – and partly the attitude. Maybe it was also the fact that, deep down, I suspected he was telling the truth – that he hadn't killed her – and the possibility bothered me.

I settled back in my chair.

'I didn't kill her,' he said. 'I was at—'

'Yeah, you said. Shut up.'

Gregory had already given his whereabouts the previous evening to the officers who'd arrested him earlier on. He'd then given them to us as soon as we'd walked into the interview suite. He'd been in O'Reilly's bar from six until throwing-out time, somewhere between two and three, before leaving in the company of a middle-aged woman from the eastern quarter. He'd spent the night at her flat. We'd picked him up at the end of his walk of shame, assuming he was capable of that emotion.

On the face of it, it was a solid alibi. He certainly stank of alcohol, and none of his clothes were bloodstained, despite it being obvious he'd been wearing them for a good twenty-four hours. O'Reilly's was a shitty, bare-boards half-club – a bar, pool tables and a floodlit dance floor by the toilets – but it saw enough trouble for the owner to have installed CCTV. It was also a fair distance from the grids. The address he'd given for the anonymous lady of spectacularly poor taste was even further away. I knew that area, and many of the blocks of flats there had cameras too.

So it was either a very good alibi or a very bad one indeed.

I said, 'You were drunk last night.'

'Yeah. So? That's not a crime.'

'But you managed to get through the evening without the red mist descending, yeah?'

'Yeah.'

'You sure about that?'

He didn't reply.

The door opened then, and a young WPC pushed her head in and jutted out her chin, indicating that she'd like a word. Laura and I pushed back our chairs. But I didn't need to speak to the WPC to read the expression on her face.

Tom Gregory had a very good alibi.

In the observation room, I ran my hand through my hair and stared at the small monitor, which showed Gregory still sitting in the interview suite. Needless to say, my hair didn't fall back down anything as neatly as Laura's would have done. I don't primp for such eventualities. I rarely face them.

'He *has* to have done it,' I said. 'He *has* to.'

'But he didn't. Face facts, Hicks. We have camera footage of him being everywhere he claims to have been. Putting it all together, it makes it impossible he did it.'

'He could have paid someone.'

But that was grasping at straws. Deep down, I knew my theory was wrong, and I was going to need to rethink this whole thing.

'He can barely pay his rent,' Laura said. 'Besides, the whole point of his record is he does things like that himself. He's a creep, don't get me wrong, but his violence is all impulsive, spur-of-the-moment stuff. He's not the type to hire someone to do his dirty work.'

'No, I know.'

'Plus, why would that same person kill our homeless John Doe as well?'

'All right, Laura.'

'Hit men not being in the habit of throwing in a second, random victim for free. I feel the need to hammer these points home, so I know we're on the same page.'

'Unfortunate choice of words, but yes. We are.'

On the screen, the same WPC who'd given us the bad news entered the interview suite, preparing to escort Tom Gregory out and back to the holding cell.

'One killer,' I said. 'Two victims. The connection between them as yet unknown.'

'I agree.'

I turned to her. 'But there will be a connection, Laura. Nobody kills two people at random like that. There's a reason. Something we're not seeing.'

'Ah. But you said before it was unlikely there was a connection between them.'

'It was unlikely before. Now it's the most likely explanation. You see how this works, right? It means I'm not technically wrong. I'm just altering my theory to fit the presently available facts. You should try it.'

Laura smirked. 'What about him?'

I looked back at the screen. Tom Gregory was gone now, so I reached out and flicked off the feed switch, and the screen went blank.

'No reason to keep him in,' I said.

'No.'

I checked my watch.

'But we've got another sixty-eight hours before we need to charge him with anything. So let's keep him for a bit.'

'Why? What's the point?'

'Because I don't fucking *like* him.'

I turned away and walked towards the door.

'That's the point.'

Five

The General surveys himself in the bathroom mirror.

His short hair is combed and gelled neatly; his face blank but stern. It is the face of a capable man: not someone to catch · the eye of, not a man to be crossed. A soldier's face – finally.

Below the shaved-red flesh of his throat, the uniform is green and straight; the red tassels at the shoulders stand out as bright as berries on sunlit grass. He holds the cap in his hands, clasped before him, and stands with rigid legs, feet shoulder-width apart. His black boots are polished enough to glint back the overhead light.

He can stand for hours like this on a night. He stares at his own reflection for so long that the face dissolves and re-forms, becomes that of a stranger. Until, in fact, he feels oddly threatened by the man looking back at him. Frightened of the figure he sees, but also in thrall to the superiority there. Other times he feels disgust for him.

Often, the feelings vacillate, and that mixture of sensations, that internal conflict, can send him curling towards an unfathomable part of himself. He becomes lost in this image that encapsulates him. Hypnotised by the half-glimpsed, winking face of his soul.

But tonight, it is getting late. He has work to do.

So the General nods to himself – *dismissed* – then leaves the bathroom and moves through the silent house to his office. It is a small room. At one side, there is the terrible, half-formed thing that both repulses and fascinates him, but he ignores that for now and turns his attention to the opposite wall instead, where he keeps his desk and computer.

Work to do: always more work. But although it has been a busy day, he has enjoyed the clamour his actions have created. He is excited that his plan – finally – is beginning to unfold. Everything, so far, is going as it should. Why would it not, though? He has been careful. He deserves to succeed. He is a soldier.

The General slips on gloves and retrieves the document he typed and printed days ago from the locked drawer in the desk. Then he places it on the computer table beside the monitor, and reads the first few lines, even though he already knows them off by heart.

Dear Detective

I don't know who you are yet. And at the time of writing this letter, you don't know who I am either. You have no idea of my existence and no inkling of what I am about to do. The truth is, I still don't know quite when it will begin myself. That is why it's going to work. That is why you'll never catch me.

And the rest of it.

It is all true. It's beautiful, actually.

On the floor by the desk, he has today's evening paper. He picks it up now and scans the news report on the first killing, finding the section he's interested in. There it is. The man who will fail to crack his code. His opponent, as much as the figure in the mirror is. The General takes a blue fountain pen and amends the printed letter.

Dear Detective *Hicks.*

Six

'You were in the paper today,' Rachel called through.

'I was? Shit.'

'It's over there on the table.'

'Thanks.'

She was in the kitchen, preparing dinner. I could hear her moving pans, occasionally wincing as an ache travelled through her. Even so, I knew better than to offer to help. This far into the pregnancy, I had a tendency to fuss – attempting to lever every possible task out of her hands as quickly as I could – and it annoyed her immensely. *I'm not an invalid*, she kept telling me. *I'll be off my feet soon enough*. I kept trying though; it seemed the least I could do. The kitchen was one area she refused to give up, though. With my culinary skills, that was probably a good thing for both of us.

'Smells great,' I said.

'Thanks.'

I picked up the copy of the *Evening Post*.

Vicki Gibson was front-page news. There was a full-colour photograph of her smiling face on the right-hand side. You can say what you like about reporters, but this was impressively fast work. We hadn't even released her identity officially yet, although I suppose it wouldn't have been too difficult to get it from neighbours, or some officer on scene in need of keeping a press contact sweet.

I scanned through the article. There was no mention of the

second victim we'd found; that had either come too late for filing or had not been considered newsworthy enough for the moment. No mention of Tom Gregory either, thank God. It just gave the typical line that we were pursuing a number of possible leads. I wished that were true. My name was mentioned in passing as lead officer on the investigation, along with a departmental phone number that, thankfully, wasn't mine. Small mercies.

I put the paper back down and went through to the kitchen.

Rachel was standing with her back to me at the counter, illuminated by the overhead spot bulbs, intent on slicing and chopping vegetables. She used the edge of the knife to scrape diced peppers from the chopping board into the sizzling frying pan beside her.

For a moment, I just watched her. Her brown hair was pulled back into a loose ponytail. The back of her neck, before her blouse began, was pale and slightly mottled. Occasionally the light glinted off the side of the thick black glasses she wore.

Thok thok thok.

Chopping mushrooms now, either oblivious to my presence or pretending to be.

From behind, you could hardly tell she was thirty-four weeks pregnant. She hadn't put on much weight at all in the first few months, and even now, although her belly had ballooned out in front, the gain was almost invisible from the back.

And aside from the occasional wince of discomfort and the trouble she had sleeping, it was impossible to tell from her behaviour either. Rachel had always been so resilient. Nothing ever seemed to faze her; she was a practical, *can do* person. She'd dealt with pregnancy in the same calm way she dealt with everything else, appearing incomprehensibly matter-of-fact all along about carrying a child and, now, about the fact that he would shortly be here. That it would then be our heady responsibility to look after him, care for him, shape him.

But then, unlike me, Rachel probably wasn't worried about that at all. Certainly, if she had to cope with raising the baby on her own, she would do so, and she would do so very capably indeed. This much we'd established over the last few months, as things had become increasingly difficult between us. As we'd grown apart, separating steadily out from the tight unit we'd always been.

She said, 'I can sense you there, you know.'

'You can?'

'Yes. The back of my neck is tickling.'

'You've always been ticklish.'

It was a stupid thing to say, because the exact opposite was true. I was ticklish; she was – annoyingly – totally immune. In happier times, she'd been able to reduce me to a helpless wreck on the floor or the bed – although that level of carefree intimacy was unthinkable now. I was just fumbling for something to say, and the reversal was something that would have brought a smile to her face in the old days, maybe even prompted her to prove me wrong, dinner on the go or not. Tonight, it didn't work at all. The silence that followed was flat and stiff, like I'd tried to embrace her when she didn't want me to.

After a moment, she said, 'What are you thinking?'

'I'm thinking you're beautiful.'

'Are you?'

'Yes. You don't believe me?'

She was still working at the chopping board, her shoulders moving with the knife, so I barely caught the shrug. It hurt when I did. Indifference always seems much worse than outright hostility. At least hostility implies that someone still cares.

She said, 'I don't really know what to think any more.'

'I'm sorry. It's been a rough day.'

'Yeah, I gather. From the paper. You want to talk about it?'

'Not so much.'

She nodded to herself, expecting the answer. I've never been the kind of detective who takes his work home with him. I don't dwell, not normally; as sad as most crimes are, my days are so full of them that I'd go insane if I kept hold of them. A

43

handful stay, of course, but I'm not built to carry much more weight than that, and anyway, what is there to dwell on when it comes down to it? The fact is that things topple and break; in my line of work, it's people and their lives. Most of the time, all you can do is try to sweep up afterwards and move on. What else is there to say? Somebody did something ugly for very dull and mundane reasons. We'll punish them for it if we can, and for all it will ultimately be worth.

The end.

'It is what it is,' I said. 'It is what it always is.'

'It's not really that anyway – how you've been tonight, I mean. It's not like you've been markedly different from any other night.'

That took a moment to settle, and when it did, it hurt even more than the shrug. In my head, I still saw the decline in our relationship over the last year as a blip – a rocky patch we'd weather, coming out stronger together on the far side – and I'd been imagining Rachel felt the same. But there it was: the truth. To her, this had become normal. It wasn't a dip in our life together; it *was* our life together. The way I was every night.

'And how is that?'

'Like you're not really here.'

I didn't reply. It suddenly felt so cold and empty in the kitchen that it seemed a miracle the pan on the hob was still sizzling. As Rachel stirred it, I said:

'I'm sorry.'

She shrugged again, and then, after a moment's silence, she sighed. When she spoke, she threw my own words back at me, but so half-heartedly that they barely reached.

'It is what it is.'

After we'd eaten, Rachel went to bed early.

She tended to have trouble sleeping for useful lengths of time, even lying on her side with the maternity pillow curled around under the bump and then between her legs to support her hips, so she grabbed as much as she could. She was on maternity leave from the laboratory now, so could catch up during the day. In lighter moments, she said her body was just getting in practice for what it would be like when the baby arrived.

I wasn't ready to sleep, so I took a beer on to the small patio out front of our house and listened to the neighbourhood. Tonight, it was quiet. No cars along our road at all, and I couldn't hear any human voices. In the distance somewhere, a dog barked, the noise echoing slightly between the low buildings.

It was grey and flat here: a spread of architectural convenience illuminated only by street lights and the occasional bright yellow windows of occupied houses. The roads were wide; the grass verges neat and buzz-cut. Our house was a police-issue residence on what had formerly been a barracks. Although it hadn't been in use by the military for more than twenty years now, it still retained its bearing.

But then, everywhere does. I remember, as a boy, seeing the huge trucks moving the rockets and aircraft constructed in the steel factories north of the river. The steelworks are still there, but now they put the same smelted pipes and hinges and computer chips into other things instead. Borders, technology, politics, behaviour small and large – looking back through history, all of it's shaped by violence of some kind.

In our region it's even more obvious, because military supplies form the basis of the economy, and half the men you meet over fifty will have seen service of some kind. My father was in the army, until he was invalided out. Everyone lives under the shadow of the last war; it presses us all from behind, nudges at us. Even though we're not at war now, it sometimes still feels like guerilla country – as though the arms are all just pushed under bushes, and everyone's ready to down tools at a moment's notice, pick up their weapons again, return to fighting.

Just looking for an excuse.

A *reason*.

I took a swig of beer.

I should have been thinking about Rachel, and working out some way to bridge the distance that had opened up between us. Before going to bed, she'd reminded me I had material to prepare for the next counselling session. We had to list what we'd loved about each other originally, and the things we loved now. I said I was on top of it, although right now I had no idea what to write, or how it was supposed to help. As if a list could achieve anything.

So I was thinking about the day instead: about Vicki Gibson and the as-yet-unidentified homeless man we'd found. And I couldn't shake what Laura had said.

It doesn't always make sense, Hicks.

It would, though. It had to – because here's the thing: crimes are always totally explicable. I refuse to believe in evil. The act of murder, however apparently heinous, always turns out to be squalid and small and human. There's always a *reason*.

In this case, Vicki Gibson's murder had all the hallmarks of a bedroom crime.

It does help to think of it like a building. You have the boardroom, the bedroom, the bar and the basement. Murder always originates in one of those rooms. *Always*. People kill each other for money; they do it out of jealousy or desire; they get angry and lose control. Every once in a while, a killer has something wrong with him underneath it all – down in the basement – and grows up malformed. But it's always explicable. It comes from somewhere in the building, and buildings are human constructs. That's my architecture anyway, and I'm clinging to it.

No evil. Nothing *weird*.

Glancing across the road, I thought I saw someone standing beside the street light. I made out a woman's face, framed by black hair, with skin that was fish white and bruised, one eye swollen to a slit.

But then a breeze took the figure away again, changing the

way the light had been falling on the bushes behind, which was all it had been.

I took another sip of beer.

Tomorrow, I thought.

Tomorrow we'd nail it.

Seven

Levchenko checks his watch.

It is half past nine in the evening, and he needs to be ready for ten o'clock precisely. Of course, there is no way the client would ever know if the order was completed late, but Levchenko is scrupulously professional about the special work he takes on – God is watching him, after all, even if the client, Edward Enwright, is not.

And so it is time to begin.

He checks the shop is locked, then turns off the light and retreats to the work area in the back room. Along one side are his stoves and benches, scattered with scissors, clipped wicks and opaque plastic cases of various shapes and sizes. Opposite, rickety wooden racks support hundreds of candles: blocks and cylinders, arranged in rainbow rows. There are too many smells in here to count, as though the air is made from pressed flowers.

Levchenko selects a small metal saucepan. It is battered, as though by countless hammer blows, and the base is soot-black from the soft blue flames that have licked at it from the gas burner over too many years to remember. He sits at the bench and clicks the burner on now, then lights it with a crackling match. The smell of the gas mingles with the flower scents; a gentle hissing burr touches his ears.

From below the bench he retrieves a crumpled plastic bag of thin white pellets. Nearly empty. The wax rattles into the pan, then gradually begins to dissolve into something that looks like greasy water. He adds dye with a pipette from the bench, and the liquid turns a beautiful shade of blue. Even after all these years, he is amazed by how magnificently wax takes its colour – so clean and pure. Staring into the steaming pan, he might be looking into a perfect sea or up at a cloudless sky. Not everyday examples, but the ones people see in their imaginations and their dreams.

There is a large clock on the wall, the second hand ticking silently around. It is just after quarter to ten.

Levchenko reaches out and prods a cautious fingertip into the pan.

At first, there is a mild sensation of pain: the initial half-second of burning you would get from boiling water. But wax is a precarious substance; it melts and solidifies over a smaller fulcrum of temperature, and the contrast of his flesh is enough to tilt the liquid touching his skin, so that when he lifts his finger out a moment later, the tip is covered in a soft blue case. Should he so desire, he could make himself the most brittle of gloves.

It is nearly ready.

He unrolls the wax from his finger and brushes away the rubbery scraps that cling. Then he stands up and ponders the candles on the racks behind him, finally selecting a tall white one – a cylinder. Back at the bench, he uses a nub of putty to stick the candle to the base of a small circular metal dish, using just enough to hold it upright.

There is a cracked porcelain sink in the workshop. Levchenko fills an old plastic washing up bowl with ice-cold, frothing water to a depth of about eight inches. Then he places the bowl carefully on the bench beside the gas burner, allowing the rolling water to settle.

Five to ten.

He eyes the clock as the remaining minutes pass.

With one minute to spare, Levchenko clicks off the heat and wraps a towel round the bare metal handle of the pan in order to lift it safely from the hob. Lost in his work, he sniffs loudly, up through one nostril, then pours the melted blue wax into the dish around the white candle. It stands, now, like a miniature lighthouse in the middle of a still sea.

The second hand ticks slowly round.

At ten o'clock precisely, he picks up the dish and plunges it down into the bowl of cold water, all the way to the bottom.

Liquid meets liquid. The wax splays upwards from the dish into the water around it – but cools so quickly that it solidifies almost as it escapes. It is too swift for the naked eye to catch, resembling a frozen explosion rather than a bloom. In less than half a second it is already done, but Levchenko leaves the candle underwater for seconds longer before lifting it back out and placing the dish down on the bench.

Is it satisfactory?

It is.

The original white candle still stands upright – thick and firm. But the pool of blue wax has leapt up in unpredictable swirls around it. The colours are paled and mottled; the wax is as thin and delicate as petals. And yes, it *does* look a little like a flower. But it reminds Levchenko more of the sky, the perfect blue slightly hazy now and the pure white centre the colour of childhood clouds.

The sky – he always think there is something fitting about that. After all, the weather appears random and chaotic, with small initial changes producing unpredictable and complex patterns, so much so that weather reports are only vaguely reliable for a few days at best. We cannot predict them, and yet it is only the laws of physics in action. It is all set. The world simply unfolds: a carpet that nobody has ever seen but which is already entirely made. Clouds are only one pattern upon its surface.

The same is true of his flowered candle. If you knew the exact starting conditions of every atom in the workshop – in the wax and the water; in his arms and his brain – if you could track their movements and make the impossibly numerous calculations, you could know in advance where the wax would move, how it would cool. Where each brittle pale blue tip would finish.

Levchenko leans on either side of the candle and peers down at it.

The truth is that you can know none of those things. God, perhaps, can know them, but no man. Even the act of observing the atoms and particles, it is said, can alter their course. So this candle, with its beautiful spread of wax petals, is as close to random as possible. Each one is totally unique, cast in and of its moment. A second later, and it would have been different. That is what makes them special.

Beyond the randomness, there is also the practical matter of construction. Levchenko knows from experience that customers often look at these special candles and wonder how exactly they were made. They are puzzled because, in their own experiences of the world, candles must be formed with moulds rather than by the eddies of chance.

That is the appeal of these, after all.

DAY TWO

Eight

'Extraordinary,' I said.

Laura just grunted in reply, but I knew she agreed with me.

We were both in early, working through the vast swathes of witness reports that had been collected by the door team yesterday. Anything out of the ordinary was usually flagged up for immediate attention, but Laura and I were both of a mind that details could easily be missed and preferred to scan as much as possible ourselves.

So we'd been sitting in relative silence in the small office we share, heads bowed over documents. The only sounds were the whirring ceiling fan, the occasional sniff from one of us, and the constant turning-over of pages. The coffees in front of us trailed steam into the air.

'Nothing,' I said.

'No.'

'Nothing.'

'You said that already.'

'Did I? Perhaps I can't believe my eyes.'

There are a number of ways to proceed with an investigation like this. One of them is forensics. The post-mortems would be performed first thing; in the meantime, everything else was either being analysed or waiting to be. In reality, forensic results tend to be of most use when you have a suspect to test them against. Unless someone with a criminal record sticks their fingerprint on a victim's forehead, forensics leaves you with a shadow but no body to cast it. A good clear outline, for sure, but only really useful when you have someone to compare with the shape.

Another way is by looking at the victim's past. Leaving aside our as-yet-unidentified second victim, how had Vicki Gibson found herself in her killer's sights? She hadn't been robbed. She hadn't been sexually assaulted. Perhaps someone hated her for some reason we'd yet to ascertain. The clearest candidate for that position – still kicking his heels in a cell downstairs – looked to be in the clear.

The third way – as old-fashioned as it gets – is witness statements. It's actually very hard to commit a crime in public without being caught *somehow*. CCTV is rare in the grids, but it is a highly populated area and Vicki Gibson had been murdered in plain sight of several windows.

All the people who might have been looking out of those windows had been interviewed, and yet, according to the reports in front of us, nobody had seen anything.

Laura picked up her coffee and took a sip.

'It's not so unusual,' she said. 'It's the nature of the area. People often turn a blind eye in the grids. We both know that from bitter bloody experience.'

'Not so much on the outskirts.' The central areas were full of illegal people, illegal trades, and people who were notoriously reluctant to talk to the police. 'And that's almost always drug-related. I don't see this as that sort of attack, do you?'

Laura shrugged. 'Not on the surface. But you never know.'

'She had two decent jobs under her belt.'

'Exactly. We know she needed the money. So it could be drug- or debt-related.'

I thought about that. It was a possibility. Take a loan from the wrong people and it wasn't unlikely you'd meet with reprisals if you failed to repay. Anyone who saw the murder would probably decide there were far better things to do than get involved by talking to us about it, like absolutely anything at all.

A boardroom crime.

'Okay,' I said. 'We can look into that. Who are the street merchants in that area? I don't know off the top of my head.'

'Me neither.'

'I don't know if I buy it though.'

Laura sighed. 'Me neither.'

'And it wouldn't explain our second victim, would it?'

'No. Unless he wandered past, drunk, and the killer followed him to make sure he hadn't seen anything.'

'That's a theory?'

'Sort of.'

'It's weak as a kitten, that one.'

She sighed again. 'I know.'

I picked up my own coffee, and we sat in silence again for a few moments. Nobody looking out of their windows. Apparently nobody around on the street at the time. I didn't buy the debt idea, but there had to be some explanation for it.

There was a rap at the door. An officer opened it immediately without waiting to be invited.

'Do not disturb!' I shouted.

'Sorry, sir.'

'We were deep in conversation there. *Deep.*'

Laura gave me a withering look.

'Shut up, Hicks,' she said. 'What is it?'

'Simon Duncan's downstairs. He wants to know whether either of you is attending the post-mortems?'

Laura looked at me. I held my palm out.

'Not me,' I said.

'All right, I'll go.' She stood up. 'What are your plans in my absence, then? Going to sit there and pout?'

'Nope,' I said. 'Troll East. Try to identify our homeless victim.'

'Lovely.'

'It's a dirty job but someone's got to do it.'

Laura gave me a half-smile as she headed to the door. Compared to Troll East, the autopsy was the easy option.

'Might as well be you, then, eh?' she said.

Nine

Our city has an underground system with six stops. It runs for several miles below the southern half of the city, under the picturesque old town and business sectors, basically tracing the curl of the river, and is used primarily by tourists and professional sorts. You can travel the entire juddering, clacking line in about twenty minutes. The trains move fast enough between stations that you wouldn't notice the open pipes and passageways you're passing. Tunnels under the earth that aren't entirely as abandoned as you might imagine.

The underground was originally planned to have eight stations, but due to budget miscalculations – or, more cynically, budget misappropriations – only six were ever completed. So there are two unfinished stations, one at either end, and they aren't abandoned either. They're the first official stops on the city below the city: one to the east and one to the west.

Because our second victim had been found much closer to the east, that was where I was heading.

The rush hour slowed me down, but I reached the dead station before nine. All that remained of the original building was a black door with a rusted chain hanging across the centre and a red circle daubed on at head height. A much grander entrance had been absorbed by the shops to either side, which were typical of the area: shuttered off-licences, bookies, a drab post office. Bin bags clustered against the walls, huddled together for warmth. There were more pigeons around right now than people, most of them pecking inexplicably at dirty stretches of pavement.

I drove a little further on, then parked up on a road close to the river and walked down to the water. From here, I could see all the way across to the northern bank, to the empty bays where we'd found the second victim. There were no boats in sight today, just the white crosses of gulls turning lazily over the river. I doubled back on myself to find the large circular tunnel leading down under the road above and into the depths of the earth. It was half grilled over, the fractured side ending in hundreds of tiny rusted fingers.

I kept my gun clipped in its holster, but took out a Maglite torch, clicking it on as I eased around the broken grille and stepped into the tunnel.

It wasn't silent inside, but there was an immediate and pro-found change to the quality of sound. The world felt compacted; existence had shrunk its parameters to the seven-foot-diameter pipe I began walking down, feeling as much as hearing the insistent hiss of pressure in the air. The pipe was built from enormous arching stone blocks, all thick with green lichen and damp. The torch cast meagre light, only ever revealing a few metres ahead, and I kept it mostly on my footing. Beneath my feet, the dank stone ground was strewn with a thatch of twigs and branches that had blown down here from the river. As I walked, the heavy hush of underground air was complemented by the steady drip of water, and the air grew colder.

After a time, the tunnel reached a larger space: a square room with pipes curling from one wall and then disappearing into the ground, as though they'd poked their heads out and immediately burrowed down out of sight. In another corner, the water was dripping down more profusely, landing on a slumped pile of pale, congealed slime. Puddles of stagnant water sat in pits in the stone floor. The room smelled of mulch and rotting vegetation, like a breeze drifting through an abandoned vegetable stall.

At the far end, a doorway led into something that more

approximated a normal corridor: perhaps it had once connected maintenance areas around the station. That was the way to go – I'd been here before.

Barely a minute later, my torch caught movement up ahead and then a torch belonging to someone else was shining in my face.

I held my forearm over my eyes.

'Ow.'

A voice boomed out, jovial and theatrical: 'Who goes there?'

'Police,' I said. 'Get that light out of my eyes. I'm not looking for trouble.'

'Okey-dokey.'

The torch beam immediately dropped down to the ground, and a figure up ahead approached.

The splay of light revealed a large man, with a barrel of a body that seemed to be made primarily from rags. He was bearded, with wild black hair and a red face, and smiling like a loon.

'What can I do for you, Officer?'

'I'm looking for someone,' I said.

'I can possibly help you with that.'

The *possibly* was to be expected, of course. The people down here had nothing to gain by annoying the police, but that didn't mean they'd openly co-operate if it meant selling out one of their own.

'This particular person is not alive any more,' I said.

'That doesn't mean they're not here!' His voice echoed in the enclosed space. 'We're full of ghosts, Officer. You know that. That's all some people down here ever talk to.'

'He may be one of yours,' I said. 'We found him upside and need to identify him.'

'Description?'

'Not so much. But I've got these.'

I took out some photographs of the clothes and items we'd found on the second victim. A lot of them were generic, but I held out some hope for a necklace we'd found, wrapped away beneath his clothes. There was an old wedding ring on it.

The man took them one by one with gnarled fingers wrapped in wool gloves, shining his torch over each of them before passing them back. He paused at the ring.

'Yeah,' he said. 'He's passed by, on and off, for years. Jesus nut. That's all I know. Don't know his name, but someone will.'

'All right. Can I . . . ?'

'Go in?' He moved to one side and shouted: '*Be my guest!*'

I walked a little way on, him following behind, muttering to himself. After a minute, he stepped into an alcove where a three-seater settee had been lodged, next to a packing crate with a candle burning. A battered old paperback was lying splayed out on the settee, and a sleeping bag was rolled up neatly at one end.

A little further on, I reached what had once been intended to become Foxton underground station. It was an echoing hexagonal space, every surface tiled, every wall filled with empty poster grids. Where the ticket machines should have been, there were racks of bunk beds. Graffiti covered the walls. There were a handful of rusted metal barrels that in winter would be full of burning wood, but now they were dark and dead. Everything was bathed in amber light from the countless candles.

People everywhere: hunched shadows, either slumped in place or meandering around erratically. There were also a number of corridors running off the central area. Doors that might once have been labelled 'No Entry' were now propped open with large chunks of rock. Every conceivable space down here had been colonised. Along all the corridors, I knew, there were fenced-off sleeping areas. Televisions flickered in the darkness, powered by the electrics that had been developed down here: snaking rubber cables that connected junction boxes and ended, occasionally, in rubber plugs in archaic boxes in the walls. There were toilets and shower stalls.

I worked my way through, showing my photos here and

there to people whose faces I couldn't see. Despite what the watchman had said, all I got was shakes of the head and shrugs.

I was beginning to despair slightly until I wandered down a stationary escalator and found a small church. It had been built in a storage area below one of the railway arches. Two metal bins were burning brightly on either side of the entrance, the flames crackling, the metal as thin and fragile as charred paper.

I peered inside. A number of benches had been arranged roughly in lines, and hooded figures were dotted here and there, elbows on knees, heads bowed, facing a wooden table at the far end. The stone wall above it was daubed with various religious symbols. The air was hot in here, and perhaps because of the silence of its small congregation, the room felt as though it was waiting for something – some boom or clank from the bowels of the surrounding tunnels.

A Jesus nut, the guard had said.

If anyone would know our John Doe, it was someone here.

I approached a man at the back of the room. He was dressed in jeans and an old black hoodie, but it was easy to tell he was fat and saggy beneath it.

'Police,' I said. 'I'm trying to identify someone. You recognise any of these belongings?'

I was already holding out the photographs when he looked up at me, revealing a bearded face mottled with red veins, and eyeballs as yellow as butter. Greasy flecks of black hair poked out from beneath the hood like spider legs. I recoiled slightly. He stared up at me, and his bleary eyes seemed to focus.

'Do I know you?' he said.

'No.'

The man shook his head, confused. 'You put me away once?'

'Not that I remember,' I said.

He stared at me for a few seconds longer, still trying to work out whether I was a real figure from his past or just a stranger overlaid with a ghost. Then he looked down at the photograph I was holding, which showed the wedding ring on the necklace.

He nodded slowly to himself.

'Yeah, I know him.'

'Okay,' I said.

I waited some more, but he didn't volunteer anything.

'And?' I said. 'What about a name?'

'Fifty.'

'That's a weird name. Parents are cruel, right?'

'I meant—'

'I know what you meant.'

I looked around. Just outside the entrance, the flames were crackling louder than before. I had that same impression that something was waiting down here in the shadows. The pressure felt like it had gone up a notch. I wanted out of here; my forehead was suddenly damp. But instead, I reached into my back pocket for my wallet, and tried to smile.

'You do receipts?'

Ten

'Derek Evans,' I said.

Laura glanced up as I walked triumphantly back into the office. I didn't know how long she'd been back from the post-mortems, but she still looked a little pale. Still managed to whip out the sarcasm, though.

'You've got the wrong office then. This is Laura Fellowes and some jerk called Hicks.'

'Lame.' I closed the door behind me. 'That's the name of our John Doe. Derek Evans.'

'Okay.'

She began typing. As she pulled the name from our files, I told her what I'd found out in Troll East.

According to the guy I'd spoken to, Evans was somewhere in his fifties and had been a squaddie when he was younger. After leaving the service, he'd wandered for a bit, never landed fully on his feet. Dragged a troubled history underground with him and found some kind of god to help salve it with. He was a big guy that nobody messed with.

'Nothing on the files for him.'

'No convictions,' I said. There were a dozen other databases we could check. Evans was bound to show up somewhere, especially having served. And despite my unease about the man I'd spoken to in the tunnels, the details all fitted. 'He hadn't been seen around for a few days, but that's not unusual. Evans liked the open air, apparently – liked to sleep outside when the weather was good enough. So that seems right.'

Laura nodded.

'Where does this leave us?'

'We'll need to check for connections to Vicki Gibson. Seems unlikely, but you never know. What did we get from the post-mortems? You still look a bit green, by the way.'

'Mmm. I think you got the better deal after all.'

'Glad to hear it.'

She told me what the autopsies had revealed, although a lot of the information remained provisional and tests still needed to be run. The upshot so far was that Dale was convinced the same weapon had been used in both attacks – or, at least, the same type of weapon.

'A hammer, he guesses.'

'That fits.'

'Time of death is also roughly what we were expecting. Sometime between two and three in the morning, although it's hard to be totally sure. He can't say what order they were killed in. Well, not from that, anyway.'

I frowned. 'Not from that. Explain.'

'There're two things. The first is the ferocity of the attacks. It's not conclusive, but a lot more damage was meted out on Evans. That might indicate that after Gibson, the killer wasn't . . .' she grimaced, '*spent*.'

'Nice.'

'That's Dale's choice of words.'

'Dale needs to see a psychiatrist,' I said. It didn't seem all that conclusive to me, not necessarily. 'What's the other thing?'

'The other thing is what makes it almost certain that we're dealing with the same killer. Dale found traces of polythene in both bodies.'

'*Polythene?*'

'*Traces* of it,' she said. 'In their wounds, to be precise. And there was much more of it in Evans's skull than in Gibson's.'

She let that sink in.

'A carrier bag?' I said.

Laura nodded. 'That's Dale's guess. Still to be confirmed. But it looks like the hammer was in a bag when the killer hit the victims with it. It must have got slightly damaged while he used it on Gibson, so he left a lot more behind during the assault on Evans.'

I blew out slowly.

The horror of it was one thing – the imagery it conjured up – but I tried to concentrate on what it meant. Had the killer been attempting not to leave evidence behind? That didn't make much sense.

'He wanted to keep the weapon clean?'

'Could be,' Laura said. 'Or else he wanted to carry it around without arousing suspicion. Beforehand, obviously. Not much chance of that afterwards, I'm guessing.'

'Unless he turned the bag inside out.'

Laura grimaced again. 'You have a sick mind, Hicks. But that's also true. The river search has turned up lots of old bags, so that'll keep us busy. I've also ramped up the search of bins in the vicinity. It's possible he abandoned the bag when he was done with it, especially if it had ripped that badly.'

'Maybe.'

I didn't think we'd get that lucky, though. I leaned back in my chair, thinking it all over. Our killer had come prepared to attack Vicki Gibson; he'd been successful enough in that – but then he'd wandered a reasonably short distance, found Evans asleep on a bench, and killed him too, even more viciously.

I said, 'We need to find the connection between them.'

'If there is one.'

'There must be something. If not, it means we've got a guy who attacks people at random. And that doesn't make any sense to me. None. At. All.'

'Maybe not entirely at random,' Laura said.

'What do you mean?'

She sighed, then gestured vaguely at the piles of paperwork on the desk. The witness reports – the interviews that had got us nowhere because, for some inexplicable reason, nobody had seen anything at all.

'Explain?'

'Maybe she was just the first available person, and Evans the second.'

I looked at the statements. And thought about it. A killer carrying his hammer out of sight in a carrier bag. Just wandering. Innocuous. Someone who didn't stand out.

Laura said, 'We were wondering how he'd managed to catch Vicki Gibson at a time when nobody was around and nobody was looking. But maybe that's not what happened at all.'

'He didn't find her deliberately,' I said. 'He just happened to be in a place without witnesses when they crossed paths.'

Laura nodded. 'I think that's what might have happened.'

'That would mean it could have been . . .'

'Anyone,' she said. 'Yes. I think it could have been anyone. Anyone at all.'

Eleven

Kramer's heart is thumping hard as he walks.

His breath clouds in front of him. The night is cold, the sky overhead clear of clouds. You can't usually see the stars here in the city, not with the light pollution, but a few have prickled through. The moon is bright and full, a worn silver coin hanging over the city.

He shivers as he walks, his teeth chattering.

It's partly the cold, but most of it's adrenalin.

That's okay. When he first started working the doors, Trevor told him it was natural to be scared. Everybody is scared of physical confrontation. On the door, you have to hide it, but only on the surface, only ever from your opponent. If you hide the fear from yourself, it fucks you over, but if you're canny you can use the adrenalin. That's what gives you the edge.

Ideally, though, he wants to dampen it down a little before he reaches his destination, so he rolls saliva around in his mouth. That's another piece of advice Trevor gave him: control the fear by rolling spit. It works too, although he doesn't know why.

So he walks, trying to stay calm but ready. Trying to keep everything coiled up for when he needs it.

Not far now. Not long.

Kramer checks the carrier bag he's holding. If there was anyone around, to all appearances it would just look full of laundry. That will be his immediate explanation if he's stopped by the police. It's unlikely they'll search the bag. If that happens, he's in deep shit. Hidden beneath the clothes, there's a ten-inch double-bladed machete, a luminous-green water pistol full of ammonia, and a hammer.

Not that he's spotted any police so far, mind, and he doesn't really expect to round here. So he won't see those items again until he reaches the house he's heading to, on the edge of the Fairfield estate.

Kramer leaves the main street and heads down a ginnel, lined on either side with tall wooden fences. It's the quickest cut-through. A few bends and he'll be out on to the edge of the waste ground, then just across to the estate beyond. He's been there before, from time to time, calling up debts. It's certainly the place for them: a maze of grey one-storey blocks, with lots of little alleyways in between; all feral kids, barking dogs, and bins lying in the middle of the streets. The whole place is one big fucking debt.

He doesn't think too much about what he's going to do when he gets there. It's pointless to get ahead of yourself. Knock on the door. When it opens – or if it doesn't, kick the fucking thing off its hinges – go in. A faceful of ammonia to put anyone down, then it'll be hammer in one hand, machete in the other. That's as far as he's thinking, because when you get hung up on a plan, you get strung out when the plan goes wrong. He's seen it with traditional martial artists on the door. In the dojo it's all straight lines, but there aren't any straight lines when you're rolling around on the fucking pavement. You need to adapt.

But he knows this: a message needs to be sent.

The first time it happened on the doors, it was some dealers trying to muscle their way in, figuring they were fifteen strong and the door team were five. Trevor explained to Kramer what would happen and asked whether he was cool with it, and Kramer said he was. They picked out the main guy and, the next morning, staged a little home invasion: smashed his knees and elbows with a hammer and put the machete up his arse. He didn't die. Didn't tell the police either. But most importantly, he didn't turn up at the club again. None of them did.

The difference tonight is he's doing it alone. But that's okay – and even if it wasn't, it's the way it needs to be, because the slight was personal: the black bodybuilder, Connor, mugging him off in front of everyone last night. Making threats, fancying himself. Kramer isn't the biggest guy, and probably looks like an easy mark to make for a guy on the up. Of course, anyone who's anyone knows Kramer behaves badly out of hours. Maybe Connor has been told since, as he didn't turn up at the club tonight. But that isn't good enough.

All it took was a few discreet enquiries to find the guy's address.

He steps out of the end of the ginnel.

It's four in the morning, so the wasteland looks deserted. The ground is pale and dead-looking; what isn't open is just patches of shivery grass and larger clumps of night-black bushes. Even a dumping ground like the estate needs one of its own. The wasteland is the kind of place you find burnt-out cars and illegally tipped rubbish – piles of counterfeit CD cases and ragged bags of old torn clothes. Kramer picks his way carefully along one of the makeshift paths that leads across its heart. He can see the sprawl of the estate in the background, the houses as dull grey and dead as teeth in the dark.

His breath still fogs, but he can hardly see it now. His trainers crunch softly on the gravel and dirt. At his side, the bag rustles.

Kramer follows the path through a cluster of bushes. Up close, the leaves are almost invisible in the darkness. The branches are skeletal. In front of him, it's difficult to see—

He stops.

There is someone a little way ahead of him.

He starts swirling the saliva around his mouth again. The figure is about ten metres away, but it's impossible to make out any details. Not big, not small. Little more than a silhouette of a human being against a silhouette of bushes.

But facing him. And standing very still.

For a moment, Kramer does the same. Neither of them moves.

Then the figure turns around and walks away, disappearing off to the side, round the back of the bushes.

Kramer remains standing in place, but a few seconds later, relief floods him, and he almost laughs at himself. It was just someone doing the same thing as him – taking a short cut across the waste ground, coming the opposite way. The guy saw Kramer, froze up, and decided it was sensible to back off and go a different way.

Obviously he doesn't look like someone to mess with. What's that saying? *Wouldn't want to meet him down a dark alley*. That's what the guy is probably thinking about him right now.

Kramer shakes his head and starts walking again, slightly annoyed. Despite the fact that nothing really happened, the encounter has given the adrenalin a little kick and brought it to life: started it working before he wants it to. He feels invincible right now, but that's—

He stops again.

Someone *else* is standing there, backed into the bushes where the stranger was. Kramer can see the red glow of a cigarette in the darkness.

Two guys meeting up out here? Well, there's certainly an explanation for that. Not one he cares for exactly, but not one he's scared of either. He'll just walk past – he starts doing so – and ignore the man . . .

But it's not a cigarette, he realises. The light from it doesn't fluctuate. Doesn't change.

As he reaches the spot, Kramer peers into the bush and sees the red LED light burning small and intense between the leaves. Then the black circle of a lens. A camera, pointing into the bush on the opposite side of the path.

He turns.

There's a small clearing. There is a chance – briefly – to see the woman lying on her back there, and to see there is something *wrong* with her. To realise, just, that she is far too still and that her face isn't where it should be.

But there is not time to put all the facts together in his head and make sense of what is happening. Because right then, he hears the quick, heartbeat punch of feet in the gravel behind him, and the whipping, wing-like sound of polythene cracking the night-time air.

And then nothing.

DAY THREE

Twelve

The next morning felt colder than it should, even though the sun was as bright and warm as it had been when I'd driven up Mulberry Avenue two days earlier, listening to Carla Gibson's screams.

Nobody was screaming here on the wasteland. It felt like a pocket of silence: the eye of a storm, maybe. We'd set up a perimeter around the entire waste ground and a couple of the surrounding streets on the Garth estate – nobody in or out that didn't need to be – so the area was still, disturbed only by the quiet, diligent work of the SOCOs as they moved between the bushes. But it also felt like there was a cold presence here, one that chilled the air simply by preventing the sunlight reaching the ground.

Ridiculous, of course.

But it felt that way all the same.

'Our guy,' Laura said.

'Yes.'

We were standing at the end of one of the paths that snaked across the waste ground. Next to it there was a tiny clearing, surrounded on three sides by prickly bushes, and just large enough for the three bodies we'd found, lying side by side. They had been laid out as if sleeping peacefully next to each other. They couldn't have died peacefully; their killer must have arranged them the way they were for some reason.

I glanced around, and then overhead. No tents had been

erected so far. They'd be tough to construct in the undergrowth, but we'd need them shortly. It wouldn't be long before the news 'copters started circling overhead – searching for a shot that would be of no use to them anyway, one that they would have to blur extensively if they even used it at all.

What would they see? Two women and one man – although from high above, that might not immediately be obvious. You would be able to tell they were fully clothed, but above the neck there would be nothing but red smudges staining the dirt. You would be able to tell that something awful had happened to them, but it wouldn't prepare you for what you'd see where Laura and I were, standing on the path itself and staring down at what was left of their faces and heads.

Beyond the bushes, residents of the estate would be lined up against the cordon, craning their necks, trying to see. They'd been there when we arrived; they'd still be there now. They weren't the types to be dissuaded by the police. Clusters of kids in too-small tracksuits stretched over thin shoulders, smoking roll-ups, strolling here and there. Older people remonstrating, wanting to know who we'd found – whether any of the bodies belonged to one of theirs. Getting the same answer each time: *we can't say right now.*

Not least because we couldn't tell.

Laura said, 'Trying to show us how powerful he is?'

'What?'

'Come back to earth, Hicks. The way's he's left them.'

'Yeah, maybe.' I looked at the three bodies, lying side by side, as though they'd all lain down there and gone to sleep, and he'd killed each in turn without waking the others. As though it had been easy for him. 'He's made it look like he could kill three people without any resistance at all. Without them managing to fight back.'

I shook my head.

'But?' Laura said.

'But they couldn't have died like that. And he couldn't have killed them all at once.'

'Unless it's more than one killer.'

'It's not.'

'We can't say that for sure.'

I didn't reply. It was possible, but it didn't make sense. It was rare – practically unheard of, in fact – for two people capable of this kind of horrific violence to find each other and work together. Not impossible, but . . . no. It was one person and we were missing something.

Come back to earth, Hicks.

It was difficult, though; my head was all over the place. Under normal circumstances – or as normal as it ever gets – I'd have been on top of things, but this was quickly moving far out the other side of normal, and it was unnerving me. The cold and the quiet were getting to me, when I wouldn't normally have paid any attention to them, and certainly wouldn't have put any stock by them even if I'd noticed. I wasn't superstitious. Things didn't get *weird* for me.

And yet . . . this whole case felt different.

'Hicks?'

'Okay,' I said. 'Possibly more than one killer. But that would be unlikely, wouldn't it? The probability is that it's one guy, working alone.'

'Go on then, Sherlock.'

I glanced to either side, up and down the path, still feeling the atmosphere of the place. The waste ground had already been dead and barren, and somehow he'd left it feeling even more so . . .

Already dead and barren.

'All right,' I said. 'So this could be the same as the Gibson scene – what we were saying about it yesterday. It's not the victims themselves, it's the place. He picked an isolated place and waited.'

'Somewhere he wouldn't be disturbed.'

'No,' I said. 'Somewhere he'd be disturbed just often enough.'

Laura was silent. It was a horrible idea, of course, but it felt right. I looked up and down the path again. *Yes.* I was sure of it. Our guy had waited here during the early hours of the morning and killed people as they came along. Ambushed them – struck out at random. Just allowed . . . what, fate? Fate to choose his victims for him.

I remembered what Laura had said yesterday.

'It could have been anyone,' I said.

Laura glanced overhead.

'No helicopters,' she said. 'Won't be long, though. We need to get the tents up.'

I nodded absently. Still thinking.

'That's why they're arranged the way they are,' I said. 'He's not showing off to us, or at least that's not all he's doing. He just put the bodies in there to keep them off the path. And he lined them up the best way to leave space for the next.'

'Christ,' Laura said.

I stared at the bodies, neatly filling the alcove.

'And maybe that,' I said, 'is the only reason he stopped at three.'

Thirteen

We held the early-afternoon briefing in the largest operation room on the first floor of the department. There were white-boards and projectors, twenty desks, room for rows of seats. Laura and I had also moved down there. Young had relieved us of extraneous cases; we would work from desks in here for the foreseeable future. He had also granted us ten extra sergeants, and them as many officers from the grunt pool as they wanted. As of today, this case was the department's number-one priority.

Because we had a serial killer.

We waited for the room to settle, and then Laura led the briefing.

'As of today,' she told the assembled officers, holding out a splayed hand, 'we are working on the assumption that we have *five* victims. Vicki Gibson and Derek Evans were killed two nights ago.'

She gestured at one of the whiteboards, where photographs were pinned along the top. We had a former photo of Vicki Gibson, but not Evans. The crime-scene photos for both were pinned below, standing out stark red against the white background.

'Details are below the photos, and on the information we've circulated, which you'll all be familiar with by now.'

I watched the room as she spoke. Many of the officers were making notes. That was good: I wanted everyone one hundred per cent intent, everyone alert. I also wanted *ideas*. I still had the same feeling I'd had back on the waste ground. A kind of dazed, sleepy feeling, but somehow also on edge. As though at some point I was going to start shaking slightly.

'As you'll be aware,' Laura said, 'this morning three further victims were discovered on waste ground beside the Garth estate. The first is believed to be Sandra Peacock, a working girl from the estate. The second is John Kramer, a door supervisor from the Foxton area; we'll come back to him in a moment. The third victim is yet to be identified.'

She moved to the projector and then clicked through a series of photographs: hideous shots from the crime scene. I kept my expression implacable, but heard a few half-suppressed gasps from around the room. For many of them, this was their first encounter with the extent of the violence close up. The victims' heads had almost literally been smashed to pieces.

'Injuries are consistent with those inflicted on Gibson and Evans. The likely weapon is a standard hand-held hammer. As you can see, the victims have been struck so many times that their features have been obliterated.'

She flicked through most of the photos quickly, but paused on the final one, which showed the carrier bag believed to have belonged to John Kramer. Inside, hidden beneath tangles of tatty old clothes, we had discovered a machete, a hammer, ammonia and a ski mask.

'As of this moment,' Laura said, 'we have no explanation for these items being in John Kramer's possession. One of you will be following that up, but in the meantime, it's important we separate them out. None of the weapons were used in this attack. As far as we can tell, the killer didn't even look beneath the clothes.'

A hand shot up: a male officer at the front.

'Shout out,' Laura told him. 'This isn't a schoolroom.'

'The blood on the clothes?'

'Yes. As you can see, there is a substantial amount of blood on the clothes Kramer brought with him in the bag. We believe – though again, this has yet to be confirmed – that the blood belongs to one or more of the victims. We believe the killer used the clothes to clean his own weapon following the murders.'

The same officer: 'You say he didn't look in the bag. So no robbery at all?'

'Nope. Not only does robbery not appear to be our killer's motive, he doesn't seem to even consider it. As far as we can tell, nothing has been taken from any of the scenes. By that, I mean we've uncovered several valuables in addition to the weapons believed to belong to John Kramer.'

'Do we have any motive at all?' A different officer – a female sergeant.

'Not yet. Detective Hicks may have more to say about that, but so far there is no obvious connection between any of the victims. No real similarities in their profiles. What's most important is the locations of the murders.'

Laura explained our working theory that the killer had chosen isolated locations rather than specific victims. She didn't need to spell out the implications of that – that our man didn't want to kill anyone in particular; he just wanted to kill, and it didn't seem to matter to him who his victims were.

So what are you getting out of it? I wondered.

Laura said, 'If you don't know the Garth estate, it's in the north-west of the city, approximately eight miles from the grids, the location of the first incident. Here.'

This time she gestured towards the enormous map of the entire city that was stuck to another of the whiteboards. We had a number of locations pinned, but most obvious were the three red markers over the murder sites we'd found.

'Normally at this point, with five victims, we'd have five big red crosses and be able to think about triangulating a working area that our killer is operating in. As things stand, as you can see, we have three points, two of them very close together. Which isn't helpful.'

An understatement, and the people in the room knew it. Our killer had attacked men and women, across a range of ages and social classes, at three separate locations. With no obvious connection between the victims, location was key – and yet there was no way of looking at the map and having the slightest idea where he might strike next.

Only that, most likely, he would.

Laura glanced over at me, and I took that as my cue. I slid off the desk I'd been perched on and stood up to address the room.

'All right,' I said. 'What we are dealing with here is a serial killer. And actually, it's worse than that. Because we're also dealing with a mass murderer. You all know the difference, right?'

A few of them nodded. It was a small distinction, but an important one. Serial killers usually take individual victims – at most, families – over the course of a number of separate incidents, whereas mass murderers kill multiple victims at a single time. It's important because the two tend to have very different psychologies underlying them. Serial killers, for example, are almost always sexually motivated, and they usually keep killing, gradually escalating their attacks until they get caught or life intervenes in some way. Mass murderers – school shooters, for example – generally combust in a single incident, often taking their own lives to avoid an inevitable capture.

Serial killers have *types*. In most cases, there is something about the victim that makes the act meaningful for the killer. Multiple murderers open fire indiscriminately, but don't take as much care to get away. One is slow-burning. One is a flare.

I said, 'What we're dealing with here appears to have elements of both. There have been similar instances in the past – spree killers, to an extent – but I've never heard of someone doing this. Our perp displays the kind of pathology and violence consistent with a psychologically malformed serial killer. But he kills multiple, apparently unconnected victims in bursts.'

I let that one sink in around the room, ignoring the thought that pressed inside my head.

And that doesn't make any sense.

After an uncomfortable couple of seconds, the female officer who'd spoken before spoke again.

'So how can we get this guy?'

I nodded. It was an entirely reasonable question to which I didn't, as of right now, have an answer.

'We've got a number of strategies to work with. We've already looked at door-to-doors in the grids, and we got nothing from them. Those are ongoing in the Garth area as well. Perhaps we'll get something from there instead. But even if we don't, let's not lose sight of the fact he picked these places for a reason. He knew they were isolated enough for his purposes. Even if they seem unrelated, they aren't.'

It was something small to cling to. The killer had some connection, however oblique, to the places he'd chosen so far. If he'd had a GPS device fitted that recorded his every movement, the data would show that at some point in the past he had been to those places for some reason. His movements formed an unbroken ribbon through history, and at some point that ribbon had touched the grids and the Garth estate. For now, those might be the only two pieces of the ribbon we could see, but as the investigation progressed, we would start to fill in more. We would begin to get a clearer picture of the man that ribbon represented.

That was the hope, anyway.

'Aside from that,' I said, 'we'll have to see what the forensics turn up. We also need to identify the third victim. My hunch is that asking around the estate, giving some information on her clothing, will get us an ID before too long. Chances are she's local.'

A third officer, a man, said, 'Interviewing all the families?'

'And friends and associates. Like Detective Fellowes said, everything so far points to these victims being randomly targeted. But that isn't necessarily the case. Perhaps – and we're stretching here – perhaps last night he only intended to kill the first woman, and the other two just happened on the scene and he felt he had to take care of them too. Or perhaps there is some connection between all the victims.'

There were a few blank looks at that. Understandably – but

again, it was *possible*. Regardless, as unlikely as it might be, it was a more comfortable proposition than the alternative: that the killer had casually waited there all night with bodies cooling beside him in the bushes. Squeezing as much fun as he could from his night's work.

Back to earth, Hicks.

'All right,' I said. 'You've all got the files. If you haven't familiarised yourselves, then do. In the meantime, let's run through tasks and who's doing what.'

But that feeling remained with me as I handed out the assignments: the sensation that these weren't normal murders. That even though they had to fit into my architecture of crime, somehow they did not. That there was something . . . *different* about them. Something I didn't want to believe was possible.

Something weird.

Something evil.

Half an hour later, most of the sergeants had dispersed to deal with the jobs they'd been allocated. A couple remained, stationed at desks on the far side of the room, co-ordinating their actions from here for the moment.

I'd worked major operations before, as a sergeant, and more recently as a detective, and it's always the same. A large, echoing room that officers drift in and out of, picking up actions or dropping off reports. Phones ringing constantly. People talking quietly behind small partitions. Despite the nature of the underlying investigation, a major incident room often has a weirdly positive feel to it. It's the energy; it rubs off. Everyone is working hard towards the same end, generally making some progress. As a team, even a fragmented one, you drive each other onwards.

Laura and I worked quietly. At three o'clock, an officer dropped off the afternoon post: he had bundles of mail tied with string in a battered green trolley. There were several envelopes for me – notifications of upcoming court appearances for minor crimes – and then one letter that caught my eye.

Addressed by hand. A vaguely childish script, written in blue ink.

Even so, I ripped it open without really thinking. It was only as I unfolded the single sheet of A4 inside that I realised what I was looking at and placed the torn envelope carefully to one side.

'Laura,' I said.

'What?' She shoved her chair back and walked round to stand beside me. 'Oh. Shit, Hicks.'

It was a typed letter, beginning: *Dear Detective*.

And beside that, in the same blue fountain pen, the same handwriting, the sender had added the word *Hicks*.

Fourteen

Dear Detective Hicks

I don't know who you are yet. And at the time of writing this letter, you don't know who I am either. You have no idea of my existence and no inkling of what I am about to do. The truth is, I still don't know quite when it will begin myself. That is why it's going to work. That is why you'll never catch me.

Randomness has fascinated me since I was a child, right from the moment my father brought home the simple computer on which I first learned to program and code. I was only five or six years old at the time, but already I understood the machine and how it worked: that it was just an elaborate calculator, one that would perform whatever operation I told it to and nothing more. Inside its cheap plastic shell, one thing led to the next in a blind, obedient process. Every single output was created entirely by the inputs. It followed orders.

Except that one of the first commands I learned was to generate a random number. How could that be?

Even as a child, I understood it had to be an illusion. As I grew older, my father taught me, and I made further studies of my own: of sequences and codes. I learned how computers use pseudo-random number generators to hide their logical patterns. A unique seed number, derived from the exact date and time, is fed through a complicated equation to produce a new number that, while derived solely from the first, appears unconnected to an untrained eye. That new number, fed back in, creates a third.

And so on.

In such a way, a string of apparently random numbers is generated. If you know the pattern and any single number, you know the whole sequence, but for most purposes, the illusion of randomness is sufficient.

That wouldn't be good enough for you, would it?

I've spent a lot of time thinking about the problem: how to generate a code even you won't be able to crack. A string for which the underlying pattern cannot possibly be discerned. That is what I have spent months working on. That is what I believe I have achieved. And it is finally time to test it. On you.

As I write this, I am still waiting for the right moment to begin. The right initial seed. I do not know where or when it will be. I do not know who. That is why it will work: because I do not know yet who will die first.

But I do know it will be soon.

Fifteen

'So,' Young said. 'This letter.'

Laura and I were sitting across from him in his fifth-floor office. We might have relocated to the main operations room downstairs, but Young certainly hadn't. I didn't like being taken away from the heart of the investigation, even momentarily, but the flip side was it at least enabled us to run our own ship. Young was big on that. While he needed and wanted to know of every development, he wasn't bothered about being seen to be. For all his hardass reputation, he was a good boss.

The letter was the first item on the agenda.

Laura said, 'I think Hicks wrote it, sir.'

'Ha ha,' I said.

'Seriously, sir – his prints will be all over it.'

I leaned forward. 'As I've said a hundred times, I could hardly have discovered this potential crime scene *without* contaminating it, could I?'

'If you say so.'

'Give it up, you two.' Young sniffed. 'Other prints?'

'Ongoing, sir.' I leaned back. 'But so far we've got standard cheap eighty-weight paper that appears to have been untouched by human hands. Other than my own. There's a load on the envelope, but that's to be expected. They're being processed now anyway.'

He nodded. 'Okay. On a practical level, what else?'

There are plenty of traps people can fall into when sending

things to the police. Dropping a letter into a postbox might feel like an anonymous, unobserved act, but there are hundreds of potential mistakes we can look into.

We caught a blackmailer once who included a printout of a Streetview map to show where he wanted the money dropped. In terms of prints and DNA it was totally clean, and he was probably congratulating himself right up to the moment we knocked on his door. How did we find him? Because to print the map you had to access it online, and his was the only ISP address to look at that particular page in years. People rarely think of everything.

'Prints aside,' Laura said, 'the envelope was sticker-sealed, so we won't get DNA from that. We've already followed up the postmarks though.'

That was normally one of our best chances: that it was possible to trace the path of the letter back through time and space. We already knew the letter box it had been posted in, and the collection batch. That gave us a window of time in which our man had definitely been at a specific location – another cross on the map, albeit a much more tentative one this time.

'It's a box on Main Street, old town,' Laura said. 'CCTV only gives an oblique view. It's probably not good enough for any kind of pre-arrest identification. Maybe useful afterwards, though.'

Young frowned again – more of a scowl this time. I felt the same way. After an arrest was all well and good. What we needed, more than anything else right now, was something to help us find the guy in the first place.

'And the timing?'

I said, 'It was sent yesterday afternoon, between the lunchtime and evening collections. A five-hour period. The IT people are already pulling images for us. I don't know how many we'll end up with. Obviously it's a busy area and he posted at a busy time. We'll get something, though. It'll be fuzzy, but one of those people will be him.'

Scant consolation, but still true. We *would* have a photograph of the person who'd sent the letter – even if we wouldn't know for sure which of the people he was.

Young tapped a pen on his desk absently.

'He posted it *after* the murders of Gibson and Evans.'

'Yes, sir.'

'Do we think it's genuine?'

'I don't,' Laura said. 'Hicks isn't sure.'

Young looked at me. I shrugged.

'Not really,' I said. 'There's nothing in there that couldn't have been gleaned from the news reports. But at the same, if it's someone pranking us, there's also a whole lot *less*.'

Young nodded. 'That's what's giving me pause too.'

'I mean, he doesn't even describe the victims, when he could have done. If it's just some nut looking to troll us, he could have made it much more convincing.'

'But if it's real . . . ?'

'If it's real, the contents still don't make any sense. He claims to have written the letter before the first killing. He's even pre-printed it and written my name on by hand. I don't know how to explain that.'

'Well *try*, Hicks.'

'The only thing I can think is that he wanted to emphasise the . . . randomness. Because it's a challenge, isn't it? The way it reads, he wants to test us. So perhaps it's important to him that we're in on it from the very beginning. That we know he was planning it long before he started killing.'

'And that he genuinely doesn't know who his first victim will be.' Young rubbed his chin, considering it.

Laura leaned in. 'Assuming this is him, I'd add that it's very worrying. There's every indication that he intends to continue. It's not clear what exactly he's planning to do next, but he seems confident that we're not going to catch him.'

'*That is why it's going to work.*' Young nodded. '*A code even you won't be able to crack.* But why?'

He looked at me again.

'I can't work out what it means,' I said. 'Presumably he's

bragging that he can get away with the murders, and challenging us to stop him. But it's like he has some reason above and beyond the killings themselves. The way it reads, they're almost secondary to him.'

'Yes. There's certainly a degree of intellectual egotism there, isn't there?' Young was still looking at me. 'Do you know what that means, Hicks?'

'I do, sir. Thank you.'

'I thought you would. Forget the letter for the moment. Do we have any indication of how he's choosing his victims?'

'Right now,' I said, 'it seems more like *they're* choosing *him*. He plots up somewhere isolated and waits. We haven't found a single connection between any of the victims. Or the places themselves. So far. It seems . . .'

'Random.' Young nodded to himself, then sighed heavily. I knew from experience that that meant a conclusion was imminent. Sure enough, a moment later, he placed his hands flat down on the desk. 'We sit on the letter for now. Right? Let's see what prints come back. In the meantime, we keep it between ourselves. No press mention.'

'Yes, sir.'

'Just briefly, how do you feel about it, Hicks?'

'Sir?'

'Are you *okay*, is what I'm asking. Beneath all that irritating bluster?'

I blinked at him for a second – and then realised what he was talking about. If the letter was from the killer, he'd addressed it to me personally. Which meant he had my name. Perhaps he saw himself as communicating with me directly.

'I'm fine, sir. Obviously I very much appreciate your concern.'

'It's not concern. Just watch yourself. If he's interested in you for some unknown reason, then there's a chance he might try to establish contact some other way. Keep an eye out, is what I'm saying.'

'I will, sir. And for the record, I'm happy to consider myself as bait.'

'We all are. Now go.'

Outside, Laura and I waited for the lift

'He's right,' she said. 'Are you sure you're okay?'

I thought there was another question below the surface. *Because you've been a bit weird recently, haven't you, Hicks? Like this investigation is getting to you.*

And yet actually, in an odd way, the letter had put me back on steadier ground. It didn't make sense right now, but if it was real, it at least indicated that the guy had a motive. A basement one, perhaps – and a fucking odd one at that – but a motive nonetheless. There was something vaguely settling about that.

And if he wanted an intellectual game, then he was going to lose. Not because I personally was smarter than him, but because collectively we all were. There were too many things for him to think of, and he only had to get one of them wrong: just like Mr Streetview, he'd mess something up eventually. Maybe he already had and we just needed to figure out what.

A code even you won't be able to crack.

Yeah, well. We'd see about that.

'I'm fine,' I said.

'Sure?'

'I'm all over it.' The elevator pinged to announce its arrival. 'I'm just getting started.'

Sixteen

'It's beautiful,' the man says.

'Thank you,' Levchenko tells him.

The man's name is Enwright, and he only just made it to the shop in time to collect his order. Levchenko's wife, Jasmina, was at the door, in the process of locking up for the night, when he arrived, breathless, and rapped on the glass. It is half past five; Enwright has rushed to get here – a businessman, just finished for the day – and his neat grey suit is fit for work, not running. Levchenko can see beads of sweat in his hairline as he leans over the counter and peers into the box.

'Beautiful.'

'I'm glad you like it.'

The candle he prepared is inside, with its random sky-coloured arrangement of thin spread petals, as unique as the clouds in the sky. It sits snugly in the centre of the box, surrounded by scrunches of tissue paper.

'I've packaged it as carefully as possible,' Levchenko says, 'but obviously it is very fragile. You will need to take care in transportation.'

'Oh, I will. Don't worry.'

Levchenko suspects he will. Nevertheless, he always makes a point of showing these special candles to customers before they leave the shop. That way, there can be no complaints or disappointments later on, when the buyer arrives home and finds damaged goods.

Because the candles are very fragile indeed, and that is part of their charm. They are of their moment, and moments by definition are fragile. All things that occur in the world are the result of countless invisible processes, the removal of any one of which would alter the outcome beyond recognition. This candle, cast at a different moment, in different eddies of water, would not be this candle – and the candle that it is can never be reproduced. In wax, just as in the moments of life itself.

This is one of the reasons why Levchenko, despite the depth of his religious faith, has never been quick to discount certain types of supposedly lesser superstition. The *I Ching*, for example – he understands and appreciates that. On the face of it, reading messages from a pattern of thrown yarrow stalks is madness. And yet that pattern, much the same as his candles, is distinct to the moment of casting. In a different set of circumstances, tossed at another moment, in a varying breeze, the stalks would yield a different result. The pattern is unique, as is each of his candles.

Perhaps many customers do not think of them in this way – though he knows many do – but the *fragility* appeals nonetheless. These are not candles that can be sold far and wide. They cannot be mass-produced and shipped overseas. No, Levchenko sells only locally, only to a specific order, and always by hand, like this. Cynically, he knows there is a market for authenticity, and if Enwright regards himself as slumming it somehow – as buying something with a stamp of poverty to it – then Levchenko does not blame him for that, and at any rate is not in a position to mind.

'I'll tell my friends about this.' Enwright is peeling bills from a thick wad he had stuffed in his baggy trouser pocket. 'I'm sure I can send some business your way.'

Levchenko nods once. 'Thank you.'

He looks at Jasmina. She is busying herself tidying the displays on the far side of the shop, but she shoots him a quick, secret smile, which he returns. Even at fifty years of age, with so much suffering shadowed behind them, they remain playful with each other. They are happy. But yes, they are poor, and so he does not mind Enwright's attitude.

Levchenko unravels more tissue paper from the roll he keeps on the shop counter, then carefully packs it around the candle, as tightly as he dares, and fits the lid in place.

'If I may ask . . . ?' he says.

'Yes.' Enwright smiles brightly. 'The answer was yes.'

Levchenko smiles in return – although of course if the answer had been no, he doubts the man would be here now. On the lid of the box he has hand-written a label that gives the precise time and date the candle was cast, as requested by Edward Enwright when he placed the order. The date and time correspond to the moment, two nights before, when Enwright proposed to his girlfriend.

Levchenko has no idea whether the couple will ever burn it. That does not matter to him. Not many people are as perfectly suited as he and Jasmina have been, so it is more than possible that time and life will burn it for them. In some ways, an engagement gift of this kind is a hostage to fortune.

But then, he thinks, many things are.

So many things.

'I'm very happy for you both,' he says, pushing thoughts of his daughter from his mind.

'Thank you.'

'Very happy. All the best to you, Mr Enwright. Indeed, all the best to you both.'

It was thirty years ago, now, when he died.

Lying beside his wife in their small, threadbare bedroom, he remembers – as best he can, anyway, because thirty years is a long period of time. When marking out the life of a man, that is a significant block, so much so that it often feels like his death occurred in the life of another man entirely. He was twenty then, a different person in countless ways, and the memory itself is hazy. He knows he was a driver, and that his work consisted of transporting goods from the city to elsewhere and from elsewhere back again. He knows he worked long hours, slept in his cab in bays, and saw too little of Jasmina and his baby daughter Emmeline, and he knows now that the money he made was too little to compensate for that lost time.

Sometimes now he looks around at the city, at men such as Edward Enwright, and thinks that money is the only value anyone has any more. *What will it earn?* they ask. *What is it worth?* Questions of worth and value should have more than financial answers; they should not be composed entirely of currency. But as a younger man he did not understand that, so he worked those long hours, thinking that was what it took to be responsible, to be a good husband and father, to wring chance and success from the dirt-scrabble hand he'd been dealt.

One night, he crashed his truck.

Nobody could ever say for sure why it happened. Levchenko had never remembered the minutes leading up to the accident, but that did not, he was told, mean he had fallen asleep at the wheel. What happened to him was so dramatic that memory loss was to be expected regardless. A mental blank, in fact, might have been the minimum lasting damage anyone could have hoped for.

Despite his inability to recall the accident, certain things were a matter of record. For some reason, close to midnight, his truck left the road on the Esther bypass, which was normally empty at such a time. The cab clattered swiftly down an embankment, cracking through trees, overturning as it went, and came to rest in a subsidiary of the Kell, three feet underwater on the driver's side.

Levchenko, unconscious, was pinned in place by his seat belt, submerged wholly in the ice-cold water.

It was luck that saved him.

Luck that someone had been driving along a short distance behind him and seen his vehicle swerve off the road in the manner it had. Luck that the man driving was a paramedic.

Even before the cab had hit the water, the man had been radioing the emergency services. Then he had parked up and come down on foot, slipping and sliding down the embankment, and somehow managed to pull Levchenko from the cab and on to the riverbank.

Levchenko was dead; his heart had stopped beating.

The paramedic worked on him ceaselessly, refusing to give up, pressing down on his chest, thump, thump, thump, pumping the water from his lungs, breathing air into him, thump, thump, thump on his breastbone. Over and over. For seven whole minutes, Levchenko, dead, did not respond.

And then he did.

But he was dead for that time.

Far more than the moments immediately before the crash, Levchenko wishes he could remember those lost seven minutes – that he could see what, if anything, might have been there. He is a religious man and always has been, and the blankness taunts him. After all these years, the question remains. Does he remember nothing from those minutes of death simply because there *is* nothing to recall?

Because of what happened to Emmy, he does not want to believe that.

There is one saving grace for his faith: the matter of how random his survival was; the fact that on a road never normally heavy with traffic, the right man happened to be the right distance behind him. His present existence – all the good and bad of it – rests entirely on that coincidence. That coincidence, in turn, rests on many others before it. And so everything he does have feels inordinately precious. Every single moment since the accident – even the worst of them – has been a gift of sorts, and he accepts each as graciously as he can.

But there is a flip side to that:

He is living on borrowed time.

What happened can sometimes make him feel lucky, but a part of him wonders if there is more to the clockwork of the universe than that. When you have faith, you can see the unlikely as fragments of a larger plan: one that belongs to God, and is only ever revealed to you piecemeal, if at all.

So he is in a spiritual quandary. He wants to believe in God for the sake of Emmy. He wants to believe that on another plane of existence, a young woman of almost ephemeral beauty is existing, smiling. He wants to believe that God sees all images of her simultaneously, a flipbook of pictures of a little girl's beautiful smile and an older girl's delightful laugh, and that He took her to a better place where she is laughing and smiling still. Part of His plan. Smelling in heaven of the honey-flavoured perfume she always wore.

But if that is true, what of Levchenko?

Why has his life been allowed to continue?

If his survival is part of some unseen plan, it has never been revealed to him. He has achieved nothing special with the years since, beyond fanning soft, quiet happiness into the embers of his life with Jasmina after Emmy was taken from them. Surely God would not have kept him alive simply to endure the agony of living to see his daughter die?

No. There must be something more.

He rolls over, resting the side of his face on his forearm. Jasmina is snoring gently beside him – a comfortable, comforting lump beneath the covers.

It is foolish, of course, to think of these things. If God has a plan, then any revelation – or not – of its purpose is out of his hands. If there is anything he is meant to understand, he will do so at the right time.

Sleep gradually unravels upon him, pulling its misty blanket up to cover his restless thoughts, patting itself gently down over his mind.

His eyes flicker open briefly as he goes under.

The last things he sees before a dream is the nightstand. He sees the photograph of Emmy. And beside it he sees the old candle, its petals frail and dusty with age. It is purple and blue and red – but he knows there are tears and more besides mixed into its waxen randomness, for this is the candle he cast eight years ago, in the hollow hours after his daughter's murder.

Part Two

It was late. After midnight, I think.

And so the boy begins his story.

He is in the bedroom he shares with his older brother. It would be cramped with just one of them; with two, the room is rendered impossibly tiny. It is the length of the bunk bed and only twice as wide. All their clothes are piled under the lower bunk. The only other furniture is a battered wooden bookcase filled with cheap paperbacks and a row of tatty comics, stuffed in so tight that the paper has bunched and torn. There is no window.

The door opens directly on to the dim corridor running along the centre of the small house. It is shut, but – suddenly – outlined with light. Their mother has been in bed for hours. This is their father arriving home.

The boy holds his breath in the dark. Lying on the bed above him, he knows his older brother is doing the same.

Together but separate, they wait.

The boy is used to judging the world, on occasions like this, by noises. When his father is whistling, there is a chance everything will be all right. When he is talking to himself under his breath, it means someone has annoyed him at the pub: someone larger than him with whom he cannot pick a proper argument, so that he now needs to find someone with whom he can.

The little boy knows that his father is a bully, just like the children at school. When he told him he was being bullied, his father tried to teach him how to box. He took him out front and kept yelling at him to keep his hands up as he slapped him.

There is a clatter from the hallway, a stumble, and a thud against the wall. Tonight, his father isn't making any other sound at all, and the boy's heart is like a frightened bird trapped in his chest. That is always the worst. It means his father is very drunk indeed, that the bitterness he carries inside him will be tight against the surface. Every time he thuds drunkenly against the wall, it will feel instead like someone shoving him. When his father is this drunk, everything feels like a shove to him. Everything is against him.

The boy hates him.

A shadow drifts across the base of the door.

Pauses.

The boy, already not breathing, somehow holds his breath deeper still.

BANG BANG BANG.

His father's fist, rapping on the door.

From the corridor, there is a laugh, and then the shadow passes. He listens as, further along the hall, his father shoulders the wall again – or, as he will experience it, the wall shoulders him.

The boy lies there in the darkness for a time, picturing him. Yes, he is *Father*, never *Daddy*. He cannot remember ever hugging him. He cannot picture his father smiling. His face is an ugly thing: red and weathered, like a troll in one of the storybooks on the shelf. His hair is brown and curly; he wears fluffy old paint-stained jumpers and brown cords. His body is small and slumped. The only big thing about him any more is his forearms and his knuckles, like an ape. All the failures and disappointments of his life are there to see.

At the far end of the house, the bedroom door slams.

The boy wants to lie there, but he can't. He sits up in the dark and rests his bare feet on the carpet, clenching his toes against its wiry texture. And when the noises start – the other slamming, his father's raised voice, his mother's muted shouts and cries – the little boy pushes his fists into his eyes and rocks back and forth, concentrating on the sensations of his feet.

He begins crying silently, the way he's learned to cry over the years, limiting the inward breaths to hide the sniffles from his thick nose.

After a while, he realises his older brother is sitting beside him. He had not even noticed him clamber down the red stepladder. But John puts his arm round his shoulder, leans into him. They are both very small, hugging each other in the dark.

The policeman listens carefully to this story, and although the boy's face betrays no obvious emotion – no sign of either sincerity or guile – he finds himself believing that this much is the truth. Having met both boys, and seen the house itself, he can picture them sitting there like that together. He can imagine the desolation and fear.

He says, 'And then what happened?'

For a long moment, the boy does not reply. But then he gathers himself. And once again there is something there in his expression. Something that seems older than the child.

'And then what happened?'

The boy begins to tell him.

This is the point, looking back, when the policeman will be convinced the lies begin.

DAY SIX

Seventeen

David Barrett is sweeping his yard.

For many people, this would be a mundane, boring task – but not for him. Behind him, lit bright by the sun, is the farm he has built over the years. It began life as a detached house, two up, two down, with a scratchy field and dirt land attached. Even back then, it was expensive to buy, but it had always been his dream to own a small farm, and the property was ideal. In the decade since he and Kate moved in, he has extended the house itself to one side and carefully cultivated the land around. They have chickens and sheep. They have rows of crops. For most things in life, they are self-sufficient.

And it is lovely.

Swish. Swish.

The broom makes a comforting noise as he methodically pushes the dust from the front of the house. It billows across the quiet road outside the property, cast into gentle rolling swirls by the warm breeze. Swish. Swish. Other than that sound, the world is almost entirely silent.

And then—

'Mama!'

He glances up to see that Robin is running across the field on the far side of the road, arms and legs working in what seems to David more of a controlled fall than a run. His son is a little bundle of energy, and it often threatens to overtake him. He is still discovering the bounds of his small body, and constantly testing them.

'Robin,' he calls. 'Be careful.'

'Mama!'

'Mama's at the shop.'

Robin keeps running, legs and arms pinwheeling.

'Mama!'

For a moment, David is not even sure if Robin means Kate or not. The little boy has been slow to walk and talk, and whereas he's made up for the former since, his language remains underdeveloped for a child of three. 'Mama' was the first word he ever managed, and one he's stubbornly clung to since. For a while, everything was 'mama', from the bookshelf to the chickens, and even now it's still the first word to come to mind when the boy is excited. David supposes that's natural enough. Kate certainly never minds.

'Just be careful.'

He doesn't shout loud enough; the breeze takes the words. And anyway, Robin is already halfway across the field and showing no signs of slowing down or being remotely careful.

David puts the broom down on the yard, his hands in his pockets, and sets off after the boy. The field is about a hundred metres long, where it meets another curl of the road he crosses now. There are bushes there, another field beyond the road. There is no real danger – it is too quiet here; there is rarely even any traffic – and Robin often plays there, but he doesn't want him out of sight.

'Robin,' he calls.

'Mama!'

The word drifts back, as small as the little boy himself. David can see the bottoms of his tiny sneakers as he runs, like white balls being juggled in the patchy grass.

He isn't too far from the bushes now.

David speeds up a little.

'Robin,' he shouts. 'Come back!'

If the boy hears him, he doesn't show it. But now David can

hear something else. The whine of a scooter: a constant nasal burr, growing gradually louder.

Maybe the kid's psychic, he thinks – because Kate is back after all; he can see her scooter puttering along a loop of the road in the distance. Her skirt is fluttering slightly, revealing rigid calves, and her hair and scarf are rolling out behind her. She is a stiff but careful driver, and takes the turning slowly that will bring her to the line of bushes Robin is still careering towards.

As she drives along, she glances his way, and David waves a big arm over his head once, pointing down to the bottom of the field to indicate that she has a reception committee. She waves back slightly hesitantly, then seems to understand, notices her son on the field and slows down gradually to meet him.

She doesn't get that far. Twenty metres away, someone stands up from behind the bushes just as she reaches them. David can't quite see what happens, but the sound drifts across – horrifying on a subconscious level – and it's like a gunshot followed by a screech of metal. He is walking, and he moves more quickly now, even as his mind is still registering the sight of the scooter on its side, careering down the road straight past his son, who has come to a halt at the bottom of the field.

'Kate!' he shouts.

David starts running.

He's still trying to put it together in his head – the fragments of what just happened. She crashed. But she didn't. There was the man. David can't see him now. His vision of the field is juddering as he runs, but the man is out of sight anyway. Somewhere around where Kate had her accident.

Those facts gradually come together, like two lenses clicking into place, revealing a clear view of the truth. The man knocked her off the scooter.

'Robin!' he shouts. 'Get back! Get back up here now!'

He sees his son's small face turn to him, sees the look of confusion and shock. The boy is pale. He saw.

'Robin! Back to the house!'

The man reappears: standing back up, like a shadow appearing over the bush. He is dressed entirely in black and wearing a balaclava. He sees David running as fast as he can towards him, watches for a second, then turns and makes striking motions at the ground out of sight. He is holding something, David can't see what.

'No!'

The noise of the impacts carries. David runs hard, feet pounding across the field, not noticing or caring where Robin is now. Because something has just snapped inside him: some twang of pain that leaves an empty kind of knowledge in its place. The man is hitting Kate, over and over. He doesn't know why. He just knows he has to get there, and that he won't get there in time, that he is chasing something he cannot catch, something that he has already missed.

And now the man is running up the road, towards the fallen scooter. Carrying something. David adjusts his course slightly, aiming to meet him – to come charging through the bush and rugby-tackle him. But he misjudges: the man outpaces him. As David reaches the line of bushes, he has already righted the scooter and is kicking down at the pedals, revving the throttle. David barely notices the tearing thorns as he crashes through the foliage, stumbling slightly on the sudden hardness of the tarmac, turning to see the cough of smoke as the scooter accelerates away.

He knows immediately that he has no chance of catching it. Within a moment, the man is already looping around, heading up to go straight past the front of David's white-faced, sunlit farmhouse dream.

Kate.

He turns slowly. She is just lying there, twenty metres away. There seems to be a spill of petrol all around her head, and even though he knows it isn't petrol, for a moment he still holds out hope as he runs.

For the moment it takes him to reach her.

Eighteen

There were a couple of things that surprised me about Vicki Gibson's funeral. The first was that it was held at a non-denominational chapel: for some reason, I'd had Carla Gibson pegged as a religious woman. I was right about that, as it happens, but Vicki herself had not been, and her mother had chosen to respect her daughter's wishes rather than her own.

The second was the number of people that turned up.

It was a quiet, warm morning. Gravel crunched softly beneath my shoes as I walked up the drive, which was lined on either side by luscious, perfectly trimmed green hedges. Funeral homes, even non-denominational ones, often seem to try to recreate a vision of heaven, of peace and rest. Outside the chapel itself, a crowd had already gathered in advance of the service.

I looked around at everyone slightly wonderingly. Other people's lives can be mysterious from the outside, and it's wrong to rush to snap judgements. Vicki Gibson had never been the isolated outsider that her poverty and living circumstances had led me to believe.

I circulated a little – carefully avoiding the officers who were attending more discreetly. It wasn't unusual for serial murderers to turn up at the funerals of their victims, or observe them from a distance. In the immediate absence of other lines of enquiry, the funeral was a high priority for us.

Nobody stood out.

There were a few of the regular customers at the launderette: two women and an elderly man. Vicki's co-workers from both jobs turned up, clustered together in two large bunches. Members of her extended family had travelled to be here. And there were countless friends from the community, dressed as sombrely and neatly as they could afford. Everybody present seemed to know somebody. Nobody appeared to be here alone.

After a while, the hearse arrived and a silence settled on the assembled crowd, like a blanket falling.

Six professional pall-bearers carried the coffin into the chapel, stepping forward in solemn, practised unison. Gradually the people followed in after. A few officers mingled with them, although most would remain stationed quietly in the grounds.

I went in last of all.

The chapel was a large hall with a peaked roof. It reminded me, bizarrely, of a holiday chalet: varnished wooden floorboards, clean white walls and small high windows framed with thick dark wood. Wedges of sunlight hung in the air above.

There were few seats left. I found one at the back.

The coffin rested on a series of rollers in front of a set of drawn red-velvet curtains at the far end of the room. The officiant, an old man in old-fashioned clothes, was standing on a small stage to the side of it. With his glasses and eyebrows, he looked a little like some kind of clockwork owl: bookish and well read. He kept glancing up, patient and serious, waiting for people to settle and the murmur of conversation to fade. Every now and then, he smiled gently at the front row. Through the sea of dark suits, I could make out the back of Carla Gibson's head, all but lost beneath the frills of a black lace hat.

My attention kept returning to the coffin.

It was the unspoken focal point of the room: the ghost in a crowd that everyone could sense but nobody wanted to acknowledge. Inside it was Vicki Gibson as she was now. Reduced from the attractive, hard-working young woman who connected all these people together to nothing.

For obvious reasons, it was a closed coffin, but when you see a dead body, nothing is clearer than the realisation that the person is gone. The absence hits you immediately. And it's made more striking because the thing in front of you *looks* like a human being even though it palpably isn't one any more. A dead human body is an awful thing to see. For a moment, it makes you as still and silent as it is.

Once you get past that, though, there's usually at least the affirmation that this is what we are: a piece of complex biological machinery that has stopped working – or been stopped. Unlike some officers I know, I've never had a problem being an atheist at a crime scene.

Funerals are a different matter, though. It seems to me that when people are gathered together, with all their thoughts and memories, it can somehow rekindle the essence of the person lost – almost resurrecting them, but not quite. They're not present, but it's easy to believe they exist again as an odd kind of shadow, one cast not by a presence but an absence, and that they've come alive again just enough to hear everyone say goodbye.

Rubbish, obviously – it's just an illusion. When people are dead, they're dead, and life for everyone else continues to unfold in its unpredictable manner. Nobody is paying attention apart from us. Nobody else is noticing or keeping score.

The officiant looked up, over his glasses, and smiled gently at the room. It was the exact same expression he'd given Carla Gibson, as though our loss was equal to hers. When he started talking, he addressed the assembled people like friends.

'Ladies and gentlemen,' he began. 'Thank you for coming to this, one of the saddest occasions imaginable.'

One of the saddest occasions imaginable.

Difficult to quantify that, but in some ways the funeral of Derek Evans was worse. At least Vicki Gibson had the company of her family and friends as she was laid to rest; Evans only had me and Laura, who joined me for this. None of the 'friends'

Evans had made below the city had come to bid him farewell. And the two of us weren't enough to raise ghosts, shadows or anything else.

'Ashes to ashes. Dust to dust.'

Laura and I stood side by side with the priest in the grave-yard, watching as Evans's cheap coffin was lowered into a hole barely large enough to contain it.

As the priest finished up the perfunctory service, I glanced around. The cemetery was open and sprawling, the flat ground interrupted only by occasional trees and gravestones – but not here, where the city-funded plots were adorned with nothing grander than a plywood cross and a name plate. There was nobody within fifty metres. Nobody watching. Despite the heat of the day, the breeze drifting across the grass and stone felt cold.

After the service was over, and the coffin had been lowered into the ground, Laura and I wandered away from the grave.

'He didn't show,' I said.

'You weren't really expecting him to.'

I shrugged. Not expecting, maybe, but hoping. Because serial killers often did. It was a case of playing the odds again: working the statistics and probabilities. What else did we have right now?

It had been three days since the murders at the Garth estate, and since then there had been no activity whatsoever. I didn't know what to make of it: the initial flurry of killings, the alleged letter, then silence. It didn't fit with my expectations based on the textbooks. Serial killers tend to accelerate. Spree killers continue. So there had to be some reason for our murderer turning shy, but I couldn't think what it might be. Was it deliberate – perhaps part of his supposedly uncrackable code – or was there another explanation?

'What are you thinking, Hicks?'

We sauntered along. I kicked at the gravel on the path.

'I'm wondering when we're going to hear from him again.'

'You mean a letter?'

'No, I don't mean that. He's not stopped killing. That wouldn't make any sense.'

'Not unless he *got* stopped for some reason.'

'Like what?'

'I don't know. Maybe he was hit by a truck.'

'We're not that lucky.'

'Right now, it feels like we need to be.'

I nodded. Right now, hard work alone wasn't getting us very far. The break in the killings had at least allowed us to catch our breath slightly and thoroughly investigate the victims we did have. Even without taking his letter at face value, every possible connection between the victims – every possible motivation – had to be followed up.

Sandra Peacock, the working girl who'd died first on the waste ground, was thirty years old and a single parent to two little girls. As an intermittent drugs user and a prostitute, she clearly fell into a vulnerable category that separated her from Vicki Gibson. The only connection between the two women was their similar age. Beyond that, there were no obvious parallels at all.

John Kramer was forty-three years old: a bouncer at Santiago's nightclub in the Beeston area of the city. It seemed obvious that he'd been on his way to a different type of work entirely, but discreet enquiries at the club had failed to turn up what that might be. Regardless, it was clear that the number of people who might want to hurt him was substantially higher than the other victims. That was part of the problem we had. We might find a plethora of individual suspects for a single murder, but without an overarching explanation it meant little.

The third victim on the waste ground had been identified as fifty-three-year-old Marion Collins. From what we'd learned, she'd had no enemies whatsoever. Her husband had reported her missing the same morning, but it had taken hours for the report to trickle through to us. Collins had worked the night shift as a cleaner in an office – a different one to Vicki Gibson

– and during the day was a carer for her husband, who was disabled and wheelchair-bound.

Despite the age difference, she fitted into a similar demographic to Vicki – hard-working women, scrabbling to make enough money to support themselves and their loved ones. But nothing else was similar about the two of them, apart from the devastation their deaths had left behind for their loved ones. As far as we could establish, neither woman had outstanding debts that might have warranted retribution.

Forensics had given us nothing either. Not on the victims. Not on the letter. Not on fucking anything.

'Back to earth, Hicks.'

'I'm totally on earth, Laura. I'm one hundred per cent grounded.'

'You're not. You've been doing that a lot recently – disappearing off into the ether. It's not like you to be so dreamy.'

'It isn't?'

'No. Normally you're more ambivalent.'

'Wow.'

'Not in a *bad* way.'

She meant it as a joke, but I didn't like to think I came across like that.

'I've never been ambivalent. It's just there's no point overdoing it, is there? The dead stay dead regardless. And our job is just to catch the people who made it happen. We're not . . .' I glanced behind us, back to the graveside. 'Well, we're not *priests*, are we?'

'So what's different now? Because something is.'

I shrugged. It was difficult to explain. It wasn't just the case, but it was fair to say the case had come along at the wrong time for me, what with the issues Rachel and I were having.

'Problems at home,' I said.

'Ah. Want to talk about it?'

'Nope.' I thought about it. 'Can I ask you something?'

'Shoot.'

'Do you believe in good and evil?'

'Fucking hell, Hicks.' She pulled up. 'Are you serious?'

I nodded.

'Okay.' We set off walking again. 'I suppose it depends what you mean. Personally, I don't have much of a problem using those words to describe people. I mean, they're just words. They're as good as any, for some of the things we come across, aren't they?'

I didn't say anything.

'But then, there have been some occasions when I've had my doubts.' She shook her head. 'Like when you see some bastard crying over what he's done, not understanding how it happened. It's as though someone stepped in and did it when he wasn't looking. You know?'

I nodded. 'Do you think people can be born evil?'

'Oh, Christ. I don't know. No. I think people can be born *empty*. And have shit lives. But that's not the same thing, is it? It's like you always say. It's cause and effect.'

'Yes.'

'But it's all bullshit, Andy. Like you said, we're not priests. We just have to catch the bastard, not explain him. And we will.'

'Yes. We will.'

'And when we do, there'll be something. He's not a force for evil. There's something. There's a reason.'

'Because there always is.'

'Exactly.' She elbowed me gently. 'You taught me that. Most of the time I despise you, but deep down I know you're right about that. You should have more confidence in yourself. I need you on full power right now.'

'You really hate me most of the time?'

'It's more mild irritation.'

'That's more what I aim for.'

We walked along a little way. I wanted to believe what Laura had said, but I wasn't sure I did.

Up ahead, I spotted a groundskeeper. He was an overweight

guy in blue overalls, raking the path free of a vague scattering of leaves that had fallen from the trees.

'Wait here a second,' I told Laura.

He looked up as I reached him, squinting from beneath a blue baseball cap. He was in his sixties, at least, with skin that was worn and reddened by the elements and by alcohol.

'Hey there,' I said.

'Hey.'

'You're the groundskeeper, right?'

'One of 'em, yeah.'

'I'm Detective Andrew Hicks.' I showed him my badge. 'You work here most days?'

'Yeah.' He leaned the rake against a tree. 'What's this about?'

'Not about anything in particular. What's your name?'

'It's Henderson. Stephen Henderson.'

I made a mental note.

'Okay. Here's my contact card. It's got my direct number on it.' He took it, albeit a little reluctantly. 'It's probably nothing, but you ever get any vandalism here?'

Henderson looked around.

'Not much. Every now and then, you know. The Jewish graves get done over sometimes, but that hasn't happened for a while.' He sounded almost accusatory. 'We called you about that, though.'

'Sure,' I said. 'I just want you to keep my card and let me know if anything happens in the future. Okay? Anything at all. Will you do that?'

Henderson frowned.

'Don't worry,' I said. 'I'll be talking to your management too. It's just that a guy like you, you might notice something that other people don't. So, anyone hanging about who shouldn't be, any vandalism, I'd like you to call me. Okay?'

'Okay.'

'Thanks for your co-operation.'

I walked back to Laura.

'What was that about?' she said.

'Just thinking on.' We started walking again. 'Just thinking on.'

Nineteen

We held the press conference in the middle of the afternoon, which wasn't ideal for the evening paper but worked well for the broadcast news. By now, the nationals were picking up on us as well, of course: a serial killer always delivers the requisite headlines. Several news teams had set up camp outside the building, and whenever I ventured through reception, there always seemed to be reporters either leaving or arriving.

I did my best to avoid them; I wasn't entirely comfortable with the attention – with being the ostensible face of the investigation. Not because the letter had been addressed to me, as such, but because I'd never been happy in the press spotlight.

I'd had to get used to it.

The press room was packed this afternoon, the air hot and still. I sat at the end, behind a small table, speaking into a microphone, a dark blue banner behind me. Laura was beside me, silent for the moment. The pre-prepared statement was mine today. In front of us sat rows of journalists, taking feverish notes on their laptops, maybe even writing copy live for website feeds. Cables spooled across the floor. The whole time I spoke, I was assaulted by camera flashes from the photographers crammed in at the sides of the room.

'We are now sure,' I concluded, looking up, 'that Marion Collins, John Kramer and Sandra Peacock are the victims of the same killer as Vicki Gibson and Derek Evans. We encourage anyone with any information relevant to this inquiry to come forward at the earliest opportunity. Thank you.'

I leaned back slightly, signalling that my part was done.

Laura took over. 'There will now be a few minutes for questions.'

A dozen hands went up at once. She signalled to one person at a time, and I listened to the questions and her measured responses. Laura was much better at handling the media than I was, even though she disliked them at least as much as I did. Blood sells, and a lot of papers aren't shy about splashing the lurid details around, so when you've sat with the grieving relatives, when you've invested in the lives of the victims, it's difficult to feel much love for the parasitical fuckers.

'Do you believe the killer was known to the victims?'

'That is something we cannot say for sure,' Laura said. 'It's certainly possible, and it's one of the avenues we're pursuing.'

Bullshit, of course – I was increasingly certain that if we could rewind Vicki Gibson's movements alongside those of the killer's, the time and place of her murder would be the only real connection they shared. The same with the other victims. I didn't think he scoped them out in advance. But of course, we couldn't be sure. Maybe he was each and every one of them's best friend, and we'd somehow missed it.

So you never say anything definitive to the press. It's a balancing act – a weird kind of arms race. You need them and they need you. You need to get information to and from the public; they need a story to shift units. As an investigation progresses, they need new angles. It's inevitable that, having drained all other resources, the angle that 'the police know nothing' appears eventually. Regular as clockwork, usually – you can time an investigation by it. You get to expect certain questions. *Reporter bullshit bingo*, we call it in private.

'Have you any suspects at this time?'

'We have spoken to a number of people in the course of our enquiries. We will continue to do so.'

The woman pressed it. 'But nobody in particular?'

She wanted a quote on Tom Gregory, obviously, who'd been smeared in more than one of the papers and then predictably outspoken in others upon his release. Not our fault. Scenting blood, the press had just leapt ahead of us like a pack of hounds.

Laura said, 'Several people have been questioned and those people have subsequently been eliminated from our enquiries. We are grateful for their assistance.'

The reporter seemed unhappy with that answer. She looked down at her laptop and began typing something.

Another hand.

'Are you happy with the way the investigation is progressing?'

Out of sight beneath the table, I made a little ticking gesture on an imaginary scorecard. There it was. A stinker of a question too. What were you supposed to say? Yes? No?

'We are not happy,' Laura said slowly, 'that the individual responsible for these horrific crimes remains at large. But our team is working hard, round the clock, in an attempt to apprehend him. We will continue to do so. Everything that can be done is being done, and I am confident that results will be forthcoming.'

'Should the public at large be scared?'

Another tick there – because the one thing that sells newspapers even better than a serial killer is a serial killer who might theoretically come after you. It makes it very important you buy the paper to find out about him, and whether the police investigation is going well or not.

'We are advising the public to be mindful,' Laura said, sounding cautious. 'We have more officers on the streets than ever before and are doing everything we can to safeguard the public. Where possible, we do advise people to avoid isolated areas, and to travel in groups whenever they can.'

Laura spun it out a little longer. Experienced as she was, she knew we were dealing with time here rather than a set number of questions. So she ran with that one. It also helped her avoid answering the question directly.

Should the public be scared?

Yes.

They certainly should.

'But as we have said, the most important thing the public can do right now is *come forward* with any information they might have. Someone out there knows this man.'

'Is there any connection between the victims?'

'At this stage, we can't comment on that.'

Another hand.

'Have you had any communication from the killer?'

I did my best to remain implacable. It was too hot in here, and I wanted to loosen my shirt collar, but the cameras pick up everything.

Laura said, 'Any communication?'

The reporter looked a little sheepish.

'It's not unheard of for killers of this type to communicate with the police, is it? Given the apparent lack of any motive for these attacks, I was wondering whether you were considering the possibility that he was enjoying the attention.'

Been reading too many books, I thought.

But he was right, of course. We remained undecided as to whether the letter was genuine or not. With an operation like this, you deal with cranks. Aside from the letter, the front desk had received three confessions in person and eight over the phone. All turned out to be impossible, but each had to be followed up, and everyone involved would be charged with wasting police time. It sounds frivolous, that charge, but time is all we have.

'Firstly,' Laura said, 'I would say it's far too early in the investigation to speculate on what the killer's motive might be. And as I said, we are discounting nothing. We are pursuing all possible lines of enquiry. As for communication – no, we have received nothing specific.'

Nothing specific. If the letter was fake, it was of no consequence. If it was real, perhaps not mentioning it would encourage the killer to write another. Or do something else.

I thought about that as Laura moved on to the next question, indicating that it would be the last.

Or do something else.

That was another balancing act.

Twenty

Back in the operations room, Laura and I slid into plastic seats on either side of the sergeant in charge of scanning the nationwide databases.

Her name was Alison Pearson, and she was the officer who'd asked the question about the killer's motive during our initial briefing three days ago. She was only young – not yet in her thirties – but had seemed focused and on-task from the beginning. Her role was multifaceted: analysing missing person reports, both on and off the system, and searching for any past murders with similar specs to our current series, as it seemed more than possible that, despite the assertions in the letter, this was not our man's first experience of killing.

We had a mounting pile of mis-pers on our desk, and had looked over a steady stream of possibly connected earlier crimes. Each one had been followed up as extensively as manpower allowed and come to nothing. Frustrating work, but necessary, and if there was anyone in the room who was not going to miss an important detail, it was Pearson.

'I found this report on the system an hour ago,' she said. 'It was only added in this afternoon, so I pounced.'

The report was up on the screen, and I scanned the details quickly. On the far side of Pearson, I could see Laura squinting at the monitor too. Pearson talked over us as we read.

'Victim is Kate Barrett, thirty-one years of age. She was killed

this morning during what appears to be an aggravated robbery in which her scooter was taken. Bludgeoned to death.'

'Christ,' I said, more to myself than anyone else. The report indicated that her husband and son had observed the attack, but had been unable to reach her assailant in time.

Laura nodded. 'Witness – her husband – says the killer hit her more than was necessary in order to steal the bike. Like he murdered her out of spite.'

'No post-mortem yet,' I said. 'So we don't know the weapon. Who's in charge of this?'

'Nobody here.' Pearson tapped the screen. 'It's in Buxton.'

'*Buxton?*'

Pearson nodded. 'It's about thirty miles south—'

'I know where it is.'

Of course I knew. It was where I'd grown up – and I didn't have particularly fond memories of the place. The name was just another random little dig in the mental ribs, as if the case wasn't bothering me enough as it was. But Pearson looked put-out, and I realised I'd been too sharp with her.

'Sorry, Alison. I'm just stressed out at the moment. It's hard enough handling all this here without having to factor another bloody town in.'

Factoring it into the alleged pattern, of course, but I was thinking mainly of the inter-departmental work it would entail if the cases did turn out to be connected. We were the bigger city, at least, so we'd have primary, and we might blag a few officers by pooling efforts, but it would still be a massive headache to be co-ordinating investigations at this point. We were drowning in paperwork as it was. Drowning full stop.

'It still might be nothing,' Laura said. 'As far as we know, robbery's never been a factor before.'

'No.'

'And we don't know the weapon.'

'PM's set for tomorrow morning.' Pearson sounded a little brighter now.

'Good.' I stood up. 'Can you get us a printout of this, Alison? Thanks again. Sorry for being snappy.'

'Of course, boss. No problem.'

Back at our own desk, Laura sat down opposite and peered across at me.

'What's up, Hicks?'

'Buxton. If this turns out to be true, it's going to be a fucking nightmare.' I held up a basic A4 printout of the city with the five known victims marked on it, along with various pencil swirls where I'd doodled prospective patterns, to no avail whatsoever. 'Call stationery. We're going to need a bigger bit of paper.'

Laura pulled a face.

I put the sheet down. 'Also, I suppose I was hoping that this was over. But it's never over, is it?'

'Look. It might not be connected.'

'No. But that man, the husband, he still saw his wife being murdered. So if it's not our guy, it means someone killed a woman for a fucking scooter. I'm not sure which is better.'

'This case is getting to you.'

'Obviously.'

'And it's not like you at all.'

'Yeah, we discussed this earlier.' I sighed. 'It's not just that anyway. Like I said, it's Rachel too. We're supposed to go to counselling tonight.'

'Counselling?'

'Marriage counselling.'

'Shit, Andy.' Laura leaned back. 'I'm sorry. I didn't realise things had got that bad.'

'We've been going for a few weeks. It's rubbish, but I'm trying to – you know – *show willing*.'

'Things are really that serious?'

'Things are really that serious. And before you say it, I would have talked to you about it, but there's nothing much to tell.'

'What's the problem?'

'We've just grown apart, I suppose.' There was more to

it than that, of course, but not that I wanted to talk about. 'Honestly, either we'll work it out or we won't. Right now, I don't know if we can.'

She looked a bit awkward. 'Well . . . you sort of *have* to, don't you?'

'Because of the baby?' I gave a hollow laugh. 'Try telling Rachel that. You know how much of an asshole I can be, and you don't have to live with me.'

Laura grimaced at the thought. 'Yuck.'

'Thanks.'

'You're welcome.'

Pearson arrived with the printout of the report from Buxton. Laura held out a hand for it.

'I'll take that. Thanks, Alison.'

'No problem.'

As Pearson retreated, I reached out for the sheet, but Laura slapped my hand.

'Get out of here.'

'No.'

'*Yes.*' I was about to protest again, but she didn't give me a chance. '*I'll* handle this for now. Like we both said, it's probably nothing at all – not connected, at least. So I'm just going to make contact, get more info. Maybe arrange to attend the PM tomorrow. The sight of a corpse will help cleanse my mind of the thought of living with you.'

I said nothing. Eventually, she looked up.

'Seriously, Hicks. Get the fuck out of here.'

She stared at me, not blinking, until I stood up.

'Thanks, Laura.'

'I was best man at your wedding. You do remember that, don't you?'

I nodded. It hadn't been because I had no male friends who could have performed the role, but simply because I'd asked Laura. Aside from Rachel, she was the person I was closest to in the world. I'd stood at the front of the hall with the two people I exasperated more than anyone else.

'Yes,' I said.

'So I won't forgive you if you fuck this up. Go. Go save your marriage.'

I nodded and left.

Go save your marriage.

I wished it could be anything like as easy as that.

Twenty-One

'How has the last week been?' Barbara said.

Barbara was our marriage counsellor, a softly spoken, gently overweight woman in her fifties. Every Wednesday we attended an hour-long session in her office in The Croft therapy centre. It was a flat, sprawling building housing a number of practitioners. In addition to basic counselling, the centre offered services like homeopathy, acupuncture and fucking Reiki, all of which had underwhelmed me from the start.

I wanted to show willing, and I wanted to save my marriage, but I couldn't shake the feeling that we'd now spent close to a hundred pounds in order to tell a stranger all the things we *should* have been able to say to each other, and none of the things we needed to.

Which was my fault, I knew.

Rachel and I sat either side of a coffee table, facing Barbara. Out of the corner of my eye, I could tell Rachel was slumped in her seat, arms folded, reluctant. Something about the atmosphere in the office made it difficult to look at her directly, as though there was a curtain hanging in the air between us.

'Andy?' Barbara said. 'Do you want to start?'

No, I didn't want to start. *How has the last week been?* Obviously she meant in our relationship, but a few other answers suggested themselves far more readily.

Another part of the problem.

I said, 'Not so much.'

'Rachel then?'

Rachel shrugged. 'I suppose.'

Despite my own response, my heart bit slightly at that, because, as with the shrug in the kitchen, it was as though she'd already given up. I didn't want that to be true. But there was nothing I could do to change it. That's the main problem with trying to solve your problems by talking: you have to want to, and you have to be able to.

'It's not been a great week,' Rachel said. 'I suppose it's not been helped by Andy's work, which has been very busy.' She half turned to me. 'Hasn't it?'

'I've been out more than I'd like. I've not had much choice.'

Rachel turned back to Barbara. 'Yes, and I do know it's not his fault. What he's doing is important. I suppose that's what I have to accept. That it's more important to him than our marriage.'

'That's not true.'

'It feels like it is. And you've been busy in the past without it feeling like that. Perhaps things are just different now. Perhaps I just feel it differently.'

Barbara said, 'Because of the baby?'

'Yes.' Rachel's hand moved over her stomach. 'And it hurts because I know it's selfish, but I can't help it. Does that make sense?'

Barbara looked at me. 'Andy?'

'Yes,' I said. 'Would you like me to leave my job?'

Rachel sighed. 'Oh, don't be—'

'No, in theory. Would that help?'

The sigh expanded through her, as though my question was a new exchange in some exhausting battle, designed to wear her down. But it didn't seem like the most ridiculous suggestion to me. A part of me knew it wouldn't solve anything, but – a sudden, bright realisation – it would be *something*. A gesture I could make that, no matter how problematic, was actually far easier than untangling the threads of what was really bothering me. Far easier than sharing them.

'It wouldn't do any good if you weren't happy,' Rachel said. 'I don't want you resenting me more than it feels like you already do.'

'I don't resent you.'

'What you do is a part of who you are, a part of the man I fell in love with. I don't want to change that. I want *that man back again*. I want things to be like they used to be, when we were happy. It doesn't seem like so long ago in some ways. But then, in others . . .'

She started to cry. Barbara skilfully slipped a tissue from a box on the table beside her and passed it across, but Rachel shook her head and composed herself.

'I want that too,' I said. 'We used to be so happy. I want that back.'

'But maybe things are different now. Maybe we're not two people who should be together any more. Despite how good things used to be. Because they're not like that now, are they?'

I blinked. None of this was new to me, of course, but still – it stung. Rachel was normally so reserved and controlled that it was unsettling to hear her so emotional, so fierce about everything. Worse, actually, than the indifference, because she sounded so . . . resolved.

Already resolved to being on her own.

'I don't want us to not be together,' I said. 'I still love you.'

'And I love you. But that's not the point, is it? I love my friends. And lately, it feels like that's all we are. We're not a couple. You don't talk. You just don't talk any more. And if it's over, if it's not going to work, then I think we both need to accept that sooner rather than later.'

I shook my head. Didn't say anything.

After a moment, Barbara leaned forwards.

'Well, that's what we're here to find out, isn't it? Did you bring your lists with you?'

Rachel nodded. 'I did.'

She plucked it out of her purse: a folded sheet of A4. The list of the things we'd loved about the other person in the initial flush of romance, when we'd first got together. The list of what we loved about each other now.

I reached into my pocket and pulled out my own piece of notepaper.

Rachel blinked. 'You did it?'

'Yes. Of course.'

She looked at me a little longer, then down at her sheet of paper, and then to Barbara.

'Shall I start?'

'Go ahead.'

'Strong,' she said. 'Dependable. Funny. Quiet but not shy. Good-looking. Sexy. Relaxed. At ease with himself.'

As she went on, I forced myself not to say anything. Rachel wasn't speaking to me anyway; she was speaking to Barbara. That was the idea: for us to use her like some kind of totem pole, allowing the other to overhear.

'Determined. Rational. Logical. Athletic.'

In her tone of voice, I heard all the things that were lost. Over the last few months, such a counterweight had been added to our relationship that the good things no longer rested down heavily enough to maintain balance, never mind tip the scales in their favour.

'Humble. Self-deprecating. Loving. Caring.' Rachel looked up. 'That's the end.'

'Well.' Barbara seemed pleased by that. 'And what about your "now" list?'

'Strong. Still athletic, good-looking. Still sexy.' She didn't blush; Rachel never blushed. 'But then . . . well, he's still quiet, but it's not the same. Before it was like he didn't speak unless he had something to say, and now it's like there's something he wants to say and won't. He doesn't talk to me any more. He doesn't seem relaxed or at ease with himself either. *And I don't know why.*'

This time, when Barbara offered her the tissue, she took it.

I sat motionless.

It's like there's something he wants to say and won't.

135

'Andy,' Barbara said. 'I'd like you to read your lists. Is that okay?'

I nodded.

'Okay.'

I met Rachel ten years ago, when I was a twenty-five-year-old grunt-pool officer. She was two years younger and doing a PhD in microbiology.

I met her online, out of necessity. Grunt-pool work mostly involves door-to-door work, research and dogsbodying, and the kind of people you meet are not the sort you generally either want or are allowed to date. Police work, in general, is very insular; cops quite often end up dating cops. But that wasn't something I wanted.

So: what made me fall for Rachel?

Beautiful.

She only had one photo on her profile: a head-and-shoulders shot. Her hair was pulled back in a tight ponytail, and she had a bit of a smirk on her lips. She was attractive without being conventionally stunning, but didn't seem like she gave much of a shit about the matter one way or the other, and I liked that a lot.

Intelligent.

Obviously we exchanged a few emails in advance of meeting up, and she did her best to explain the subject of her PhD to me. I'm not as stupid as I look, but I understood about one word out of every ten. I couldn't even pronounce some of them. She kept apologising for it sounding so dry. But she didn't need to, because, as incomprehensible as most of it was, her passion for the subject still came across clearly, and I liked that a lot too.

Confident.

The other thing I liked before we met in person was that she didn't get hung up on the cop thing. She was politely interested, but certainly didn't go gaga over it. Some cops lap up that kind of attention, but not me. And I found it appealing that

Rachel wasn't immediately asking for war stories or telling me how interesting the job must be. In fact, I got the impression it would take a lot more than a uniform to impress her. That's a good thing.

Our first date was . . . interesting.

It was a bit of a haphazard arrangement: a rushed meeting. She was organising a postgrad meet-up night in the basement of the university union and said she could get me in past security. She was already out there when I arrived, smoking and chatting with the guards as though she was friends with them. I smoked back then too, so lit one up and introduced myself.

She was smaller than I'd expected, wearing a top low-cut at the back that revealed a stretch of fairly ripped muscles, the kind a climber has. She also wore glasses in real life, but beyond that she looked and came across exactly as she had in her profile and emails.

As we went inside, she said, 'You're taller than I expected.'

'Six two, as advertised.'

'Yeah, but that site has a few trade-descriptions issues.' She signed her name on the guest sheet against mine. The guy manning the table peeled off a sticker and she slapped it hard on my chest. 'A lot of those profiles don't exactly match reality.'

'Mine is all true.'

'Good start, then, Andy.'

I followed her downstairs. 'Have you met a lot of people online then?'

'Enough that I was about to give up.'

'I guess it must be difficult for women on there.'

She shrugged without turning around.

'Difficult anywhere. What about you?'

'A few. None that have ever really gone anywhere.'

'Must be just as difficult for you to meet people in your line of work.' She threw a smile over her shoulder. 'The *right* sort of people, I mean.'

'Yeah. You can say that again.'

Downstairs, we entered an L-shaped bar full of shadowy

people. It wasn't an ideal scenario. What wasn't pitch black was illuminated with green neon, and the sound system was pumping so loud it was strictly mouth-to-ear in conversation terms. Even harder, it turned out Rachel was responsible for the gathering, so she kept having to flit off and talk to groups of people, making sure they were okay, circulating. So for most of the next two hours, I was basically propping up the bar: just another person there she knew who she'd talk to every so often – apologising every time she did.

Caring.

Considerate.

'Sorry, sorry, sorry.'

'It's okay.' I sipped from my bottle of Corona. 'We sorted this on the fly. I knew I wouldn't have your full and undivided attention.'

'At least you know what you're letting yourself in for.'

In truth, I didn't mind watching her circulate. I was quietly noting the groups of people, and there wasn't a single one she left out or didn't touch on at some point. It was like a military operation. She was very organised, very in control. Rachel has always been ultra-efficient, and this was the first time I saw it in action. Despite not being the centre of her attention, I liked it a lot. I've never really minded being on the periphery, especially when I'm on the periphery of someone very interesting.

Organised.

Efficient.

About ten o'clock, the bar began to empty: groups of people disappearing, leaving the coloured strobe lights increasingly tracking bare patches of stone floor, as though searching for something. In between saying goodbye to people, she dashed over and touched my arm.

'You got to run off?'

I checked my watch. I was on early shift in the morning, but I hadn't drunk so much that getting up was going to be a big deal.

I shrugged. 'Not really.'

'I've got to head to the lab; I've got an experiment running. Fancy prolonging this hideous torture a little longer?'

'It's not torture,' I said. 'But yeah, sure.'

It was cold outside by that time, and we walked side by side, slightly hunched in our coats, misty-breathed and chatting about some of the other people who'd been there – a lot of foreign students, she explained, which was why she'd felt compelled to make sure everyone was feeling comfortable.

'And I figured you were comfortable enough,' she said.

'You figured right.'

Intuition.

Kindness.

Her department was a ten-minute walk across campus: a faceless building lined with implacable walkways and wide, heavy red doors. Rachel had a large collection of keys, and she worked through them as we went through various security doors, each one closing with a heavy thud and a click behind us. At this hour, the place was deserted; the run-down corridors were all but interchangeable, and the doors leading off were distinguished from each other only by tiny steel plaques.

The lab itself reminded me of school science classes: rows of benches divided into stations. A lot of them were covered with equipment – microscopes and tissue boxes full of dishes and pipettes – but Rachel's was predictably pristine and polished. She collected a sheaf of papers from the neat pile at the back, then opened one of the cupboards above, revealing further carefully arranged rows of material.

'Follow me,' she said.

She led me through to a back room, where one wall was taken up by an enormous bulk of metal and glass. Inside, a circular rack of sealed beakers was spinning around astonishingly quickly.

Rachel checked the display and frowned.

'Not done.'

'Problem?' I said.

'I wanted to get it done, but never mind. It's just mixing my samples for me, and somebody else will probably want it first thing.'

She put the papers down and pulled the top off a biro with her teeth, then started making a few notes, glancing occasionally at the display on the machine.

Then she topped the pen again.

'Okay. That's that, then. Sorry again, by the way. This is what it means to date a geek.'

'It's fine,' I said. 'I'm just concentrating on not knocking over a Petri dish or anything.'

She looked at me, suddenly all science-serious.

'You know what will happen if you do?'

'No. Tell me.'

'The apocalypse.'

Serious but funny.

'Shit,' I said. 'Well, you know, I was hoping more for "you'll develop superpowers, Andy".'

'Useful in your line of work. But no. A deadly strain would be released. We'd probably have to quarantine ourselves in here for a while.'

'Really?'

I knew she was kidding, but suddenly I couldn't take my eyes off her. I was aware of her body and how close it was, and the way she was looking at me. The slight, playful smile on her lips.

'We'd be locked in,' she said.

Sexy.

Forward.

Rachel glanced down to where an empty pipette was resting on a desk. She reached down and knocked it on to the floor.

'Whoops.'

'And now?'

I turned the piece of paper over, although there was no point; I hadn't written anything on the other side, because I didn't need to.

'All the same,' I said.

It made me feel sad. Nothing had changed. It wasn't about her, the things I couldn't say. I loved her more than ever, even as I was losing her, and there was nothing I could do about it.

'All the same things.'

Twenty-Two

Later that night, when we got back home, Rachel went straight to bed. She'd cried more in the car, but quietly and to herself, in a way that made it clear she didn't want to talk about the counselling session. Or at least not right now.

The atmosphere had been miserable anyway, as though the conversation was playing out silently in the air between us without either of us having to speak out loud. I could sense the questions, the repercussions. If my feelings hadn't changed, did that mean it was somehow her fault? That it was up to her to figure out why her feelings had?

After she'd gone upstairs, I took a beer outside and sat on the patio overlooking the old barracks.

No pale ghosts forming in the bushes tonight, but there didn't need to be. I could feel one anyway.

Her.

Emmeline Levchenko.

I do my best not to bring my work home with me, it's true, but still. Some cases stay with me all right.

And now, a tickle at the back of my mind, there was Buxton to think about too.

I took a swig of beer.

Whatever I told myself about nothing being weird, I couldn't escape the feeling of storm clouds gathering. A *tightening*, almost: the sensation that there was more going on with this case than I realised, and that as time went on, I was going to become more and more entangled in it. Buxton meant nothing, of course; it was just a coincidence. But there it was, all the same, and it was making me uneasy.

Irrational, Andy.

Remember? Being rational was one of the things Rachel loved about you.

Which brought me back round to the counselling sessions. They were a waste of time as things stood. What was the point, if I wasn't going to engage? If I wasn't going to tell her the truth?

I finished off the beer and stared out into the darkness. At the empty bushes across the street. *It's like there's something he wants to say and won't.*

Intuition, all right – but she wasn't entirely right.

Not won't say, but can't.

DAY SEVEN

Twenty-Three

Blinking against the heat of the morning sun, Billy walks up Killer Hill.

It's a name the children have passed down between them over the generations, mainly because it's so steep it kills you to run up it – and even at a gentle pace, in this heat Billy is already sweating. Killer all right.

As far as he knows, it doesn't have a real name; it's one of those places marked out by children as important but ignored by adults. The older boys and sometimes girls used to get drunk at the top and have campfires and things like that. One time, Carl told them all, he was there and some of the older kids had a cat in a cage. One of them poked it with sticks. Carl was laughing as he explained how it had hissed and squawked at them, until eventually they had got bored and set fire to it.

The other children didn't believe Carl, but Billy did. He snuck there the next day and saw the scorched ground and the cage, buckled with fire, with what looked like burnt branches inside. He passes it now, and the scorched patch has grown back over, as though it was never there at all – or as though, as Carl had laughed, it was only a cat so why should anyone care?

Billy doesn't like coming this way, but it's the quickest route into the woods, which are his favourite place to play. The path at the top runs between the dark trees like a doorway.

He wanders half a mile through the woods. The trees here are enormous, like the pillars in some dusty museum, supporting a canopy of branches and leaves that fractures the sunlight high above. Nevertheless, the ground has been baked dry by the summer heat. In places, it is as cracked as old clay. Roots stick up like frayed, rusted pipes, hooping back into the ground, as though once upon a time the trees were padlocked in place by giants.

Sometimes dirt-bikers come growling and buzzing through this part, chasing each other over the undulations of the hardened earth. The sound is always abrasive, nasal and angry. None today – all Billy can hear is the gentle ticking of the forest. But he wants to make sure he is alone, so he takes a tight, rustling path through a sprawling patch of bright green ferns, some as tall as he is. The air flickers with midges. He wafts and splutters them away, bending fronds to one side as he goes.

This is a secret route he doesn't think anyone else knows: a route not even known to most children.

Once he is clear of the ferns, there are a number of older trees, then a broken-down stone wall. Beyond that, a stream trickles through the wood. Stepping stones dot it, polished slippy and smooth by the burbling water. Beyond that, the trees get thicker and more tightly packed, gradually condensing into the deep forest that bases the mountains in the misty middle distance.

At school, children are warned about straying too far here. There are wild animals, for one thing. For another, it is deceptively easy to get lost. A few walkers every year end up missing, and not all of them are found again. But the wood will look after Billy, he thinks; it won't let him lose his way. And as for wild animals . . .

Well.

He stops by the stream and unfolds the sheet of instructions, then clicks open his penknife.

Let them try.

*

He is going to build a bow and arrow.

Well, he is going to have a go.

The instructions have been torn from a page in the army survival handbook. As well as that and the penknife, he has a ball of string; all he needs from the forest are suitable pieces of wood to work with. The principle is easy enough: a supple length of wood for the bow, sterner shoots for the arrows. You just carve the correct notches and cut the string to the right length.

Of course, he could just buy one. Many of the boys at school have weapons – lock knives and catapults they've either bought from illicit market stalls or passed between each other. Carl even has a throwing star that he showed them all round the corner in the playground, winging it at a tree. Everyone had a go except Billy, because then someone said a teacher was coming.

But he doesn't want to buy a bow and arrow.

At school, the boys probably wouldn't sell him a weapon anyway, and might even laugh at him if he asked them. The market is out for similar reasons: the big men in the bulky coats would probably not even laugh, just ignore him altogether.

The main reason, though, is that deep down, he doesn't *really* want one.

He just wants to play.

And the woods are, for want of a better word, Billy's best friend. He feels at home here, playing in the trees and discovering paths through the undergrowth. All woodland has secret trails, and it is always delighted when little boys care enough to discover them. That is how it seems – that there is a benevolence to the forest. He plays in it and, after a time of watching and wondering, it begins playing back. Despite always being by himself here, it is the one place in the whole world he feels least alone.

And that's also why he's not afraid, even though the news on the TV has been saying not to go to isolated places on your own. He can't explain it, but he feels the wood will look after him somehow. That if this murderer is around, it will like Billy more than it likes him – that in fact it probably won't like *him* very much at all.

Billy understands the sort of man they're looking for. Sometimes he fantasises about killing some of the boys who bully him at school, but that's not evil because he wouldn't do it. If he had them in his power – like a cat in a cage – he wouldn't hurt them. He might poke them with a stick *once*, just so they knew how it felt, but he would stop when they started crying. It would be too upsetting to hurt something helpless. Evil is not getting that, and that is what the man in papers is like. The killer. He is like someone who could torture a cat to death and then laugh about it afterwards, and there are loads of them about.

Half an hour later, Billy has built the bow and sharpened a single arrow. He isn't sure what wood he's used for either, but both are certainly fit for purpose. He's pleased with himself. The bow is supple enough to bend into a semicircle without it snapping, and the string is tied carefully into the notches he cut. It took a while to find a branch straight and thin enough to carve into an arrow, but he scavenged around the base of the tree and found one that would do: chopping it off flat at one end and drawing a ridge with the knife to fit the bowstring, then sharpening the other end like a pencil.

He loads the bow now and holds it out in front, aiming at the ground, then closes one eye as he draws back on the string – it's surprisingly fiddly to keep the arrow level, but he tries to rest it on his fist. The string slips out of the end a couple of times, but after a minute he gets the hang of it.

Twang!

It goes fast, but doesn't fly straight and stick in the earth like it did in his imagination. Instead, it lands at an angle and scatters the other twigs around, like a fish squirming suddenly on a seabed, then lies across a thatch of them. It forms a nice pattern, he thinks – an angle crossing three straight branches beneath. Neat.

He picks it up. He's ready.

He glances across the stream.

Ready to go hunting.

There are no wild animals to be seen.

Billy runs through the trees for a while, resisting the urge to whoop like an Indian, occasionally stopping quickly – *ambush!* – and firing the arrow at a tree, and pretending it's one of the boys at school. In real life, it never sticks in, mainly just clatters sideways against the trunk, but at least he nails a couple of dead-on shots, so much so that the arrow gradually dulls at the tip.

He stops to sharpen it, hunkering down in the bushes, his heart thudding in his tiny chest and the blood pulsing in his ears.

Then he's off again, running and ducking.

Deeper into the woodland.

After a while, he catches sight of a cluster of birds in the branches of a tree overhead, little more than larger, darker leaves amongst the green. He stops and takes aim, closing one eye. Letting the moment pan out as long as he can. Imagining scenarios: needing to bring food back to a camp; needing to hunt to survive. But he knows that he doesn't, and the birds are low enough to be vulnerable, despite the awkward trajectory, so he doesn't fire, just lowers the bow, keeping the string tense.

And then he hears something.

The sound makes the fine hairs on his arms stand on end.

At first he thinks it's a wild animal he can hear – an animal in distress – as there's nothing remotely human about it. It's a birdlike cawing. But then again, it's not like any bird he's ever heard, and right now it's the only real sound in the forest. None of the usual birdsong. Even the ticking of the undergrowth has fallen silent here.

The sound is coming from just up ahead, over a ridge in the earth topped by a row of bushes.

Another sound: *thud, thud, thud.*

The cawing disappears. But then, after a second or two of silence, it is replaced by a rattling, gurgling noise, like someone trying to suck up the remains of a milkshake through a straw. And that sound continues.

Suddenly it feels as though Billy is very far away from civilisation: that, aside from whoever – whatever – is beyond the ridge, he is totally alone here. He looks around, feeling helpless. If the forest was his friend before, it has deserted him now. Every instinct in his body tells him to turn around and run away, back through the vast expanse of wood he can feel behind him

And yet slowly, ever so slowly, Billy creeps forward up the slope. He knows he shouldn't, but he can't turn around. Something draws him on.

As he approaches the bushes, he checks the arrow is still tethered in place on the string. It is, and that makes him feel a little more fierce. He isn't scared – or rather, he is, but he is also brave. Even if he can't fire straight, whoever is here won't know that.

Just as Billy reaches the bushes, the gargling increases in pitch, becoming sharper and more urgent.

He uses the tip of the arrow to move a branch – ever so carefully – to one side.

There are two men. One is lying on his back, just a few feet past the foliage. His bright red face is bubbling angrily from the remains of his nose and mouth. One arm is casually tracing an arc through the dust, like a lazy snow angel. The second man, wearing a black balaclava, is crouched over the legs of the first, poking him leisurely in the stomach with a screwdriver, as if attempting slowly to stir his insides.

Billy's heart stops.

Then starts again.

He is stuck in place, unable to retreat. He doesn't *dare* move. For the moment, the man is intent on torturing the victim on the ground – poking into his intestines almost inquisitively – but he could look up at any moment.

Billy swallows.

Too loud.

The man's head turns, and their eyes meet.

For a second, the forest is entirely frozen and Billy still doesn't dare move. And then suddenly everything comes to life. The man goes from crouching to upright in one motion, as though it's on film and some frames have gone missing. And Billy fires the arrow at him, then scrambles up, not even waiting to see if it hits, just turning and running back through the vast, empty woods.

As fast as he can.

Twenty-Four

'It's definitely one of ours,' Laura said.

'Fantastic. Tell me everything.'

She'd just got back from a briefing with the police in Buxton, after which she'd attended the post-mortem of Kate Barrett. And she had returned bearing gifts.

The first photograph she slid across to me made me wince inside, and regardless of anything else she was about to tell me, I knew she was right, that this was our guy. The photo had been taken at the scene. It showed a close-up of the remains of a woman's face, hair splayed out on the blood-soaked tarmac on which she was lying.

The damage wasn't as extensive as to our victims, but it was close enough. The killer had been interrupted, after all. I pictured David Barrett, a man I'd never seen, plummeting across a field in an attempt to reach his wife – and the whole time the man ahead of him was just striking her repeatedly in the head.

It was more an emotion than an image: a frantic, keening sensation of desperation, anguish. Because he had not been in time. Most of the injuries were to the right-hand side of her head and mouth. The latter hung open, the destruction obvious. Her right eye was lost under blood; her nose hung off, leaning away from it. The remaining eye stared upwards, as clear and empty as the sky it must have dully reflected.

'Okay,' I said.

'From the full report alone, it's him.' Laura took the photo away again. 'Her husband managed to give a full statement, the poor bastard. He didn't understand. He said the guy could have easily got away with the scooter, if that was what he wanted. There was no way he needed to do what he did.'

'Because he never wanted the scooter,' I said.

'My guess too. It wasn't about that.'

I shook my head.

Laura said, 'I know.'

'Show me the rest.'

She passed me more of the other crime-scene photos. I flipped through them one by one, then put them down on the desk, feeling numb.

'Full results of the PM aren't in yet, obviously. I left halfway through.'

'But?'

'Polythene was found in the wounds.'

I nodded. I'd been expecting that – or something, at least. If Laura had left halfway through, it must have been because she'd seen enough to be satisfied.

'Not been confirmed as that yet,' she said. 'But I'm convinced. This is our guy.'

'Okay.' I leaned back in the chair and put my hands behind my head. Stretched. 'So now what?'

'I've left Buxton to it for now. They're keen to follow up everything at their end – which is good for us, obviously. As things stand, they've only got one to deal with. But we'll be co-ordinating from now on. Young's negotiating, but I don't see any problems.'

'Can't they just take the whole thing off our hands?'

Laura gave me a sly smile. 'No such luck.'

'What are they like?'

'The Buxton PD? They're okay. Seem sharp enough. The DCI in overall charge is a guy called Franklin.'

'Franklin?' I said. 'What's *he* like?'

'Seemed on top of things to me. Reiterated the need to work

together. Pool resources. That side of things will be okay, I think.'

'Are they asking for anything?'

'Not so far. Co-operative, like I said. They're going to come over tomorrow for the daily briefing: bring us what they have and take a little of what we've got. Share it all and see if anything leaps out.'

I nodded slowly.

'In the meantime, we need to get all the data relating to Kate Barrett factored in to our investigation. In case it's part of the pattern.'

'If there is one,' I said.

'Yeah.'

But even if there was, how were we supposed to make sense of it? It was hard enough thinking in terms of our city, never mind expanding the investigation to neighbouring towns. Was he going to take it nationwide? Had he left us for now – possibly even for good?

And then there was the Buxton connection, which was definite now. Who was Franklin? Had I ever encountered him before? The name wasn't familiar, but I wasn't sure.

That tightening again. The storm clouds gathering.

Laura misread my expression. 'I know.'

I nodded, but thought: *No. You don't.*

Twenty-Five

'Okay, Billy,' I said. 'We'll take this at your own speed, in your own time. If at any time you get scared or upset, you just have to say and we'll stop for a while. Is that all right?'

Billy Martin nodded – a little too quickly. I was sure he was feeling both scared and upset, because anybody in their right mind would be, never mind a twelve-year-old boy. But he was obviously determined, in the manner of twelve-year-old boys everywhere, not to let it show.

'All right,' I said.

We were sitting in the comfort suite: the room on the department's second floor that was reserved for the more fragile interviewees we encountered. Laura and I were stationed on a two-seater settee opposite Billy and his father. A child support officer was seated away to one side.

The room was set up more like a living room than an interview room; all the normal accoutrements were hidden as far out of sight as possible, so that the most ostentatious thing was the black-ball camera up in the corner. Billy didn't seem to notice that anyway. His gaze kept darting between me, Laura and the floor, as though he didn't want to meet anyone's eyes long enough for them to notice how scared his own were.

I felt sorry for the kid. He looked even younger than he was – just a skinny rake of a thing with messy brown hair and an old T-shirt that looked hand-me-down and two sizes too big for him. His jeans were ragged and tattered at the bottoms, where his cheap trainers had scuffed away the fabric, turning the denim there into muddy strings.

The pity was mainly because of his father, though, who didn't seem concerned enough about his son's ordeal to me. He was just sitting there, fat arms folded over a fat belly, his face reddened by annoyance – for all the world as though he'd been summoned here because his son had done something wrong. We were compelled by law to have the man present, but I think all of us – including Billy and his father – would have preferred to do it without.

'All right,' I said again. 'Can you tell us why you were in the woods in the first place?'

He shuffled awkwardly. 'I was playing.'

'By yourself?'

'Yes.'

'Do you often go there?'

'Sometimes.'

Beside him, his father snorted slightly.

I said, 'You knew to take care though, didn't you? With the things in the news recently?'

'I guess.' He shrugged slightly, embarrassed. 'But I thought it would be okay.'

'I know. What were you doing?'

He hesitated.

'Go on,' I said. 'It's fine, honestly.'

'I wanted to build a bow and arrow.'

'What?' This time his father's snort was actually angry. 'A bow and arrow? What on earth did you want to do that for?'

Billy slumped further into the settee, as though wanting to disappear entirely inside it. Obviously at his age – on the cusp of adulthood – it was a humiliating thing to admit, and yet his father's response was to compound that.

It was already entirely clear that Billy Martin was a kid without many friends or much in the way of confidence. It was now becoming obvious what the root cause of that was. Honestly, it might well be the single most depressing thing police work teaches you: some kids never have a fucking chance.

I said, 'You wanted to play cowboys and Indians? Something like that?'

'I guess.'

'That's okay. It's a good game. I used to play that myself when I was your age. I didn't have many friends, and I got picked on. So I used to imagine I was shooting the kids that picked on me.'

His father snorted again. I ignored him, because Billy looked up at me a little more hopefully. What I'd said was true, and it wasn't hard to remember how I'd felt at his age: gawky and awkward and lonely. You never forget these things; you never forget how it feels. There's nothing wrong with finding play wherever you can when you're a kid . . .

Buxton.

I shook that thought out of my head.

'So you were in the woods. We know whereabouts. We've just come from there.' I nearly said *the scene,* but corrected myself just in time. We'd get to that soon enough. 'What happened then?'

Billy took a big inward breath. 'There was a horrible noise up ahead. I didn't know what it was, and I went to look. I know I shouldn't have, but I did.'

'And what did you see?'

The upset finally surfaced properly.

'Okay,' I said quickly. 'We know what happened, so I don't need you to go through everything you saw. It must have been horrible.'

He nodded. Not crying, but almost.

'How long were you watching?'

'I don't know,' he said. 'It's hard to remember. Maybe . . . a minute?'

Christ. Given the way time expanded in horrific circumstances, I guessed it probably hadn't been that long. But even so, it must have been more than enough.

We'd already identified the victim – a twenty-eight-year-old male named Paul Thatcher. That portion of the woods had a slight association with cruising, although we had no way of knowing whether he was out there for that or something else. I'd seen the body and what had been done to it, though, and I wasn't sure I could have watched for more than a second or two. The poor kid must have been frozen in place. Out in the middle of nowhere, not knowing whether to run or hide or what.

'This is going to be a difficult question,' I said. 'But was the man alive when you saw him? The man on the ground, I mean.'

Billy took another deep breath.

'I think so,' he said. 'Sort of.'

Sort of. From what we'd found at the scene so far – and that was obviously ongoing – *sort of* made an awful kind of sense. Because, yes, Paul Thatcher was dead when we got there, but from his injuries he'd clearly been *sort of* alive for a considerable amount of time beforehand. Billy's answer mattered because of what it implied. That even though he'd been observed torturing Paul Thatcher, our killer hadn't panicked, hadn't run, hadn't even chased after the witness.

Instead, very calmly, he'd carried on with his work.

'Can you describe him? Not the man on the ground. The other man.'

'He was all in black and he had a mask on.'

'What kind of mask?'

'A balaclava? Like in the army. All black, just with the eyes showing.'

'That's good. Can you say how tall he was?'

'No. He was . . . crouched over him, stabbing him in the stomach. Or doing something, anyway. When he stood up . . . I don't know.'

'He saw you?'

'It was like one second he wasn't looking at me and then he was. Staring right at me.'

Even second-hand, I felt a chill. At that point, the kid had been a good mile from any help, and he'd locked eyes with a grown man who'd tortured and killed several people. A monster armed with a hammer, a screwdriver and God only knew what else.

'His eyes were just . . . empty.'

'Empty?'

'They reminded me of . . . this story. The kids at school. They told me about someone who killed a cat. I couldn't imagine what sort of person could do that. But when I looked into his eyes, I realised . . .'

'*This* type of man?'

Billy nodded.

'So you ran?'

He nodded again, but then hesitated, perhaps realising that it didn't sound as brave as he so obviously wanted to be.

'Don't worry,' I said. 'The kids at school, they would all have done the same. Hell, I probably would. You did the right thing.'

'I fired at him first, though.' Billy leaned forward, suddenly emphatic. 'I fired at him.'

His father snorted again. 'With your bow and arrow?'

'Mr Martin,' I said. 'Do you want to shut the fuck up?'

The man stared at me, jaw falling slack.

'No, seriously,' I said. 'Shut the fuck up.'

Laura tapped my knee. I leaned back, and let her take over for a moment.

'Mr Martin,' she said. 'What my partner is trying to say is that we need Billy to feel free to give his own account of what happened.'

I was about to interrupt, because, no, I was trying to say that I wanted the man to shut the fuck up, but Laura tapped my knee again.

'Personally, I think he's been very brave.' Laura smiled at Billy. 'You ran. Like Detective Hicks said, that makes total sense. Trust me, it's fine. But then what?'

'I ran for a long time. I didn't dare look behind me until I got to the stream.'

'And what did you see?'

'Nothing.' Billy looked miserable. 'Just empty woods. He wasn't chasing me or anything.'

It had apparently taken the last few seconds for my insolence to land in Billy's father's head. He unfolded his arms and leaned forward and was about to assert his authority on the situation.

'Listen—'

'All right then,' Laura said, sounding breezy. 'I think we're done for now. Let's leave it there. Thank you all for your time.'

She glanced up at the camera in the corner as we stood up. The child protection officer would deal with the additional details. Laura and I headed for the door.

But as I got there, I hesitated, and then returned to where Billy Martin was sitting and knelt down in front of him. Didn't even glance at his father beside him.

'Billy,' I whispered. The interview was over, but I didn't want the camera to pick up the lie I was about to tell him. 'I want you to know something.'

He looked at me nervously. 'What?'

'I shouldn't tell you this,' I said. 'But just between you and me. You hit him. Enough to slow him down.'

He stared at me.

'I did?'

'You hit him.' I smiled. 'Good job. That's why you got away.'

Twenty-Six

Dear Detective Hicks

I notice you have failed to acknowledge my previous letter. Obviously, I did not expect you to reply directly. I was far too careful to allow you to trace my message, as I'm sure you will have discovered. You will find similar efforts have been taken with this one, although no doubt you will be compelled to check. That is one of the reasons I will stay ahead of you. You have too much to do, while I have only one thing. So far, my code is unravelling exactly to plan.

But you told the press you have received no correspondence from me. If you are 'holding back details', I quite understand. However, it may be that you are unsure whether I am the man you are looking for. If that is the case, I am enclosing proof that should satisfy even you. I would hate to think you weren't taking me seriously. I want to beat you fair and square.

So let me help you, as much as you deserve.

The people who have died mean nothing to me. By now you know that they are strangers to me, that they have done me no personal wrong, that they have no obvious connection to me. But I am telling you something else. Their deaths mean nothing. The murders are irrelevant to me. What I am interested in is the pattern below the surface. Can you break it? That's what matters.

Why murders then? Because the stakes are very high, in ways you cannot possibly understand. And I want the finest minds concentrated on cracking my code. Challenging the police, on their own ground, is the ideal solution. After all, you are soldiers of a kind. You have enormous resources. If anyone can do it, it will be you. If not, I win, don't I? I beat you. You don't seem to be doing very well so far. But please keep trying. A hollow victory is no victory at all.

In the meantime, as mentioned above, I enclose proof that I am the man you are looking for. It should be incontrovertible. It will also reveal something that will surely be of interest to you, something it is only fair you know.

You haven't found most of them yet.

Twenty-Seven

Half an hour after reading the second letter, Laura and I were seated in a suite in the IT department.

It was a long, narrow room that reminded me of a university computer lab – rows of benches covered with terminals, interspersed with bulky printers, photocopiers and cabinets full of spare cables and hard drives. It was lit, dimly, by the thin remains of daylight coming through the open slatted blinds, and it smelled of carpet cleaner and electricity, like ozone in the air before it rains.

We were sitting at one of the terminals with a techie called Garretty, waiting as he took all the necessary precautions with the item the killer had sent along with his second letter.

A CD.

I could sense Laura fidgeting beside me: biting her fingernails and shifting slightly on her office chair, rotating it back and forth with her heel. I was doing my best to keep still. Inside, though, I was doing the same.

'Maybe it'll be music,' I tried. 'We can get him for copyright infringement too.'

Laura gave me an awkward smile. I returned it.

Of course, both of us had a good idea of what we were going to find on the disc. There wasn't much it *could* be other than a recording of some kind. Audio, photo or – God help us – video. Given the nature of the crime scenes so far, I imagined neither of us was looking forward to that. I certainly wasn't.

At the same time, I kept telling myself, it was more evidence. He might have slipped up. However horrible it was, there might be some detail that would prove his undoing. That was the hope here. Pretty much the only thing to cling to.

'We've got a single file,' Garretty said.

'Just one?'

'There are the usual extraneous files you'd expect to find on a CD, but only one has been written to the disc by the user. It's non-rewritable, so he couldn't have deleted or added anything after recording it. MPEG encoding.'

'MPEG?' Laura said.

I nodded, feeling grim. 'It's a video.'

'Christ.'

Under normal circumstances, you could just open the file and let it play. Under these, the techie was using various programs to deal with it. These machines were all secure environments, and the contents of the CD would be ghosted across into a virtual environment so as not to risk losing any data from the disc itself.

The internal safeguards would also take care of any malware the killer might have kindly thought to include – although I wasn't expecting anything like that. Our man was clearly malicious, but for now, for some reason, I was prepared to take the letter at face value. He wanted us to know it was him. He wanted to give us some insight into what he was doing.

But could we take it at face value? Maybe it would be a mistake to do so – to believe a single word he'd written. The thing to remember was that ultimately he didn't want to be caught, so whatever his claims, he wasn't going to tell us anything that helped us.

That was what I'd normally think, anyway. But this guy felt different. Unless I was missing something, we weren't particularly close to catching him: up until now, he'd been killing with relative impunity. Then there was the challenge implicit in his letters. And the crimes did seem to match what he was saying – that he was killing apparently at random, for some reason we couldn't guess.

Or maybe I just wanted to believe there had to be something. Some reason for what he was doing.

He's playing with you.

If so, he was doing it successfully.

'Okay,' Garretty said. 'Let's set it going.'

'This is likely to be upsetting.'

It felt only fair to warn him, but he shrugged and clicked the mouse. 'I'll take a walk if I feel like it.'

The video began playing in a window that filled most of the computer screen. At the bottom, a bar tracked the time elapsed and remaining. It was clear from this that the file was just over seven minutes long.

'Hand-held,' Laura said.

I nodded. As the footage played, it was obvious the camera was in someone's hand: the view was moving loosely and jerkily, tracking over blurred undergrowth, never settling long enough to make out any detail. The crunch of woodland underfoot came from the speakers. He was walking somewhere, dangling the camera by his side.

And then the sound fell away as the man drew to a halt and brought the camera up.

It showed a man lying on his back on the ground, surrounded by swirls of brambles and grass. The man wasn't a derelict. He was wearing an old brown suit over a white shirt that had ridden up to reveal a pale stomach, heaving slightly from the heaviness of his breathing. From his face – eyes closed, mouth working soundlessly – he was clearly disorientated, although there was no clue what had happened to him. His grey hair was in disarray, some of it plastered to his forehead with sweat.

The camera moved in to get a good view of his face, then swung quickly away, and there was the familiar crunch of undergrowth as the man stepped back.

The view steadied again, then moved from side to side, as though the camera was shaking its head. Then it tilted forward so that the display now showed the entire body of the man a short distance in front.

Laura said, 'He's mounted it on a tripod.'

'Yes. That he has.'

'A short introduction to show the victim. Then mounting the camera to leave his hands free.'

'At least it suggests he's working alone,' I said. As grim as I felt, I was trying to be professional and detached. 'If he had a partner, the other guy could film it for him. Or vice versa.'

'Do you think he filmed the others?'

'I don't know.'

'Where is this?'

'I don't know that either.'

The view remained still – the victim just lying on his back, his stomach undulating, as though he was trying to be sick but couldn't.

'I don't think it's the woodland where Billy Martin encountered him,' Laura said. 'Certainly rural, though.'

I nodded. 'Maybe north-east of the city? Lots of winding country roads out that way. Patches of forest and woodland in between them. Miles and miles of them, in fact.'

Laura didn't reply.

I knew what she was thinking, though – that the area was huge, and we desperately needed a way to narrow it down. Because what the man had written in the letter was true: the man on the floor was a victim we didn't know about yet.

The killer stepped into view.

Here he was, then. Walking across to the man lying on the floor. Billy Martin had seen him and lived. Several others – we didn't even know how many – had seen him and died. And somewhere on our board of images, we had a blurred image of him visiting a postbox. But this was a clear sighting.

Aside from a pair of white trainers, he was dressed entirely in black: jeans and a rainproof jacket. A wool balaclava. Ski gloves. It was difficult to tell, but he appeared to be of medium height and build. Nothing exceptional. Without the mask and gloves, he wouldn't have looked out of place on any street in the city.

Anybody. Nobody.

He was holding a white carrier bag in one hand. You couldn't really tell what was inside, but I knew from the previous murders that it would be a hammer, and that something awful was about to happen.

And then it did.

Standing astride the prostrate man, the killer smacked him five times straight in the face with the bag. Mercifully, the detail was obscured by the quality of the footage. All you could really see was the man's head bouncing repeatedly and his face turning steadily crimson. But the audio captured each wet collision.

'Okay,' Garretty said. 'I'll just take a walk now.'

'You do that.'

I wished I could join him. We were only two minutes into the footage. There was – somehow – another five for us to sit through.

And we did.

We watched the killer use a screwdriver on the man's lower stomach, stabbing at him like a sewing machine, and then we watched him standing on the wounds. He used the screwdriver on the remains of the victim's face, avoiding his feeble attempts to hold his arm in front. The whole time, the soundtrack recorded an awful gargling as the man failed to breathe and scream properly through a nose and mouth that were no longer where or what they should have been.

Finally, the killer beat the man about the head with the hammer until his whole body had gone floppy. Even then, it was difficult to be certain he was dead.

The killer disappeared from view again, retreating behind the camera. The view held the unmoving body for a few more seconds, and then juddered as he lifted the camera from the tripod.

'He's made a snuff film,' Laura said.

Her voice sounded odd.

I nodded. 'Are you okay?'

'No.'

'No. Me neither.'

There was nothing else to say. But we watched for the final minute as he carried the camera over by hand, zooming in to create a full, horrific record of the injuries he'd inflicted. What was left of the man's head wasn't even recognisable as a human being any more: just something red staining the bright green grass.

'Where is this?' Laura said quietly.

'I don't know. We need to find it, though—'

But then the killer moved the camera away from the dead man in the grass and panned carefully across the land around him. And my skin, already shivery, became even colder.

Because there were other bodies lying nearby.

He panned over one, two, three . . .

Four.

Oh my God.

Five.

After pausing on the fifth additional body, the camera juddered again slightly and the file stopped, leaving us in silence.

'Fuck,' Laura said.

It was so soft, I barely heard it. I didn't register how unlike her it was to swear. My thoughts were standing too still to let new ones through. The first one that made it was the realisation that our man had a killing spot. One that we hadn't found.

One that, for all we knew, he was adding to right now.

'Yes,' I said. 'We really need to find that.'

Twenty-Eight

'Welcome to the dark room.'

'The what?' I said.

DS Renton closed the door to his 'office' behind us. Suddenly he looked a little embarrassed.

'The dark room. It's just what we call it, off the record. No windows, you see, and we always keep the blinds down on the door. Plus, you know, because of what we deal with in here.'

I looked around. 'Good name.'

It was a small room, probably five metres by three. The only free wall space was to allow for the single door behind me; the rest was lined with shelves of computer equipment, reference books, files and binders, above a handful of desks and gently humming monitors. Cables snaked across the fuzzy, buzz-cut carpet.

This was the fabled LG15, then – the dark room – which everyone in the department knew of and hated the idea of visiting. Few ever had need to. It was the home of the specialised 'live IT' unit, dedicated to dealing with the murkier end of online investigations.

On the nearest wall there was something that looked like a CD rack, except the slots were slightly larger. Each one contained a naked metal hard drive with a label scrawled on in ballpoint pen. All names. Emily. Adam. Sally. Will. Every single one of the names represented a 'child' – a false identity, routed separately, that could be used by DS Renton and his small, hand-picked team of officers in chat rooms and online discussions to infiltrate paedophile groups.

There were also rows of disks used to store conversations and – worse – back up the confidential data from investigations: photos and videos. In this room, images of all types were analysed, categorised, catalogued.

Important work, but difficult and hideous – and done down here, behind closed doors, in a basement room without windows. Officers who worked here were screened more strenuously than those licensed to carry automatic weapons, and underwent more frequent psychological reviews.

Renton sat down at a desk and motioned for me to join him on a chair beside him. As I sat, he tapped a few keys and brought the monitor to life.

'I've received the file,' he said. 'Not had a chance to view it yet. Do you mind?'

'Go ahead.'

There didn't seem to be any point warning him, given the things he must have seen in his time.

He watched the video clip in silence. My own instinct was to look away, but instead, I watched it again, hoping to spot something I'd missed on first viewing. Some clue.

It was marginally easier to watch now I'd seen it once and knew what it contained, but still tough. What played out on the screen hit you in the heart as much as the head, or perhaps even somewhere deeper. I've seen a lot of dead bodies in my time, but watching someone being killed was very different. The act was alien. How could someone do that? How could someone be so vicious and empty as to cause another human being such suffering?

Do you believe in evil?

Renton, meanwhile, was professional and detached, but even he wasn't impervious. He was obviously troubled by what he was seeing – maybe the day you aren't any more is the day you leave this place for your own sanity.

When the clip finished playing, he leaned back and ran his fingers through his hair.

'Okay. Shit. Tell me more.'

'What we have here is evidence from an ongoing investigation. This recording was made a few days ago – or at least that appears to be when the copy was created. We received it, with a letter, through the post. This man is still at large.'

'This is . . . the guy?'

'Yes, this is the guy. At present, we don't know where this location is and we don't know the identities of the six victims shown. Obviously, we very much want to.'

Renton blew out.

'I can help you with that. Obviously we've done this sort of work before. The first thing we'll do is pull out the helpful frames.'

Renton explained the process. What he and his colleagues would do was scan through the file meticulously, frame by frame, and make sure there was nothing we were missing. They would get the cleanest shots possible of the victims' clothes. Coupled with missing persons data, that should enable us to identify them.

'What about finding them?' I said.

'How much scope have we got?'

He meant money. 'Given what we're dealing with here,' I said, 'as much as we need.'

'That's what I figured. Okay. Well, the obvious stuff we can do is look for landmarks. At first glance, there's nothing, but there might be something there that helps us pin down the areas to look at. For starters.'

'And then?'

'This is the expensive part. We can recreate a map of the terrain from the video. It won't be perfect, by any means, but you'll basically end up with an overhead diagram that maps the layout of the trees and the land. Geographically precise, and possible to cross-check against existing satellite data.'

'Sounds good.'

'Sadly, it's not an automated process. You'll need officers doing it by hand. And obviously, with tree cover, it won't be exact.'

'It'll give us an idea, though: maybe rule out some areas at the least.'

'Yep.'

It wasn't perfect, but it was something.

I said, 'I'm also interested in something a bit more . . . oblique. We have the what, and can work on the who and where. But *why*?'

'What do you mean?'

'Why make the video?'

'That's one for the psychologists, I think.' Renton shook his head. 'I mean, you do occasionally see this kind of thing. That's a generic "you" by the way, as this is one of the most extreme things I've come across in my whole career. But serial killers, some serial rapists, they do take videos. To relive it, I guess. And child pornography rings, obviously.'

To relive it. If his letters were to be believed, that just didn't seem like our man. He wasn't interested in the murders themselves so much as using them as a test. Why video them, then? Was it just this one, so he could prove the letters really were from him?

Or was it something more?

I said, 'Have you ever seen a snuff film?'

'No.' Renton was silent for a moment. 'Not officially, anyway. Officially, they don't exist.'

'What do you mean, "officially"?'

He gestured at the frozen image on the screen.

'Well, this is what many people would call a snuff movie. It's a film of somebody being murdered. That's rare, but not unheard of. And there are thousands of videos of people dying on film – beheadings, accidents, CCTV footage. But to be a snuff film officially, the footage has to have been filmed for distribution, for financial reasons.'

'To be sold for profit?'

'Yes. And nobody's ever found one. It's one of those myths that sounds macabre enough to be true, but obviously isn't when you think about it. There'd be too much risk involved: killing somebody on camera and distributing it. And there's no need to do it. You could create the same thing with actors and special effects. Hollywood does it all the time.'

'That's not *real*, though.'

'No, but if you want real death on camera, it's already there, risk-free. You've heard of Daniel Pearl? Or the Yellow Man? You just don't go to the trouble – the vast trouble – of creating something new and trying to find a market for it.'

He was right, of course. Filming a murder is one thing. But how the hell do you then go about selling it? It's not like you can advertise it in the back of the paper.

'At the same time,' Renton said, 'something about it rings a bell.'

I frowned. 'Pardon me?'

He frowned, then shook his head.

'The clip. I don't know what it is. It reminds me of something. I don't know what.'

I leaned forward. 'Another murder?'

'No, no. Believe me, if I'd seen something like this before, I'd remember it. No. It's something else. I'm not sure what.'

'A movie?'

'Maybe. I don't know.' He shook his head again, as though dismissing the idea, and I leaned back slightly, disappointed.

He sounded far away. 'It'll come to me.'

Twenty-Nine

It took me a long time to fall asleep that night.

Beside me, Rachel slept fitfully, snoring gently, fidgeting, her bump resting on the maternity pillow. It was a warm night too, and even lying on top of the covers I was sweating. But it wasn't really any of those things that kept me awake: it was the thought of those bodies, still lying out there somewhere, exposed to the wilds, waiting to be discovered.

That and the thought that there might be more of them now. If not yet, there would be soon. But then, maybe not. If the murders were random, there was no guarantee the dump site would be added to, and no guarantee that it wouldn't.

When I did sleep, I dreamed I was outside a house.

It was a two-storey building on a long, wide road that stretched far out ahead and behind. The homes here were all the same: wooden and rickety, hand-made almost, each one sitting in its own fenced-off square of dirty scrubland. Nothing grew out here. There was a slight breeze, and dust billowed across the tarmac around me, as though a car had dropped me off and then sped off spinning its tyres. Above me, in the sky, clouds sped past impossibly quickly.

The house was painted red, but the colour had faded. I walked up to the front door and pushed; it swung silently open and I stepped into a small hallway. To the right, there was a lounge, with threadbare settees and a wooden cabinet that seemed wrong, although I couldn't work out why. To the left, a dirty kitchen, with ridges of solidified fat on the counter curled around absent cups and plates.

In front of me, a dark staircase led up to the first floor.

I stood there for a moment, listening. *Feeling*. At first, the house seemed silent, but it wasn't. There was something. Not a sound so much as a heartbeat. A slow, thudding pressure, as though somewhere, behind a closed door, a drum was being sounded.

I started up the stairs, my skin itching.

On the landing, there was a corridor that ended in a bright, arched window that must have faced out over the rear of the property. Leading up to it was a long strip of frayed red carpet, not wide enough to meet the mouldy skirting boards on either side. In front of the window, motes of dust whirled impossibly quickly, like a cloud of midges, forming half-glimpsed fingerprint patterns in the air.

I started walking slowly along the corridor. As I did, the heartbeat grew louder.

There were three doors. The first was open on to a bathroom. Everything inside was blue and green and shimmering; it was like peering into an artificially lit underwater cave. I turned away and kept walking.

The second door, on the other side of the hall from the other two, was closed. As I reached it, I realised the heartbeat sound was coming from the room behind.

I stood there for a long time, facing it.

Then I reached out and pushed it open.

Immediately, the heartbeat stopped. Light from the corridor fell into a small, dark room that was little more than a cell. It was stripped down and empty – but only of fixtures and fittings. Sitting in one corner, hugging her knees, was a woman in a bright white nightdress. Her dark hair fell over her bare knees and thin shins.

She appeared to be sobbing, but making no sound at all, as though behind glass. When I breathed in, there was the faintest scent of honey in the air.

'Hello?' I said.

The motions of sobbing stopped. For a moment, she was very still.

'Hello? Are you okay?'

She lifted her head very slowly, revealing her face.

'Oh,' I said.

She was a very beautiful young woman – or had been once. The skin of her face was bright white, framed with black hair. Her right eye was swollen shut so badly that it looked like her eyebrow had simply been underlined.

Emmeline Levchenko. A memory or a ghost, assuming there's even a difference, finding its way into my nightmare. An image of her back when I could have – *should* have – saved her, and failed.

A still second later she came screaming at me.

DAY EIGHT

Thirty

As the coffee machine begins rasping and spitting, Jake kicks Marie Wilkinson in the stomach.

She rubs her hand gently over her belly and whispers *shush* to him, but it doesn't do any good. Quite the opposite. It feels like the little scamp starts doing cartwheels in there.

The image makes her smile.

In the first few months of the pregnancy, it had been difficult to believe there was the beginning of somebody inside her. Certainly, she hadn't been able to imagine how it would feel at thirty-four weeks: that it would be impossible *not to* imagine it, this new life inside her that was now only weeks away from being an actual baby.

Through her twenties, when she'd very adamantly not wanted children, it had been this aspect she'd always found the most terrifying to contemplate. The sensation of something growing inside her. It had made her shudder. There was childbirth itself to fear, of course, but the idea of becoming an incubator had always seemed far more alien. So it had surprised her how quickly she adjusted – how much, in fact, she'd come to like it. And although there is still the birth itself to be afraid of, she's almost come to terms with that as well. A part of her is even looking forward to it.

As she rubs her stomach, smiling at Jake's movements, she thinks: *I can't wait to meet you.* He's so active. It feels like he's full of joy, doing pirouettes in there out of sheer excitement.

When she dreams about him, he's one big smile. The aches and pains of pregnancy are uncomfortable, but she pictures her body as already holding him – embracing him, just as it will when he arrives – and it feels like she can put up with the discomfort forever if needs be.

Fortunately not.

Not long now. It's easy to imagine he can understand her thoughts. *You get yourself ready, little man, because you're going to love this world.*

As the machine dribbles out the last few trickles of coffee, she senses Tony enter the kitchen behind her. He is busy, as always, rushing to get ready for work. Hair damp from the shower, shirt slightly untucked, still doing the tie he doesn't really need for the work but wears anyway.

'Hey, sweetie,' she says over her shoulder.

'Hiya. Coffee – thanks. You're a star.'

'Well, if you haven't time for breakfast, you've got to have something.'

'Tell me about it.'

She pours him a cup. There's enough for a second in there; she might treat herself when he's gone. At first she scrupulously avoided everything she was supposed to, but she's relaxed a little as time has gone on. An occasional cup won't hurt. The advice seems to change every few weeks anyway.

'Did I keep you awake last night?' she says.

'Not that I'd ever tell you. How's Jake?'

'Active this morning. It's the smell of coffee. I told you.'

'Maybe you're right.'

Freshly brewed coffee is her favourite smell, and while it's probably her imagination, she's noticed Jake respond to it a few times too. *Confirmation bias*, Tony has told her, meaning she was looking too hard for patterns and remembering the times he started jumping inside her more readily than the times he didn't. Her husband is far too sensible, but she loves him for that almost as much as for the sense of physical security he gives her.

As if on cue, he embraces her from behind, rubbing his hands gently over her bump. This close, she can smell drifts of his aftershave, and beneath that, *him*. He has always been manly without ever seeming to try. Big and solid. The kind of man who can carry anything you set down in front of him, do any job you give him.

Jake kicks against his hand.

'Feel that?' she says.

'Yeah.'

'Going to be a footballer, I reckon.'

'Either that or a right little thug.'

She pats his hand gently, and he moves away, reaching around her to get his coffee.

'Well, I hope you and Jake are going to look after each other today.'

Marie smiles again. 'I'm sure we will.'

'Got anything planned?'

'Just pottering.'

'Good.' He looks troubled. 'Don't overdo it.'

'We won't.'

She's pleased by his use of the baby's name. The pregnancy wasn't planned, and it took them both a little time to come round to the idea – Tony more than her. To begin with he always referred to it as 'the baby', and even after the scan showed it was a boy, and they'd discussed and agreed upon a name, he still seemed to find it hard to get his head around the idea of *Jake*. It was easier for her because she could feel him in ways Tony couldn't. A few weeks ago she'd had a brainwave and invested in a home ultrasound device – just a cheap, simple thing, but using it seemed to have made a huge difference. Tony had heard his son's heartbeat properly, and after that, it was rarely 'the baby' any more and always Jake.

Tony drains his coffee almost in one.

'Don't burn yourself, sweetie.'

'I won't. Asbestos mouth.'

He kisses her on the forehead. She tilts her head back and

he kisses her more fully on the mouth. As they embrace, Jake continues his activities.

Tony says, 'My unborn son is already kicking me in the wallet.'

'Get used to it.'

'Yeah.'

It's a sore point, probably, as she knows that's his chief worry. But he stays in the embrace for a reassuring moment longer before moving away, grabbing his coat.

'Okay. I've got to run or I'll be late. You look after yourself, okay?' He frowns. 'I'm serious.'

'Me too – don't worry. I'll be good.'

'No need for that. Just be careful.'

Marie sticks her tongue out at him.

'Love you,' he says.

'Love you too.'

And then he's out of the door, closing it behind him. She hears him running down the path and the gate clattering.

A part of Marie breathes a sigh of relief. She loves Tony's company, of course, but she could certainly get used to this being-alone-in-the-house-with-Jake business. It feels like her territory now. Her maternity leave has only just begun, and it feels good. No more random hours. The house is hers. *Within a couple of weeks*, she thinks, *you'll probably be going stir crazy*. But in a couple of weeks there won't be time to do anything much other than care for Jake. And she can't wait.

Marie potters around for a while, putting away the dishes she washed the night before, washing the ones she used for her breakfast. Then she picks up the pot and pours herself a coffee, using Tony's cup. She'll have one after all – it can't hurt, can it. That's when the front door opens and the man in the balaclava comes in.

Thirty-One

In the two days since I'd spoken to Stephen Henderson at the cemetery, the groundskeeper's skin had reddened to an even brighter shade: almost sore with colour. Whether it was from working out in the sun, or the drink, it had clearly been a rough forty-eight hours.

'I probably wouldn't have thought much of it.' He scratched his forehead beneath the blue baseball cap. 'Not if you hadn't mentioned it to me to be specially on the lookout.'

'You did good,' I said. 'We appreciate it.'

I was standing by the grave of Derek Evans with Henderson and Nigel Anders, the duty manager responsible for grounds-keeping shifts. Anders was a young man in a neat, slim-cut grey suit, black hair gelled to one side in a sweep. He looked like he was going to be sick.

'We've never had *anything* like this before,' he said. 'I mean, occasional vandalism, yes. But never anything like this.'

I nodded.

'Think it means anything?'

I didn't bother answering. *Yes, of course.*

I looked down at the remains of the grave. Buried cheaply, at council expense, all he'd had was a cheap wooden cross with a name badge pinned to the upright strut. Most of the graves in this patch were identical: this was where the poor, the homeless, the elderly without families, or without families who cared, were interred. Evans's resting place stood out, however, because of what had been done to it.

I needed a timeline here.

'So let's get this straight. Mr Henderson, you're sure the grave hadn't been touched last night?'

'Yes, sir. It was fine when I did my rounds.'

Anders gave me a look at that, as though he wasn't too convinced and nor should I be. From my encounter with him so far, he didn't come across as a young man particularly impressed with the people in his employ. Or maybe he was just pissed off that Henderson had called me before letting him know about the desecration first.

'I'm sure of it,' Henderson said, perhaps picking up on his boss's vibe. 'Like I said, because of what you mentioned, I've been paying special attention. Keeping an eye out. And this plot was fine last night. This morning, on my rounds, I found this.' He sniffed, put out. 'Not even my plot this morning, but I checked anyway.'

'I believe you. You did well.' I turned to Anders. 'What kind of security do you have here?'

He bristled slightly. 'It's a cemetery, Detective Hicks. Not a bank vault.'

'I know. What kind of security do you have?'

'The main entrance is gated from six on an evening until eight in the morning. But that's not really security as such.' He gestured around. 'You can see how big the grounds are. The wall's low in places. People can get in if they want.'

'You have a watchman?'

He shook his head. 'Every now and then, if it looks like we've got a problem. Drunk kids, usually. Religious problems. But that's only every once in a while – it's not cost-effective normally.'

'Meaning, not right now?'

'No.'

I looked around the grounds, taking in the scale of them. It would indeed be a nightmare to police the whole area, although obviously we wouldn't need to do that. We just needed to watch a few graves. Not that the man would return, I was sure. He'd made his point. At the same time, he knew that we'd have to.

Playing with us.

'Any internal CCTV?'

'Only on the main gate. I don't know about the streets outside. Like I said, we don't normally have a need. Certainly not for something like . . . this.'

He gestured down at Evans's grave.

I nodded.

Someone had pulled the cross out of the ground, snapped it in half and stabbed it back in over where his body would be. As though, having graduated to using a screwdriver on his victims, our killer resented not having had a chance to do so on Evans before his death, and was making up for it as best he could now.

But that wasn't even the worst of it. The worst of it wasn't the damage he'd done to what was already there, but what he'd left in addition.

'Think that's human?' Henderson said. 'Or animal?'

Anders grimaced at the question.

I looked down at the small pile of excrement that had been left where the cross had been. Human or animal? It was impossible to say, of course, but I knew what I was betting. I thought, just as in his letter, our killer was making it very plain to us what he thought about the victims. How little they meant to him.

'I don't know,' I said.

Thinking: *human or animal?*

It seemed increasingly difficult to tell.

After arranging for scene-of-crime to attend the cemetery, and a pair of reliable sergeants to oversee proceedings there, I made my way back to the department for the midday briefing. It was already under way as I slipped quietly in at the back of the operations room, which was even more crammed than normal.

The air was stifling from the presence of warm bodies, and I faced a wall of backs, all paying attention to Laura, at the far end of the room, talking through the developments in the case.

'As you can see,' she said, 'the tech department has isolated images of the six victims from the video we received yesterday.'

She clicked through them, one by one, on PowerPoint. These were not the images that would be shown to relatives for the sake of identification – close-ups on clothes, for example – but the best full-body shots that Renton had been able to extract from the footage. The victim who was killed on camera was the clearest and easiest to look at. The others were blurred and patchy from artificial zoom, but the shots were good enough to identify things like clothes, sex and, in all but one case, hair colour.

None of the officers in the room had been forced to watch the video in full, and the still photographs were tame by comparison, but even so, looking around the room I noticed grimaces on the faces I could see and uncomfortable shuffles in posture where I could not. One officer in front of me unfolded his arms and rubbed a hand over his chin.

Of course, it wasn't just the injuries that were upsetting; these officers had seen worse, and in greater detail, over the past few days. I think it was more the same sense of horror that had stayed with me since I had first watched the clip, growing steadily. These bodies were still out there, unfound and unaccounted for. The first had lain there for God only knew how long, and then others had accumulated around it. Not only was it incomprehensible that the killer could do what he was doing, but the photographs exuded *sadness*. There is always sadness when you discover a body that has lain unattended for any length of time – a sense of loneliness, almost; an additional wrong – and that sensation came through in these images.

And of course, now there might even be more.

Laura said, 'We are cross-referencing these against the misper reports collated by Sergeant Pearson. We believe we have identified the victim in the video – the first image I showed – as

Colin Benson, a businessman reported missing three days ago. We are presently in contact with his family, and hope to identify the other victims today.'

She clicked the PowerPoint controller and the screen changed to show a number of smaller photographs side by side.

'This brings the total number of *known* victims to thirteen, if we include Kate Barrett, which for the moment we are. You've already heard the report from DCI Franklin, who will be joining our operation from Buxton and providing us with much-needed manpower, most of which will be used to search for the unidentified area in which our man now seems to be operating. We need to find that location, for a number of very obvious reasons. Yes?'

Laura took a question from someone by the wall – something about whether the killer was likely to continue at that location, given that he had sent us the video – but my attention was elsewhere. I was doing my best to scan the officers at the front of the room. I'd missed Franklin's contribution to the briefing, but he was here. I was wondering which of the backs of heads I could see might belong to him.

I settled, finally, on one with carefully groomed silver hair. That was probably him, although it was impossible to tell for sure.

I stared at him for a moment, then back to Laura.

'We also know, from the scene near Swaine Woods yesterday, that he is not *solely* using this location. We've discussed yesterday's letter already, so it's possible that alternating locations suits whatever pattern he's working from. It's also possible that there *is* no pattern. We need to keep an open mind. Regardless, we need to find this location.'

She clicked to another screen, this one showing a map of the city, with a close-up on the rural areas spreading out to the north-east. Even zoomed out, it was impossible to capture it all – the sheer maze-like mass of country lanes. Several square miles at least.

'This is the area we'll be concentrating on initially,' Laura said. 'And yes: it's an enormous task. We hope IT can help us narrow down our search areas, but for now, this is it.'

A hand shot up from the opposite side of the room.

'Press?'

Laura shook her head. 'This latest development remains strictly internal. We don't need those roads clogged with amateur search teams and hunters, trampling over everything. It's *our* job to find these people. So that's another difficulty. The search needs to be swift, thorough and discreet.'

I sensed, rather than heard, the groans in the room.

'I know, I know. We've got assignments ready to give out. In the meantime, is there anything else?'

I stuck my hand up.

Laura craned her neck. 'Yes? Oh look – it's Detective Hicks, back from holiday. Glad you could join us.'

'Glad to be here.'

I made my way through the standing clusters of officers and in between those seated in chairs. As I approached the front, I saw that Young had joined the briefing, which was unusual for him. He was sitting next to the man I suspected was Franklin, which I presumed was the reason for his attendance – interdepartmental goodwill. I reached Laura and turned to the assembled officers.

'I've just got back from Staines cemetery,' I said, 'where Derek Evans was interred the day before yesterday. As you may have gathered, we've seen some activity there overnight. SOCO are currently on site.'

I told the room about the scene that had been secured at the cemetery. As I expected, looking around, I saw predictable expressions of disgust on the faces of the officers. What had been done to the grave was the act of an animal, and I heard people muttering to that effect.

'As horrible as it is,' I said, 'it gives us another problem as well. A logistical one, you'll all be glad to hear, because we don't have enough as things stand.'

There were the expected groans.

I said, 'The funerals of Sandra Peacock and John Kramer are scheduled to take place later today. The others, over the next few days. We're going to need a presence at each.'

It seemed unlikely to me that he attended the burials in person – certainly he hadn't been at Derek Evans's – but we needed to cover ourselves.

'We'll also need surveillance on all the burial sites in case he shows up again. My guess is he won't. *Of course* he won't. But he knows this will stretch us thin, and he knows we have to do it anyway because we can't afford to miss anything. He's playing with us.'

I looked around the room, picking out faces, allowing the silence to let the implications of what I'd said sink in. There were other things to discuss – an idea I'd had on the drive back from the cemetery – but I didn't want to share them with the room yet, not until I'd talked them over with Laura.

'That's where we're at for the moment,' I said.

Last of all, I looked at Young, sitting in the front row, and then at the man beside him. DCI Franklin of the Buxton police force. He was in his late fifties, but well preserved: skin tanned and unlined, silver hair swept neatly in a side parting. He had his arms folded. Legs crossed too, so that one trouser leg had ridden up far enough to reveal five inches of black sock above his polished black shoe.

A tightening.

Storm clouds rolling ever blacker in the sky.

Because it was him.

'Earth to Hicks,' Laura said. 'Are you okay?'

'I'm fine.'

'I seem to be asking that a lot recently.'

'And I seem to be telling you I'm fine a lot, which I am.'

Which I wasn't. Not at all. After the briefing had finished and everyone in the room had dispersed, Laura had introduced me to Franklin. I'd shaken his hand, tried to look him in the eye, tried to pretend I was *fine*. I had no idea how good a job I'd done, but I thought I'd hidden the unease I felt fairly well. He didn't appear to have recognised me, but I expected, sooner or later, that he would.

Laura said, 'Are you sure? Because you seem—'

'The letters,' I said.

'Don't change the subject.'

'I already have. The subject was changed and you're too late to stop it. I've been thinking about the letters.'

'So have I.'

'Yes, but I've been thinking something different from you. Because you didn't see what the guy did at the cemetery.'

Laura leaned back and sighed, running her hand through her hair. Naturally, it fell down impeccably again.

'Go on.'

'It just strikes me that that kind of behaviour doesn't fit with the letters. With the way he comes across in them, I mean. He seems so controlled and articulate. Not the kind of man to go and shit on someone's grave.'

'He said they mean nothing to him.'

'Exactly. And he could be *displaying* that, I suppose. But it doesn't seem to me to be the kind of thing you do if someone genuinely means nothing to you. If I was going by instinct – by logic – then I'd be betting that the man writing the letters did not desecrate Evans's grave . . .'

'But?' Laura said.

'But I don't trust my instincts any more. I don't know what to make of this investigation. None of it makes sense.'

She looked at me for a while, then leaned forward again.

'What about the video? He sent us the video.'

'That's true. So maybe there's two of them working together. Or maybe what happened at the cemetery last night *isn't* connected.'

'You think?'

'I don't *know* what to think.' But I said it too hard, and I could tell from Laura's face that she was on the verge of asking me that too-familiar question again. *Are you okay?* 'I'm just throwing this out there. Just chucking ideas in the pot.'

'Okay. Listen, I—'

But she was interrupted by the phone ringing. She frowned at it, then took the call.

'Fellowes.'

I watched her, silent now, as she listened to the incoming call. A moment later, she snatched up a pen and began scribbling furiously. Her expression had turned grim. Her pad was upside down, but I could see she was writing an address and details.

Marie Wilkinson . . .

'Right.'

She sounded sick.

When she put the phone down, I didn't need her to tell me. I was already getting my jacket on. We had another. And it was a bad one.

Right then, of course, I had no idea.

Thirty-Two

Sitting in his car in traffic, the General is on fire.

Even though his arms are still trembling from the adrenalin, he feels alight with strength – all but delirious from the electricity that this day, and the ones before it, has generated inside him.

When he was planning this, he had visualised it principally as an intellectual exercise – he'd had no idea quite how *exciting* its execution would be. There have been horrors and difficulties, of course, but it has all been thrillingly unique. And he has secret knowledge now. Few people walking the earth have experienced the sights and sensations that he has. Few people have killed so many.

And he understands now how and why his father had grown into the man he remembers: that dispassionate murderer of men. The act of killing is impossible to describe: a mixture of transgression and power; the sense that you *should not* do this, quickly followed by the realisation that you *can*.

His father would be proud.

Up ahead, the traffic lights change, and the cars in front ease away. His hand shaking, the General releases the brake and moves forward with them.

The ghost of his father, now summoned, keeps pace in his head. His father never killed a man directly, but make no mistake, there was blood on his hands: blood that was inches deep, impossible to scrub away even if the man had wanted to – which, of course, he never had. The General's father had loved his stories. And he had told them far too frequently for his apparently dispassionate tone of voice to hide how much they meant to him.

One story has always stayed with him.

His father, words blurry with alcohol, would tell it to him at the dinner table while his mother washed up, pots clattering loudly in the sink, pretending not to hear. It was about the factory in Bremen that had been bombed in the war. His father's doing. *Without me*, the man would tell his enthralled son, *the war could easily have gone a different way*. It might have forked off down a less successful path.

Because his father was a code-breaker. Even now, retired and slower, he could crack any sequence his son came up with. And years before, he had broken the code on transmissions that revealed the location of the pharmaceutical factory in Bremen. Without him, they would not have been able to drop the pinpoint bomb that turned it and the village around it into a booming pillar of pitch-black smoke.

I watched it on the video, his father would say. *A lot of men'll tell you they saw faces in the smoke, but there wasn't any. Bits of bodies maybe, but nothing else. That's human nature, you see, to look for patterns. But it was just smoke.*

Even as a boy, the General was old enough to know the reputation the strike had subsequently gathered: that it had become contentious, historically. Had there really been biological weapons? *Of course*, our country said. *Of course not*, said the enemy: it was a medical facility; as a result of its destruction, thousands died, many of them children. Whatever the truth, neither side contested that the surrounding village was demolished by the bomb. Innocent lives had undeniably been lost in the strike. Vaporised bodies in the smoke, many of them civilian.

Now, the lights up ahead turn red. His car rolls to a halt and he cricks on the handbrake.

The lights change. Off he goes again.

Collateral damage, his father would tell him, raising the glass of whisky to his lips. *Do you know what that means?*

Yes.

It means it had to be done. It's not nice when you have to kill civilians, but it was worth it. Their lives against ours. It was for the greater good.

The General would ask him: *why were we at war, Dad?*

His father would often shrug, maybe grunt into the last rounded triangle of liquor in his tilted glass, but he always gave the same answer.

Who knows?

As he follows the flowing traffic – this time through a set of green lights – the General remembers that answer. As a boy, he was impressed by the ambivalence of it, the sheer matter-of-factness. It seemed like a soldier's answer. Now, as an adult, he recognises a deeper truth to the words. There will have been many decent reasons underpinning the war on both sides, and probably many indecent ones, but attempting to untangle them is impossible and pointless. The world rotates on an impenetrable clockwork of cause and effect, impervious to excavation.

Why did it happen?

We did it for resources, for territory, to protect ourselves. And so on. There are a million possible answers, but the truth is that they are never really intended to be explanations, only justifications.

Below the surface of his words, that was surely what his father meant, wasn't it. That for a child killed in the village of Bremen – perhaps tilting their head and seeing a dot in the pale sky above them; perhaps even sensing the hush of death descending – what possible use was a justification, an explanation, a reason?

Thirty-Three

We interviewed Tony Wilkinson in the suite. He sat across from us on the same seat in which we'd talked to Billy Martin yesterday. But the atmosphere was very different.

I don't think I've ever seen a man so reduced. I'd never met him before, of course, but it was easy enough to get a sense of the man from his more obvious physical characteristics. He was thirty-four years old, good-looking, broad and athletic. I imagined that twenty-four hours ago, he would have given the impression of being a strong, reliable man.

But twenty-four hours ago, he had a wife and a son waiting to be born, and while traces of that man remained, he seemed to be in tatters. Some internal clock had been wound on countless years in the last few hours, hollowing and ageing him from within so severely that his loss appeared physical, visible. It had crippled him.

He said, 'Jake.'

It took me a moment to understand.

'That was going to be his name?'

'That *is* his name.'

He shot me a look. Under different circumstances it might have been angry and forceful, but he was too drained right now – his emotions all over the place – for him to summon it properly. He was right, though. It made me realise that Rachel and I hadn't even discussed names yet. I wondered whether she had ones in mind that the gulf between us had prevented her mentioning to me. I was sure she did. That was normal, wasn't it? That was what normal people did.

'I'm sorry,' I said. 'You're right. Jake.'

'It's not you. I'm sorry. But Marie . . .'

Wilkinson shook his head and broke off, taking a few moments to gather himself together. Determined, I thought, not to cry. As beaten down as he was, it was obvious he was not a man to cry in front of strangers, not even under circumstances like these. His shoulders seemed slumped from the weight of it. Laura and I sat quietly, patiently, waiting for him to be ready to speak again.

'That was what Marie wanted to call him,' he said finally. 'It took me a while to understand, I guess. He was such an . . . abstract concept for a while. But then he was just . . . well, he was Jake.'

'I'm sorry,' I said again.

I meant something different this time: not so much an apology as an attempt at sympathy. Sorry for your loss, perhaps. Sorry for what you've been through. But, really, it was a meaningless thing to say; the words sounded empty even to me, and Wilkinson barely registered them. Why would he? I'd seen what the killer had done to Marie Wilkinson. I hadn't known and loved her, and I was in some way prepared for it by the countless horrors I'd seen in the past. And yet the Wilkinson house was still the most abhorrent, awful crime scene I'd ever stepped into.

'I can't imagine how hard this is,' I said. 'I really can't. But what I can tell you is that we will – that we *are* working around the clock to stop this man. He will not get away with what he's done.'

'No.'

Wilkinson looked at me as he said that, and a little more of the anger came through this time. Heaven help the man, I thought, if Wilkinson got hold of him. With everything that had happened – not least the indescribable, *inhuman* horrors of today – a part of me wished it was possible to make such a thing happen.

'The only reason we're asking you to go over all this again is so that we can catch him more quickly. There might be some detail that can help us. Maybe even save somebody else's life.'

He nodded slowly.

'I know.'

We'd already noted his movements over the past day, but I wanted to go over them again in case there was anything he or we had missed. Marie had made him a coffee, which he'd drunk before leaving for work at about half past eight. About quarter of an hour later, the Wilkinsons' elderly neighbour, Keith Carter, had phoned the police to say he had seen a masked intruder enter the property next door.

What happened next was unclear, but Carter appeared to have taken matters into his own hands and gone round to the Wilkinsons' house to make sure Marie was all right. Upon entering the property, he must have interrupted the murderer, and had himself been struck. At that point, or very shortly afterwards, the killer had fled the scene.

Officers had arrived at the house just before nine, where they had found Carter slumped on the outside steps with serious head injuries, and Marie Wilkinson lying on the kitchen floor. Both of the victims died at the scene. While Carter's interruption had prevented the killer committing his usual level of damage to Marie Wilkinson, what had been done proved to be enough.

Where did that leave us? For one thing, it meant the killer had probably been watching them – that he'd waited for Tony Wilkinson to leave, and then taken the first opportunity he had. Carter's involvement was presumably accidental. So if Marie Wilkinson was his chosen target, how did that fit into the pattern? Was it something specific about her, or was it the location? We didn't know. For the moment, it left us nowhere.

I was rubbing my hands together, still thinking it over. 'Have you noticed anything untoward in the past few weeks?'

'Like what?'

'I don't know. Someone hanging around? Someone who seemed to be watching the house?'

Wilkinson shook his head. 'God, no. I wouldn't have . . . left her alone if I had.'

I nodded as sympathetically as I could. But while he sounded sure, I knew it was an easy thing to say in hindsight. In reality, he might have seen something suspicious, or Marie could have mentioned something to him, and he probably wouldn't have acted on it. Because you don't. *A guy was hanging around a bit too long yesterday.* What were you supposed to do – give up your job and sit by the window?

'You're sure?'

'Yes.'

'Nothing, however small and insignificant it might have seemed at the time . . . ?'

'No.'

That look again: *I'm not an idiot.*

'I'm sure.'

'Okay.'

I swallowed the frustration. There had to be something, didn't there? Even if it was something so innocuous, so small, that he'd forgotten it – or, worse, was choosing to forget, because acknowledging it now would mean recognising that he'd failed his family in some way. If that was true, I understood and, again, was sympathetic. But the small things were exactly what we needed right now. *Anything* was what we needed right now.

So I was about to try again, but then Laura tapped my knee gently: her perennial 'can it for a moment, Hicks' gesture.

'And you can't think of anyone who might have wanted to hurt Marie?' she said. 'I know that—'

'No. Of course not. She never made an enemy in her life.'

'What about you?'

'No.' His face clenched up at that. 'What is *wrong* with you people?'

'We have to check.'

'If someone had a problem with me, they'd take it up with me, wouldn't they?'

Not necessarily, I thought. The fact is that *everyone* has enemies, at least to some extent. No matter what Tony said about his wife, or himself, somebody probably disliked them. Maybe someone even *hated* them. In a standard investigation, it was often those kinds of apparently trivial animosities and vendettas that turned out to be fertile ground to plough.

But this wasn't a standard investigation. With our guy, it wasn't personal. *The people who have died mean nothing to me.* The traditional lines of enquiry here were more a matter of box-ticking and time-wasting than anything else. Marie or Tony could have been hated by a hundred people, and it wouldn't mean anything.

So, again, that question: why had the killer chosen her? How did she fit into the code he was challenging us to break? She had been a thirty-three-year-old brunette. She had been pregnant. Was it that? Or was it nothing to do with her at all, and more about the location?

'Have you got kids, Detective?'

Tony Wilkinson's question was like a slap. I thought of Rachel again, and almost said *yes*. But she was at the same stage of pregnancy as Marie had been. Given what had happened, and how I felt about my own upcoming fatherhood, it didn't seem like a good thing to mention.

'No.'

'Well I do.'

'I know.'

And I wanted to tell him that it was something to cling to. He had lost his wife, yes, and in the most horrific of circumstances, but he had not lost his son: the paramedics at the scene had managed to deliver Jake. The little boy was now under twenty-four-hour care in the special baby unit of the hospital.

And that really *was* something. But it was not what Tony Wilkinson needed to hear right now. That it *could have been worse*.

I said, 'I'm sorry.'

'You have no idea.' This time the anger in his voice was undeniable. 'Why did this happen to us? You can't even tell me why, can you? I've seen you on the news. Why haven't you caught this fucking bastard yet? Why is . . .'

But then the words collapsed under him.

'We will,' I said. 'We're doing everything we can.'

Wilkinson shook his head and looked down at the floor for a moment. At the neat, plush carpet that I knew was designed to give an illusion of comfort to the interview suite because it might remind people of home. After a moment, without looking up, he said:

'Do you know what Marie used to tell me about Jake?'

I waited.

'She used to say that she couldn't wait to meet him.'

I wanted to close my eyes. Instead, I forced myself to meet Tony Wilkinson's gaze as he looked up at me. His face crumpled as he burst suddenly into tears. It was an awful sight and sound. The sobs seemed to rack him from head to toe, from the top of his soul to the very bottom.

'And she never got to. Oh God.'

He could barely even get the words out. Laura and I sat very still.

'She never got to meet him.'

Thirty-Four

In one corner of his shop, Levchenko keeps a small television on a stool, where he can see it from his seat behind the counter. He is sitting there now, his elbows resting on the counter, watching the press conference unfold live on the twenty-four-hour news channel.

There has been a steady stream of customers and browsers for most of the afternoon, but for the moment the shop is empty and he is alone. Jasmina is in the back room, tidying his pans and polishing away dabs of spilled wax from the gas burner. She is more fastidious than he is. Occasionally, it drives him to distraction, but he also knows it is one of the things he would miss most about her if she was gone: that ultimately we love the rough edges of people more than the smooth surfaces. He also knows that for her, cleaning has become a way of erasing thoughts, of keeping them at bay. For him, in some strange way, it is the opposite. But they are both coping strategies. One removes; the other attempts to ignore.

Regardless, he is glad she is otherwise occupied right now.

That she does not have to see this.

But then he senses Jasmina emerge from the room behind the counter. Instinctively he picks up the remote control and turns the television off, making it as natural a gesture as possible. His wife bustles past him without noticing.

'You are running low on pellets,' she says.

'Yes.'

'And red dye too. Mind you . . .' she gestures around the empty shop with a flap of her arms, as though the lack of customers is another black spot she would like to clean, 'it is not like there is any urgency.'

'No.'

He is still staring at the silent television screen. On the surface, his mind is equally blank, and by a similarly deliberate act of will. Like the television, it would take very little effort for him to bring his thoughts back to life.

'Are you all right?'

Jasmina is staring at him with a curious frown. He blinks at her and, for a moment, has no idea how to answer. It is suddenly as though this woman is a stranger to him, a person he has no idea how to communicate with. The press conference on the television – the sight of the detective – has taken him back to a time when they might easily have separated, and accelerated him forward on the path they did not take, a path where she would not be here.

He shakes his head, dispelling the image. This is his wife.

Despite everything, they have weathered their lives and managed not to come apart. His heart – his whole chest – fills with love for her, like blood spilling back into a numb arm. He smiles.

'Yes. I'm sorry, my love. I was wool-gathering.'

She harrumphs. But the look on her face says she can believe it, and that, while it drives her to distraction, it is a rough edge of his that she loves him for in return. In such ways, he realises, do relationships grow over time. We begin by looking for perfection; we end up by loving flaws.

'I am going out for a while,' she says, smiling. 'Since you are ignoring me.'

He smiles back. 'Very wise.'

'That is why you love me.'

'One of the many reasons,' he says. 'Still.'

'Still.'

Her smile takes on a slightly different character now, one

that warms him. Most of the time, the love he feels for her is so intense it is a physical thing in the room between them. When they are separated, the thing blurs and doubles, one part with each, so that they remain together. It really is something, he believes, to have shared your life with someone for so very long. Even a life touched by tragedy. As though there are other kinds of lives.

'I won't be long,' she says.

'You take care.'

'And you. Be careful with all this hard work.'

The bell tinkles as she opens the door – and then Levchenko is alone once more.

He switches the television back on. Jasmina is sensitive. Reports such as this one, on crimes such as these, would only upset her. They would bring back memories. She might even recognise the detective from his name.

As the press conference reaches its conclusion, Levchenko watches Detective Hicks and remembers. It is a name – and a face – that he will never forget. And just as he has returned the television to life, so he allows his thoughts and emotions to rise to the surface too.

What does he feel now, looking at the policeman? It is difficult to describe in words. Difficult to quantify and weigh.

Hate?

No, he thinks. Not that.

Hate is not strong enough.

Thirty-Five

'Do you want to talk about it?' Rachel said.

I was home for five hours, tops, and no, I didn't want to talk about it. What I wanted to do more than anything else was catch up on some sleep – or at least lie in bed vaguely hoping to do so. My head was so full of horror that it would be difficult, but still. I needed to try. I couldn't run on vapours.

'Not really.'

'Maybe you should.'

I didn't reply.

She said, 'I saw the news. The pregnant woman.'

I nodded. I wished she hadn't seen it.

'Andy?'

For a moment, a part of me wanted to lash out. I wanted to tell her that if I needed to talk about it, there were the usual police psychologists – the ones that flitted in and out of the department from time to time, the ones detectives were encouraged to share their traumas with. And as aggressive as that might have come across out loud, I wouldn't have meant anything bad by saying it. I wanted to keep Rachel safe from the grim details. There was no reason for both of us to carry them.

But . . .

He doesn't talk to me any more.

I said, 'Marie Wilkinson.'

'Yes. That must have been horrible.'

'Horrible.' I nodded again. 'Yes. And I spoke to her husband too. He wasn't good – obviously he wasn't. Maybe that was even worse, in its own way, because Marie Wilkinson is gone now; she's not suffering any more. But his whole world is gone, just like that. Jesus. There was nothing left of the guy.'

'Except the baby.'

'He has the baby, yes. Perhaps, anyway; that's still touch and go. But not her. He doesn't have her, and she never had the baby she wanted.'

Rachel nodded. Her hands were over her belly, subconsciously protecting our unborn child. Perhaps she was trying to imagine what Marie Wilkinson had gone through, or what it would be like for me and our child if anything happened to her. Because she sensed it, probably: how little I wanted this child. Or at least I was sure that was what she thought.

'What happened,' I said. 'Neither of them could ever have seen it coming.'

'Does anyone?'

'Yes. Everyone. Not so they can avoid it maybe. But it always makes sense, at least. There's always a reason for it.'

'Are you really so sure about that?'

'Yes. Murder's not like being hit by a truck or having a heart attack or anything. It's not some random natural disaster. People are killed for reasons, even if they're stupid reasons. Looking at the wrong person for too long. Sleeping with people they shouldn't. Pissing someone off. None of it's *right*, but it always makes some kind of sense.'

Rachel didn't reply.

'But there's no sense to what happened to Marie Wilkinson. We're sitting there, and her husband asks me *why*, and I can't tell him. I can't fucking say anything. And it's the same with all of them. They were killed for no reason at all. Not that I can tell.'

'No reason?'

'They weren't robbed. They weren't sexually assaulted.'

There's no connection between them. The bastard doesn't even seem to get any enjoyment from it.'

'He must be doing it for some reason.'

'Yes, he must. He is. We just can't see it yet. If we take him at his word, he's testing out a pattern to see if we can crack it. These people mean nothing to him. Literally. They don't matter at all.'

'I don't understand.'

'Do you want to?'

'Yes. Tell me. Please.'

So I did. The whole time, she listened carefully, not taking her hands from her stomach once. By the end, she was rubbing it gently.

'You think he deliberately targeted a pregnant woman?'

'Yes.' And I thought, but didn't say: *yes, that does mean it could maybe just as easily have been you.* 'The victims mean nothing to him, but they represent something. He has a reason. It's just a different kind than I'm used to. It's a . . .' I fumbled for a way to describe it. 'It's a dark-room crime.'

'A what?'

'A dark-room crime.'

She looked at me blankly.

'It doesn't matter,' I said. 'It's just . . . it's *evil*.'

'I don't believe in evil.'

'Me neither. Or I didn't use to. Maybe I'm starting to.'

'Well I'm not. I'm a scientist.'

'You were, yes.'

'And will be again.' Her hands stopped moving. 'You don't want this, do you? The baby? You don't need to answer that. I know you don't.'

I looked at Rachel. She looked back, waiting.

'I don't know,' I said.

And here, at last, we stood on the brink of the thing I couldn't tell her. My words teetered on the edge, but wouldn't go over, not all the way. Not far enough to fall all the way down to the truth.

'I'm scared,' I said. 'I'm scared about our child.'

'What do you mean?'

'About keeping him safe.'

'Oh.' She shook her head. *What – is that all?* 'You know, I think about that every day. I worry about it more than anything. I think everyone does, don't they?'

'Probably.'

'But the thing is, we can. Keep him safe. Most children are safe, aren't they? Even without parents as good as we'll be.'

I started to say something, but she interrupted.

'As good as *you'll* be.'

'But I can't protect him,' I said. 'Nobody can. It's not possible, is it? There are no guarantees.'

'No. There never have been. But the odds are good. You know that better than anyone, right?'

She had me there. Yes, the probability was that our son would be just as happy and protected as any child could be, and that nothing bad would ever happen to him. The world can be a good place as well as a horrible one. Many people experience the former with only brief, bitter tastes of the latter, and there was no reason to think our son would be any different.

Rachel said, 'Your job . . .'

'Makes me see the worst.'

'So you have a skewed sample to work from.'

'And it blinds me. I know that.'

I nodded, because she was right in what she said. Yes, I could keep my son safe. I could teach him how to defend himself and the kind of people and places to stay away from. Rachel looked relieved. She thought I was finally talking to her about what had been on my mind all these months. It was only a small part of what had been bothering me – the safe part, perhaps – but because this sudden bridging of the distance between us felt so good, I found myself staying there.

'I do know it,' I said again. 'But it's still hard for me. I'm scared. Even knowing all that, I'm still scared.'

'Yes. And that's why you'll be a good father.'

'Will I?'

'Yes. Because you're a good man.' She stared at me, long and hard, then sighed. 'Do you know, that's the most you've said to me in months?'

'I'm sorry.'

'You don't need to be. I'm glad – well, I mean I'm glad you finally did. But look, we'll be okay. You have to believe that, Andy. I have faith in you.'

'Do you?'

'Always have. Don't see any reason to stop now. Well, I see a few, but maybe now they're not quite as big as they were. Thank you.'

I smiled at her, and she smiled back. As nice as it was, at the same time it made me feel guilty.

You're a good man.

No, Rachel. No, I'm not.

And I almost said something – about Buxton, perhaps, or about Emmeline Levchenko – but at that moment she stepped forward and embraced me. After a second, I hugged her back, as fiercely-gently as I could manage, and whatever I'd been about to say dissolved in the feel of her, the presence of her. I couldn't remember the last time we'd hugged so easily. She felt at once like a stranger in my arms and someone achingly familiar.

'This case can't be making it any easier for you.'

'No.'

'Because this guy strikes at random?'

'We can't work out the pattern, so we can't stop him. While he's out there, we can't protect people.'

'Well then.' I felt her chin against my collarbone and her breath warm on my neck. Our son, inside her, pressed against my stomach. 'You know what you need to do, don't you?'

'What?'

'You need to catch the fucker.'

I nodded. All else aside, that much was true.

'You need to catch him.'

DAY NINE

Thirty-Six

'He's playing with us,' Laura said.

'I know.'

'There is no pattern.'

'I think you're right.'

She looked at me, surprised. 'That's not what I expected you to say.'

'No?'

'Normally, even if you did think that, you'd disagree with me on general principles.'

I shrugged. We were perched at a desk in the corner of the operations room, going through every single scrap of data over and over again. It was tedious work, but I was glad of it. Maybe I was just glad that Franklin wasn't here today. He was due back this afternoon, but until then, at least his absence had lifted a little of the pressure.

Still. We'd achieved nothing – found no pattern at all. I was becoming convinced there was no success to be had. That the bastard had always been misleading us.

'When someone's right, they're right,' I said. 'Even you. I'm beginning to think the letters are a red herring. All this talk of finding a pattern – he's using it to throw us off track for some reason. To keep us busy. Stretched too thin.'

Laura grunted at that, meaning: *it's working, then.*

The operations room around us was a hive of activity. Phones were ringing constantly, and officers kept drifting in and out, delivering reports and collecting fresh actions. As much man-power as we had, it was nowhere near enough, not for this many crimes, and the atmosphere in the room felt strained and urgent. We were all tired and frustrated. And that, of course, was what he wanted. Regardless of his real motive for the kill-ings – still clinging to the assumption that there was one – he wanted us strung out.

'It's not just the pattern, either,' I said. 'He's laughing at us in other ways too.'

'What do you mean?'

I gestured at the room. 'Look at what we're doing. We're chasing anything and everything, because we have to. And the more data we have, the worse it gets. Do you know the birthday problem?'

'Oh – more and more, as the years pass.'

'It's a maths puzzle. In a room full of people, how many need to be there for it to be likely two of them share the same birthday?'

'I'm not getting out my calculator, Hicks.'

'It's twenty-three,' I said.

'Twenty-three?'

'Yeah, exactly. It seems like it should be more, but that's the number where two of the people present – any two of them – are likely to have the same birthday.'

'Your point? Wait. No, I get it.'

'Exactly.'

It wasn't just that every individual victim needed to be scrupulously investigated in their own right – although that took enough time in itself – but the results also needed to be examined across the entire breadth of the investigation. With this many victims we were *bound* to find connections eventu-ally. And we had. Marie Wilkinson, for example, was known to one of the women who worked in the launderette with Vicki Gibson. She had been a regular customer, and it was probable that the two women had met at some point. We were sure it was a coincidence, but it had still needed investigating. Nothing.

Similarly, Sandra Peacock had often gone to Santiago's, where John Kramer had worked as a bouncer. Was that important? It turned out that no, it didn't seem to be. But we had to waste time looking into it anyway.

The missing-persons reports and the unidentified victims in the video just added extra complications. We thought we had two of them pinned down, and a potential ID on a third, but we couldn't be sure. So did we run with that data or not? Obviously we had to. Obviously we wouldn't know if we were right even if we did find something. Which we had not.

'It's a fucking arms race,' I said. 'That's what we have here. We only need him to make one mistake; that gets more likely with every murder. But the more he *doesn't* make one the busier we are and the harder it'll be to spot when he does. Perhaps he already has.' I picked up a file of reports and dropped it on the floor. 'And we're too lost in fucking paperwork to see it.'

Laura shook her head, then reached down and picked up the file and put it back on the desk on top of all the others.

'If there is a pattern,' she said, 'we're going to find it.'

I sighed. 'What time is this woman coming in?'

Given that I was in a relationship with a scientist, I suppose I should have known better than to have a stereotypical view of what one would look like. But still, I had certain expectations of the mathematician we'd arranged to see. She would be serious and austere. Logical and businesslike. Somewhat *grey*.

And as Professor Carol Joyce was shown into the small office, I realised I'd been more or less spot on. She was in her fifties, silver-haired, with rough and lined skin, wearing brackets around her mouth. But there was also an air of casual authority to her that was quite striking. I imagined that to make it as a woman for so long in academia required a degree of toughness. She looked no-nonsense. I had little doubt that every single second of this meeting would be billed to expenses, right down to the bus ticket across town.

'Detectives,' she said.

We all shook hands, and then she shrugged off an expensive handbag and thin coat, hanging both over the back of the chair across from us.

'Thank you for coming,' I said as she sat down.

'Not at all. Apart from anything else, I'm curious.' She looked around the small room, seeming almost amused by her surroundings. 'I've never been in a police station before. Not once.'

'Is it living up to your expectations?' I said.

'So far.' She glanced at me, still apparently amused. 'What can I do for you?'

'Well, we're hoping you can help us. We have a code we need to break. A possible code, anyway.'

'How fascinating.'

I slid a sheaf of papers across the desk to her, and she lifted them with elegant hands, peered for a moment, then reached down and retrieved a glasses case from her handbag. The case *pocked* shut, then she hooked on small circular spectacles and peered again, a little more successfully.

'Before we discuss any of this, I should explain that everything in there is confidential.'

She didn't look up, but raised an eyebrow. 'Would you like me to sign something?'

'Not at all. We can't, of course, stop you mentioning our conversation, but we'd appreciate it if you didn't. The fact is you'd possibly be putting lives at risk.'

'You don't have to worry. And anyway, I think I've already guessed what this is about.' She looked up. 'It's the murders, isn't it?'

I smiled non-committally.

'That's fine.' Professor Joyce waved a hand vaguely. 'I don't expect you to confirm it. I remain curious, though. I've never been approached for something like this before, and I'm not sure how I can possibly help you. I suppose it depends on what you feel comfortable telling me.'

'Let us just say,' I ventured, 'we have evidence suggesting there is a design behind the data you have there. I can't tell you why we suspect that to be the case. But we are hoping that if there is a pattern, you might be able to spot it better than we can.'

'Let's see, then.'

She turned the first page. As she worked her way through, I did my best to explain the data we'd collated. One of the problems was that we weren't even sure what kind of pattern we were looking for, so everything was potentially important. We'd included as much as we could think of.

The hardest thing had been to decide on identifying the victims. We didn't want to do that, but while it was unlikely, it remained possible they *had* been individually targeted. In the end, we'd listed the initials. The sex of the victims was M or F. Then, obviously, there was age. A basic physical description. We'd listed the dates and approximate times of each attack, along with the period between murders. The numbers of victims on the same night. Location – for the victims we had found – was described in various ways, including GPS co-ordinates and standard map references.

Professor Joyce read through all of it, her face betraying nothing. After a couple of minutes, she looked up.

'May I take this away with me?'

'Of course.'

'Because I can only give you my very basic first impressions from a brief look-through now. What I'd like to do, ideally, is feed the data into some of the programs we have in the department – code-breaking programs, essentially – and see what they come up with.'

'That sounds fantastic,' I said. 'Does anything strike you at first glance?'

'I'm not sure. You don't have to answer this, but the evidence you have that there is a pattern – what is it?'

I glanced at Laura. She shrugged.

Your call, Hicks.

'It's not conclusive,' I said. 'We have some reason to believe the data isn't random. It's an attempt to *look* random. Like a computer algorithm. A . . . pseudo-random number generator?'

'Yes, I'm familiar.' Professor Joyce pursed her lips. The lines around them deepened. They looked a little like scars, formed by a lifetime of perusing problems. 'What do you know about them?'

I felt a little helpless.

'They're complex computer programs that generate a string of data. You have one number, say, and you do something to it to generate the next. Add five, or whatever. And so on. If you know the "add five" rule, you can predict the next number.'

'Basically, yes, though it's not quite so simple. You have to bear in mind the code can be very complex. It's not just "add five" – that's obviously too predictable.'

'Okay.'

'Backtrack a little, though, and let's deal with numbers. How do you form the first number in the sequence?'

I remembered the letter. 'It's usually something unique. The date and time setting, for example.'

Professor Joyce nodded. 'Yes, that's right. If the sequence began at a different time, it would be very different, even though it followed the same rule. If you add five to one, you get six. If you add it to eight, you get thirteen. Same underlying rule, different sequence. You see?'

'The numbers in the code aren't set? They depend on the first . . . variable?'

'That's right.'

I rubbed my forehead.

Professor Joyce looked at me sympathetically.

'What I'm really saying, Detective, is that whatever the code here might be, the first variable is probably the most interesting.'

'Right.'

She was telling us we should concentrate on the first victim: Vicki Gibson. A pattern might explain where the *next* victims came from, but he needed a reason to have started where he did. So what was his secret? The problem was that we'd explored every corner of Gibson's life and found nothing to go on. And then there were the letters.

I still don't know quite when it will begin.

That is why it's going to work.

Laura said, 'Nothing leaps out at first glance, though?'

'No. That's why I asked what evidence you had to suggest there even was a pattern here to be found.'

My heart sank a little. Professor Joyce must have seen it on my face.

'But I wouldn't expect to see anything obvious. If I could spot a pattern in this in ten minutes, then you would have done too. And there is a great deal of data here: variables of different types. All I can really see immediately are the clusters.'

'The clusters?'

She looked a little awkward. 'The . . . well, the *incidents* that occur together.' She gestured to the data representing the murders of Kramer, Peacock and Collins: victims three, four and five. 'Here, for example. These variables are clustered.'

Same date, same location.

'Okay,' I said. 'Go on.'

'My academic speciality is codes: the making and breaking of them. When you're constructing a code, the aim is to make something as indecipherable as possible, and there are very sophisticated ways of doing that, involving prime numbers. It's possible to encode a message, for example, in such a way that it's practically impossible to break without the key.'

'That doesn't sound good.'

'No, but I don't think that's what's happening here. A much simpler way of coding a pattern is to include static through it. Do you have a pen?'

I passed her one. She leaned over and, without standing on ceremony, scribbled a line of text across the top of the sheet in front of her.

'There,' she said. 'What does that say?'

I turned the sheet round.

H1TCICB5MK3X7S38P

'I have absolutely no idea.'

'It says "Hicks". If I wanted to send that to someone for them to read, they'd need to know the following rule: start at the beginning, and whenever you encounter a consonant, completely disregard the next three symbols.'

I read it again, mentally crossing out.

'I just did that off the top of my head,' she said. 'Obviously you could make it far more complicated. After a vertically symmetrical consonant, like "H", ignore only the next two. And so on.'

'Okay. So the clusters are . . . the bits you ignore?'

'The static, yes. The letters of "Hicks" are all there. They're even in the right order, plain to see. What makes the sequence *appear* random and meaningless is the clusters of static in between the letters. I just picked those additional symbols at random. They mean nothing.'

They mean nothing . . .

Christ. I pictured our killer waiting by the estate that night for whoever came along. Had those murders been part of the pattern he was daring us to find? Or was it just static, obscuring the secret from us?

'So it's possible,' I said slowly, 'that not all this data is even relevant? That any pattern we're looking for might only be part of it?'

Professor Joyce nodded her head once. And because she understood what we were talking about here – that these weren't just strings of code, but people who had been murdered – her face betrayed open emotion for the first time. She looked grim at the underlying reality of what she was telling us.

'Yes,' she said. 'That's certainly possible.'

Thirty-Seven

'I knew I recognised *something* about it,' DS Renton said. 'I'm still not sure, and it might be nothing. But this is what I was thinking of.'

We were sitting in LG15 – the dark room – again. This time, rather than analysing our video clip, Renton was logging into a website. The screen was pitch black aside from grey bits of text and a header of devil's hands clutching a row of bloody skulls.

'What is this?' I said.

'It's a shock site. A forum filled with extreme images. Footage of death and torture. Suicide, rape, murder . . .'

'There are forums for that?'

The strip light in the ceiling was humming ominously.

Renton shrugged as he typed in a username and password.

'That kind of material is all over the internet,' he said, 'but this place is a bit of a hub for people. I mean, you don't need to come here to watch a beheading video, say, because they're everywhere, but this place sort of *catalogues* them. And the rest.'

'Wow.'

'Thousands of users online at any one time. Most new material of that nature gets posted here and commented on.'

Oh Christ, I thought.

'Our video's not . . .'

'No, no. Don't worry. But we scan these sites quite often – five minutes at the beginning of every day, just to keep an eye out for anything we might need to get involved with. It doesn't happen often, but sometimes someone'll break the rules and post something they shouldn't.'

I watched as the page changed to the forum listings. Still the same image at the top of the screen, now with rows of sub-forums underneath. True Gore Images. True Gore Video. The numbers to the right showed that each category contained thousands of postings.

'This place has *rules*?'

'Oh yeah. No kiddie stuff is what it mainly comes down to. Even nutters have their own conceptions of morality. But every now and then someone'll figure the secrecy here means open season. So we keep an eye out.'

'Secrecy?'

'Yeah. It used to be open, but now you need to be a member to view or post, and they're not allowing new members any more. It's a closed community of weirdos, and that allows them a certain degree of freedom. Or the illusion of it anyway.'

'Okay.'

'Here we go.' Renton clicked on a link on his profile marked 'Favourites'. 'I scanned through last night and found it again, saved the thread. It's an interesting one. Not nice. Brace yourself.'

He opened the thread and clicked on the video link in the first post. After a moment, a new window opened and the file started playing.

It showed a static image of grassland: a short stretch that ended in a line of dark, shadowy trees. The day it had been recorded, the weather had been good: the grass itself was bright and inviting, untended and shimmering slightly in the faintest of breezes, as though under calm water. In the audio feed, I could hear birdsong – and then something else. A clatter.

A hissing.

A few seconds later, a figure entered the frame, walking a little distance ahead of the camera. He was wearing blue jeans, a black coat – and a black balaclava, with tufts of brown hair emerging from the back of the neckline. In one hand he was holding a hammer, turning it round and round in his grip. And in the other – by the scruff of its neck – a tabby cat. It was twisting, jerking in his grasp.

'Oh God,' I said.

Renton nodded. 'Yep.'

The footage didn't last long – just over a minute in total. The man pressed the cat down against the ground and struck it repeatedly in the head with the hammer. The hissing and fighting ended after the second blow, but that only allowed him to let go and concentrate on hitting it again and again.

When he was done, the man stayed crouched over the animal's body for a few moments, tilting his head and peering down dispassionately at the damage he'd inflicted. For all the distress and emotion he showed, he might have been studying a butterfly on a leaf. Finally he stood up and walked back behind the camera. The screen went blank.

For the last few frames, I had been holding my breath.

'*When* was this posted?'

'Last year,' Renton said. 'It's local, too, which is what originally caught my eye. He's posted a few of them. This is the only video he took outside: the others look like interiors – a garage of some kind. There are photos too. Here.'

He opened a new window and loaded a different thread. This one contained static images. Cats pinned down like laboratory specimens and slit open. One had all its legs and its head cut off. Four or five were hanging from trees by their necks, all with a gloved hand intruding into the frame from the side to point at them.

I stared at the photographs with horror. Below, there were messages from other users congratulating him on the post. I read the first – *Great work! Can't wait to see more!* – and felt sick.

But also, just barely, a tingle of something else.

You didn't expect us to find these, did you?

I said, 'How do you know he's local?'

Renton nodded. 'He filled his location information in. Maybe he was lying, but I don't see why he would be. Plus we identified the location the first video was shot. Swaine Hill.'

Shit. *Killer Hill*. Where Billy Martin had entered the woods. Billy Martin, who'd talked about someone killing a cat. What had he said? My heart began beating faster.

First things first.

'All right. Did you ever trace this guy's account?'

'That's the down side, I'm afraid.' Renton pulled a face. 'The site's totally anonymous. The server's based abroad, and the registration shifts. That's one of the things that makes it so appealing to the users. The lack of accountability.'

'If we contact the admins?'

'Good luck with that.'

'Shit.'

I leaned back.

This was him. I *knew* it. He'd recorded these images last year and posted them online for some reason – to show off, maybe – and the whole time he'd been practising. Preparing for his work this year. A dry run of some kind.

The kids at school. They told me about someone who killed a cat.

Another realisation.

The guy hadn't bothered to chase Billy Martin . . .

I stood up quickly and pulled out my mobile. Laura took an age to answer, then:

'Hicks. What have we—'

'Laura, listen to me. Get someone round to Billy Martin's house. I think he might need protection. We've got to get him in here right now.'

I heard her typing. 'I'm on it.'

'Because I think he might have recognised Billy.'

'What? Where from?'

'I think . . .' It was hard to bring myself to say it. 'I think it might be a kid. An older teenager maybe.'

I reminded her about what Billy had said.

'I'm on it,' she said again.

'I'll be upstairs in a minute.'

I hung up. *Shit, shit, shit.* But there was hope now too – stronger than before. The guy might have hidden his identity online, but he couldn't fucking hide in real life. Not for ever. No matter how fucking clever he thought he was.

Renton said, 'Think it's our guy? Jimmy?'

'Jimmy?'

'The username.'

He tapped the screen and I saw what he was referring to. The username for the posts was Jimmy82.

'Yes,' I said. 'Yes, I do.'

Thirty-Eight

The door was answered by an overweight woman in her forties with an unwashed tangle of brown hair. She was dressed in black leggings and a sprawling white crop top, and had an angry speckle of sunburn across the top of her chest. A cigarette in one hand, trailing smoke. I imagined that was more or less a permanent fixture.

'Mrs Johnson?'

'Yeah.'

I smiled and held up my warrant card.

'Detective Hicks. This is Detective Fellowes. We're looking for your son, Carl. Is he home?'

Mrs Johnson slumped against the door frame and folded her arms. Not so much a gesture of defiance as one of familiarity, perhaps even inevitability. 'What's he done now?'

It was a reasonable question. After we'd taken Billy Martin into protective custody, he'd given us Carl Johnson's name as the boy at school who'd bragged about being present when a cat was killed on Swaine Hill. Carl had only just turned thirteen, but was already well on his way in the world. Where Billy seemed very much like a child still, Carl Johnson had lost any innocence a long time ago. Under-age drinking. An assault charge against another child at school. Truancy. Shoplifting.

But then, looking at the run-down area and the parental concern on display here, it wasn't so surprising. It was like

Billy's bow and arrow in a way – you twang the string and that's it: the arrow flies, its trajectory set.

I said, 'Is he home?'

She bellowed over her shoulder. 'Carl!'

'I'll take that as a yes.' I put my card away. 'Can we come in, please?'

'What's he done?' she asked again, taking a drag on the cigarette. 'Nothing would surprise me, to be honest. Absolutely nothing.'

'If we can come in, we can discuss it,' I said. 'To be honest, we're hoping he can help us. If he can, he might not be in any trouble at all.'

'Huh. That'd be a first.' She relaxed away from the door frame. It seemed to breathe a sigh of relief. 'Follow me. *Carl!*'

From upstairs: '*What?*'

'Get your arse down here, you little shit. *Now.*'

Mrs Johnson was trudging ahead towards a doorway on the right, trailing smoke, but I gave Laura a look as I closed the front door behind us. The stairs led straight up ahead from the front door. Carl obviously wasn't our man, but he was a streetwise kid who wouldn't have much love for the police, and we needed to talk to him right now. So without us even having to discuss it, Laura stayed by the door just in case the *little shit* decided to elope on us.

I followed Mrs Johnson into what turned out to be the living room: a small, dismal space with a worn carpet and a threadbare three-piece suite. The curtains were open, but the weak light only emphasised the misty air; it felt like the windows in here hadn't been open for a long time. The room smelled strongly of the overflowing ashtray on the small coffee table and the stale, lingering aroma of old sweat.

A moment later, Carl sauntered in, shadowed by Laura. As I'd suspected, he cut an entirely different figure to Billy Martin. He was still clearly a kid beneath his cheap T-shirt and jeans, and the hair on his upper lip was as thin as eyelashes, but he had an attitude way beyond his years. He kicked at the carpet as he walked past, head down, not looking at me but with a sly little smile on his face.

'Carl,' I said. 'Have a seat.'

'Whatever.' He could barely be bothered to form the word, and sighed as he slumped down, his body clenching at the last moment to hit the settee as hard as he could. 'What do you want?'

'Charming,' Laura said. 'Didn't your mother teach you any manners?'

Although it wasn't a genuine question, I glanced at Mrs Johnson anyway, and she shrugged. The gesture seemed to say that manners were something a little like a PlayStation 3, and not everyone could afford them.

'What can I do?' she said. 'He runs riot. Breaks my heart. It'd be different if his bastard dad was still around.'

'No it wouldn't,' Carl said.

'Shut up. Button that smart mouth.'

He chuntered her words back at her: . . . *Button that smart mouth.*

'Carl.' I stood in front of him. 'Let's start again. We're not here to cause you problems if we don't have to. If we have to, we will. You get me?'

'Like I said, what do you want?' He folded his thin arms and looked over at the window with a sigh. 'I've got places to be.'

'Yeah, that's the first thing that went through my head when I saw you: here's a kid with places to be. Well, let's make this quick then, shall we? You know a place called Swaine Hill? It's also known colloquially as Killer Hill.'

He didn't say anything.

'Colloquially means that's what some people call it.'

That got me a glare, at least. 'Yeah, I know.'

'And so . . . ?'

'Yeah, I know it.'

'Amazing. So, you go there, I take it?'

He shrugged.

228

'You go there for the parties, right? Beer. Dope. Older kids hanging out because there's nowhere better for them to go, and so on?'

'I guess.'

'It's not a quiz, Carl. You don't need to guess. Yes or no – you've been there or not?'

'Yeah. Sometimes.'

'Right. So – tell me about the cats.'

He looked at me and frowned.

'The cats?'

I sighed. 'Cats. Furry little things. People have them as pets. Most people don't put them in cages and set fire to them, though. Unlike you.'

Carl stared at me for a moment, confused, then scared. He unfolded his arms.

'What? I never—'

His mother exploded. 'What the *hell* have you been doing now, boy? I swear on—'

'Mrs Johnson.' I swivelled on the spot and held out my hand. She was out of her chair, as though about to attack her son. 'Just leave this to us for a minute, okay?'

'I never did that! That wasn't me!'

I turned back to see Carl was half out of his seat too.

'Word around the school is that you did, Carl.'

It was a lie, but I wanted to see his reaction.

'*Who* said that? I fucking swear that—'

'That's what I'm hearing.' I smiled at him benignly. 'You should listen to your mother about that smart mouth. You start using it to brag and show off and you see what happens? People take you at your word. So blame yourself. Did you or did you not say that? Don't guess this time.'

He glared at me. Folded his arms again.

'No.'

'But you were there when it happened?' I said. 'Sit back down again, by the way.'

He did what he was told.

'I don't know,' he said. 'Maybe. Who cares anyway? It was only a cat.'

'I imagine the cat cared. And I care. I like cats. Detective Fellowes?'

'I like cats too,' Laura said.

'So there's two of us who care, and we're both police, and it happens to be a crime. So it matters quite a lot. You didn't do it, is what you're telling us. Who did, then? Because it *did* happen, didn't it?'

Carl was silent. At the corners of his jaw, muscles were bunching and pulsing. His face was like a fist.

'Carl?'

'Yes. It did happen. It wasn't me.'

'But you were there.'

He nodded, looking more miserable now.

'Tell us then. *When* did it happen?'

'It was one night last summer,' he said.

As he began to explain, it became obvious almost immediately that the incident he was describing was not one of those 'Jimmy' had recorded online. Aside from anything else, the animal killings shot outside had all taken place in daylight, whereas the incident Carl was describing for us had been at night.

He told us what we already knew – that groups of teenagers gathered at the top of Swaine Hill on a night-time for all the usual types of teenage misbehaviour: drinking, smoking, partying. It was mostly older kids there, he said, but they didn't seem to mind him and a handful of his mates showing up from time to time. I imagined the older kids liked having them around – someone to look up to them – but was less sure what Mrs Robinson thought she was doing allowing a young child out alone at that fucking hour.

Carl said, 'It was one of the older guys who brought the cat.'

'Name?' Laura was writing all of this down in her notebook.

'I don't know.' He looked between us, slightly imploringly

now. 'Seriously. He wasn't from our school. And anyway, it was him that brought it, but not him who did it.'

'Age?' Laura persisted.

'*I don't know.*'

'Then guess.'

'A few years older. Sixteen, seventeen. But like I said, it wasn't him that did it.'

'So who did? What happened?'

'He sold it.'

'Brought a cat along and sold it?'

'I think his family couldn't care for it. Their own had just had a litter or something, so he was basically just getting rid of them wherever he could. I think this other guy had agreed to take it off his hands. He could have got it for free, but insisted on paying for it.'

'You don't know the guy's name either?' I said.

Carl shook his head. 'Never seen him there before. He must have been friends with one of the other kids, but he was older than the rest. Probably in his twenties.'

'Okay,' I said. 'So he bought the cat. And then what happened?'

'Well, it was in a cage. This wire cage, you know – like a carrying case, but all open. And everyone was laughing about it at first, 'cos it was scared to death. There was all the noise, and we had a fire too. We always had a fire. So it was pretty funny at first.'

'Pretty funny,' I said. 'Yeah, it sounds it. And then?'

'And then the guy put the cage down and took out a knitting needle. And everyone sort of went . . . quiet.'

'Not *pretty funny* any more?'

Carl shook his head.

I wasn't sure I wanted to hear the rest, but I asked it anyway, because I had to.

'And?'

'People thought he was just messing around at first. But . . . he wasn't.'

Carl told us the guy stabbed the kitten repeatedly through the holes in the mesh, softly at first, as though just playing with it, and then more seriously. The whole time, with this animal hissing and spitting and screeching, the guy was just crouched by the side of the cage, prodding at it.

Carl looked utterly miserable now. No longer half as cocky as he'd been when he'd walked in here. Somewhere inside him, it seemed, there was a kid after all. Not that you had to be a kid to feel sickened by what he was telling us.

'He was trying to get its eyes.'

I shook my head. 'And nobody tried to stop him?'

'Sort of. But he was a bit older, like I said – he just shrugged them off as though he wasn't interested. And for some reason that worked. I think everyone was a bit . . . it was weird to see it happening in front of you.'

'Yeah, it would be.'

'A few of the girls were yucked out. A few of the guys too. I mean, I didn't like it. I didn't like it at all. But people just walked away and left him to it. He wasn't . . . well, it was like he was in a world of his own by then.'

Carl took a deep breath.

'After a while he just got bored. There was some lighter fluid they'd brought to start the fire, so he used that and burned the thing up. The smell was fucking awful. It took ages to die.'

He fell silent for a few seconds, and I just stared down at him. Beside me, I could sense that Laura was looking off to one side.

Carl said, 'He just stood there afterwards. Grinning. He was *grinning* at us, like he expected a round of applause or something. But by then everyone was just ignoring him. I don't think anyone knew what to do.'

I knew what I wanted to do with him.

'You'd never seen him there before?'

Carl shook his head.

'And never since?'

'I never went back – I didn't want to see him again. And I

think a lot of other people didn't go back either. I don't know if anyone goes there any more. But people heard about it at school, just 'cos it was so shocking, you know? And so I was just like, "yeah, I was there".'

I stared down at him. He looked like he was going to cry.

'It wasn't me. It wasn't!'

'All right.' I sighed. 'All right. What we're going to need are the names of *everyone* you were there with. Your friends. If you didn't hear who this guy was, maybe they had better ears than you.'

'Okay.'

He started to reel off a bunch of names. Laura wrote them down while I thought it over. As horrible as the story was, it moved us another step closer to finding this guy – assuming it *was* our guy. But it had to be. He'd practised with his animals, and for reasons I still couldn't fathom – apparently not the normal basement ones – he'd then moved on to human beings. This was a break. As awful as it was, there was hope here, because some existing connection had taken him to the hill that night. Somebody would know someone who knew him, and that was about as solid a lead as we'd had so far.

'Jimmy,' Carl said suddenly.

Beside me, Laura's pen froze.

'What?' I said.

Carl nodded brightly. '*That* was his name. I remember now. That was what somebody called him.' He looked pleased with himself. 'Jimmy.'

Thirty-Nine

Levchenko would not be here now if it wasn't for the policeman.

Business has been slow today – only three customers since midday – and under normal circumstances he might have closed the shop early and gone home with Jasmina when she left, an hour before. Instead, wanting to watch the press conference on the murders without her knowledge, he decided to stay here, just for a while, under the guise of earning the money they both knew they needed.

So he is here now, sitting in his shop, watching the small television on the counter. It is a little after five o'clock, but still bright and sunny outside. Inside the shop, however, it feels gloomy and dark. Perhaps that it is simply him. Perhaps that is simply the effect the policeman has on him.

Hicks . . .

On the screen, he is sitting on the far side of the table and the camera is zoomed in so that he fills most of the frame; you can just see the elbow of the female officer sitting beside him. Hicks is reading a statement from pieces of paper in front of him. Occasional camera flashes illuminate him, but it is impossible to tell if he notices them or cares.

Of course, he does not care. He never did.

Always so detached and professional.

Even now, still so young and polished.

'We are currently looking for a man in his early to mid twenties,' Hicks says.

In his smart suit, Levchenko thinks, he might as well be working in a bank. Or a similar place – one that deals with data rather than people.

'His name might possibly be James or Jimmy, or at least people may know him by that name. He is approximately six foot tall and of average build, with sandy blond hair. It is possible he is known to older teenagers in the Farfield area of the city, and we encourage anybody with information about this individual's identity to come forward.'

He looks up from his notes. Levchenko remembers his eyes from the last time they met. Although they seem much more serious now, don't they? Tired and troubled.

'We will treat any information we receive in the strictest confidence.' Hicks puts the papers down. 'I'll now take five minutes of questions. Yes?'

A voice drifts over, barely audible.

'Tom Benson, *Evening Post*. At this point, you indicate that the killer has claimed fifteen victims, but you've only named nine of those. Is that a problem of identification?'

Throughout the question, Hicks nods seriously.

'I am not able, at present,' he says, 'to provide details on the victims whose names have not been released to the press.'

But the voice persists.

'We are aware of a number of crime scenes across the city. Were these additional victims found at those locations?'

'I am not able, at present, to provide details on the victims whose names have not been released to the press.' Hicks nods elsewhere in the room. 'Yes?'

Levchenko smiles to himself – but without humour. The detective has not changed: still stonewalling; still treating legitimate questions and enquiries with indifference – contempt, even. It occurs to him that not only is he here in the shop right now because of Hicks, but at this place in his life as well. And that due to the spread of cause and effect that ripples from even the smallest actions, at least one other person is not.

Emmy.

Lost in memories, he misses the question. On the screen, Hicks stares out at his unseen audience.

'We are pursuing several lines of enquiry. But I reiterate: I am not able, at present, to provide details on the victims whose names have not been released to the press.'

Because you haven't found them, Levchenko thinks.

That's the subtext of the detective's words, isn't it? Surely everybody in the room there can pick it up if he can? That must be why they're pecking at him, like chickens scrabbling at dirt.

'Over a week into the investigation,' a reporter asks, 'without an arrest. How close are you to identifying the suspect you've described?'

It might be Levchenko's imagination, but he thinks he sees Hicks's expression drop slightly. That makes sense, doesn't it? The detective wouldn't like to be criticised. Too sure of himself for that.

'As I've said, we are pursuing several lines of enquiry. We encourage anybody with the information I've indicated to come forward. We're confident that an arrest will follow shortly.'

Are you?

Another smile without humour – though a small part of Levchenko is enjoying seeing the detective floundering under pressure. But there is the fact that people are dead. That is nothing to celebrate. And the fact that whatever happens to Hicks, nothing can change the past.

Nothing can bring her back.

Levchenko shakes his head.

It is true, of course, and he experiences a moment of guilt. What is the point in the vague thrill he feels at the detective's troubles? God would not approve – yet he feels it anyway, and suppresses the shame that accompanies it. Why not? Surely God does not approve of Hicks either. Just as we are judged for what we do, so must we be judged for what we do not. *Will you allow me this?* he asks God. *Nothing can bring her back now, but something at the time might have stopped it.*

Hicks could have saved her.

Levchenko could have . . .

But he clamps down on that.

It is important to remember this, to repeat it: there was nothing he could have done beyond what he did. He is a good citizen, so he reported his concerns to the relevant authorities – to the people who *should* have done something, because that is the point of them – and so the blame lies with them.

The blame *has* to lie with them.

He stares at the television screen.

With him.

The bell above the door tinkles.

Levchenko looks up suddenly. An old lady is pushing her way in, with some trepidation, as though she isn't sure whether she's allowed to.

'Hello?' she says. Her voice trembles. 'Are you still open?'

'Yes. Please, come in.'

Levchenko uses the controller to switch off the television. He wants to see the end of the press conference – wants to see the detective squirm – but he can hardly turn down the business. And even if he could afford to, manners forbid it. He can hardly send this old woman away now she is inside the shop.

'What can I do for you?'

'Your candles,' she says. 'The special ones you make?'

'Oh yes.' Levchenko nods, pleased. 'Yes. How can I help you?'

'It's short notice.'

'That's all right,' Levchenko says, although he wonders whether it is. It depends on how short the notice is. His stock of standard pre-made candles is plentiful, but he is out of wax pellets and certain shades of dye for the base.

The elderly woman unfolds a piece of paper.

'It's for one of your special candles,' she says. 'One cast at the moment?'

'Yes. I know the ones you mean. When is it for?'

The woman smoothes out the crinkled paper.

237

'Tonight,' she says. 'The time does not matter, but it has to be today. It would be my daughter's birthday.'

Levchenko pauses. Normally, he would refuse – but with business the way it has been, that is hard to do. Besides, something about her troubles him. The way she is shaking slightly. And her choice of words, too: it *would be* her daughter's birthday. It makes him think of Emmeline, which spurs him on.

He says, 'Let me check.'

He picks up the phone and calls the warehouse where he buys his wax supplies. It rings for a few moments – the woman before him fidgets nervously – and is answered by Robi, the shipping manager. He sounds harried, and Levchenko talks to him in his own language, detailing what he needs.

'I cannot have it in the post tonight obviously,' Robi says.

'That's okay. I was hoping to call in.' Levchenko checks his watch and calculates the distance involved. 'I can be there in a little under an hour?'

'That . . . should be okay. Who am I fooling? I will be here all night anyway. I will have it waiting.'

'Thank you, Robi.'

'You are welcome, Gregor.'

He puts the phone down and thinks – he has no intention of being here that late himself, so he will cast the candle in his garage. From the warehouse, taking his bicycle, he will have to circle round the top of the city slightly, but the evening is warm and fresh, and the country roads in that direction are pleasing. He likes it out there a lot.

He smiles at the old woman, as kindly as he can. 'Let me have the details, please. What is your name?'

'Carla Gibson,' she says.

Forty

There was a buzz in the operations room. With the developments of the past twenty-four hours, it felt like we were closing in. That, at least, was the feeling amongst the officers present, and they were giving it their all – putting in an extra few hours now at the end of a long, complex task, convinced that it might be all it took to get it done.

I understood the attitude, but didn't share it.

Partly it was just a hangover from the press conference, which had continued the trend of increasing belligerence from the media. But it was also the feeling that, despite recent developments, we were still a long way from ending this.

We'd moved fast. Officers had already interviewed all the kids that Carl Johnson had named as being in attendance at Killer Hill that evening, along with others who might have been there other nights. None of them had been able to help us much. The ones who'd been there on the evening in question *remembered* it, of course, but, just like Carl, none of them knew who 'Jimmy' was.

So we'd widened the net, tracking down older teenagers at schools within the general vicinity of the incident. They'd given us other possible names, and so on. Nothing concrete so far. It felt like we'd interviewed every kid who'd ever been at one of those outdoor parties, and the guy who'd killed the cat was a stranger to all of them.

So all we really had was a first name – one that might not even be real.

In terms of IT, DS Renton was keeping us updated on their findings, and we kept passing them on to the search teams. We had officers trawling the north-east areas of the city, the country lanes out in the sticks where the video had most likely been shot. But what we still had amounted to hundreds of miles of winding, intertwining country roads to search.

And then there was Franklin.

He'd arrived sometime while we were out interviewing Carl at his home, and been present ever since, kept here by the activity: the sense that we were on the verge of some kind of breakthrough. I'd spoken to him a few times already, and each time I imagined he was looking at me more curiously than he should have been.

Do I know you?

Have we met somewhere before?

We have, haven't we. But where?

He drifted around the operations room drinking coffee. Although I did my best not to look at him, I could feel him looking at me. The whole time. Like a painted portrait, wherever he was in the room his eyes seemed to be on me.

I knew it was only a matter of time.

'Okay,' Laura said. 'For a moment, let's forget about *how* he chooses them.'

'All right.'

I put Franklin out of my mind, and tried to concentrate on the matter at hand. The pattern. I still kept oscillating between believing there was one and being convinced there was not. Whichever was true, however many times we looked over the data ourselves, there appeared to be nothing to see.

'All right,' I said again. 'What else, then?'

'*How* does he kill them?'

'We know that.'

'Yes, but step back from it a pace. His victims so far have

tended to be fully grown adults, and some of them have been male. Look at John Kramer, for God's sake. Not only was he handy in himself, he was *armed* when he was attacked.'

I saw what she was getting at.

'You mean, how does he get into a position where he can kill them? He has to overpower them somehow. Or else take them by surprise. I guess that must have been what happened with Kramer.'

'What about the others, though? The ones we've not found yet.'

I thought about that. Obviously we didn't have any evidence from the bodies themselves to work with, but we had the evidence in the video. Six bodies. All of them in a spot so isolated we'd so far failed to find it.

'How did he get them there?' Laura held up a still from the video he'd sent us; it flapped slightly in her hand. 'We know he films the murders – or this one, at least, but it seems likely he films them all for some reason. He did with the cats. But the point is, we know the victim in the video was killed *at that location.*'

'And so the question is . . .'

'If the spot is so isolated, how did he get the victim there?'

'And not just him,' I said. 'The others too. Whether he killed them there or not.'

We were both silent for a moment.

There were two possibilities, as far as I could see. The killer could have subdued the man in the video – and presumably the other victims – at a different location and then taken them to his nest in the woods. That would involve a hell of a lot of risk and effort, but it was possible. Alternatively, it could be similar to the crime scene on the edge of the Garth estate: that he simply waited patiently somewhere out on those isolated country roads. Not finding a victim so much as waiting for the next victim to find him.

Either way, it implied the *location* was important to him. If there was a pattern to his crimes, it had to have some kind of geographical basis.

I said, 'We know he doesn't leave anything to chance.'

'No.'

'So he has to know this place, doesn't he? It's isolated enough to allow him to do what he does. Either he can take them there without being disturbed. Or else . . .'

Laura waited. I was thinking about the way he'd worked at the Garth estate. And the way he'd messed up in Buxton while killing Kate Barrett. He hadn't wanted to be seen. Quite the opposite: it was out in the middle of nowhere, and he hadn't counted on being spotted.

'Or else,' I said, 'the place is quiet, but still busy enough to supply him with victims.'

Laura stared at me for a moment, not saying anything.

'He's waiting there,' she said finally.

'Yes.'

'So it's a place where people go.'

'No, it's not.'

I looked at the map, with its networks of roads. I'd been out there myself. The country lanes were narrow and quiet, edged by green fields and woodland. Little copses. Traffic was sparse. There wasn't much out there. Nowhere that people would actually *go*. It was more a place to pass through.

'He waits by the roadside,' I said.

'What?'

'He waits by the roadside. Maybe flags down cars for help. Maybe knocks cyclists over.'

I stared at the map.

I was sure of it.

Forty-One

It is nearly seven o'clock, and the day is beginning to settle down. The world has darkened a few shades. In the woodland Levchenko passes, shadows are rising between the trees. The sun still makes it down to the road in places, dappling the warm tarmac and creating a camouflage of brighter shades in the canopy of overhanging leaves, but evening is arriving. Birds flit low over the occasional fields, darting in and out of the clouds of midges itching above the hedges.

The purr of the bicycle tyres is all he can hear.

At some point, he slows, then stops, taking a moment to absorb the world around him. The complexity of light and shade, the contrast between the grey road and the shredded greens and browns of overgrown woodland.

The world is beautiful here, he thinks, because there is too much for the eye to take in, so much lovely detail that you glimpse only a part of it and catch the barest sense of an impossibly intricate whole. He gets the same sensation from some paintings, where an abundance of colours and patterns, built with countless brushstrokes, awes the eye, overwhelming it. It seems unimaginable that a human mind could have conceived something so complex and then created it, inch by inch, with nothing more than an accumulation of small, simple human movements.

But then, beauty can also be found in simplicity.

His daughter, Emmy, was beautiful – and yet her face was

plain and unlined. Her beauty stemmed from the absence of complexity: the lack of guile and anger and hatred. She had been beautiful because, despite everything, she had always appeared undamaged by the world. At least until the end.

There are two types of people in the world, he believes. There is good and, yes, there is evil. Some people see such simple, innocent beauty as his daughter possessed and they wish to protect it, recognising how fragile and precious it is. But there are those who resent it and seek to corrupt it: to bring it down to their level. People who cannot bear the presence of such beauty outside of them when it is gone from inside, or perhaps was never present at all.

Ugliness, then, is easier to define – and the world is full of it. Sometimes it is all you can see. And so he enjoys coming out here, into the countryside, and taking in a brief sip of its opposite. A reminder that the world can be beautiful, albeit almost always when people are not in it.

Levchenko puts his foot back on the pedal and kicks off again.

The tyres whine along the country lanes. The sack of wax pellets he has collected is strapped to the back of the bicycle. Home is mostly downhill; he rarely has to pedal at all.

As usual, once Emmy has entered his thoughts, she refuses to leave. It is her loss that causes him to question everything. Why was he spared in that accident? There has to have been a reason, and it cannot have been to see his daughter die. What kind of God would countenance such a thing? So there has to be something else. Something he was saved in order to do; a role he will play in a pattern that has not yet been revealed to him.

Unless that moment has already passed . . .

And this is his deepest fear: that God kept him alive so that, years later, he could save Emmy. If that is the case, he failed long ago. The thought is unbearable, but it would explain why, despite his most fervent prayers, God has fallen silent ever since. While He remains real to Levchenko, perhaps Levchenko is nothing more than a husk in His eyes, devoid now of purpose and passing his remaining years much as he rides his bicycle, permitted only glimpses of beauty and understanding.

But no. That is intolerable.

If any number of things had been different, Emmy would still be alive today. Her murder was the effect, but his own actions were only one of the causes; there were others. He cannot bear to blame himself.

And so he chooses, instead, to blame the detective.

Hicks.

An image drifts into Levchenko's mind: not the officer he's been observing on screen, grappling with the spate of murders, turning awkwardly like a worm on a hook, but the younger man. The constable, brash and polished and indifferent. The one he met all those years ago.

He remembers sitting in a room with Hicks, cowed by the man. Levchenko had been raised to respect and believe in authority; that was the reason he was there. He could have taken care of her boyfriend himself – warned the man away from Emmy and made sure he took the warning. Instead, he was here, talking to the police, because the police were meant to deal with things like this. They were meant to take care of people and make sure they were safe. They were meant to be good. So Levchenko had been certain the police would help him. That they would save her. And yet, as he explained the situation, Hicks had practically yawned.

'Please, sir,' Levchenko remembers saying. 'I am scared for her life. She will not leave him; she does not dare. He will surely kill her eventually. That is my fear.'

'I understand.' Hicks leaned back in his chair. 'But there's not a whole lot we can do unless she's prepared to press charges.'

In desperation, Levchenko slid a photograph of his daughter across to the officer. He had taken it himself the night before, during the brief time Emmy had fled to their home before returning to his.

'Please,' he said. 'Look at her.'

And Hicks did. He stared down at the black-and-white photograph of her bruised face for what felt like an age, and that age seemed full of possibilities – of hope, hanging by a thread but still hanging. He was horrified by the image, but trying, professionally, to hide his reaction. And for that brief time, Levchenko remained convinced that Hicks was a good man, and that he would do what was right, what was necessary.

'He did this?'

Levchenko nodded.

Hicks looked up from the photograph. 'She told you that?'

'Yes.'

'Will she tell us?'

Levchenko did not reply.

Hicks nodded and slid the photograph back across the desk.

'I can't tell you,' he said, 'how often we see this. And it breaks my heart, believe me. More than I can tell you. But ultimately, I have to say, there probably isn't much we can do. We can proceed, but if there is insufficient evidence, it will go nowhere.'

'Nowhere?'

'Our hands are tied,' Hicks said. 'The only evidence we'll have is her word, and without that we have to weigh up the likelihood of a successful conviction against the cost of the investigation.'

Cost.

Levchenko stared at him, a sinking sensation inside.

'There is also a danger,' Hicks said, 'that our attention might make the situation worse. Do you understand? He might take it out on her.'

Levchenko shook his head.

'Please. You must protect her. Please. You must.'

There was a long silence, during which Hicks stared at him. Then he slid the photograph back and looked at it again. Levchenko saw his eyes flicking from bruise to bruise.

'All right,' Hicks said. 'I'll talk to him. To both of them. I'll try, anyway.'

'Yes?'

'I'll see what we can do.'

'Yes.' The tension burst in Levchenko's chest, hope spreading like blossom. All was right with the world again. 'Please. Yes, you will do that.'

'But I have to warn you . . .'

'You will keep her safe.'

Hicks did not reply to that, and his expression was unreadable. Thinking back, Levchenko would identify the look on the man's face as boredom. He would decide that Hicks had only ever been humouring him – that he wasn't going to do anything at all, and his promise was an empty one, designed to get this awkward and naive visitor out of the room as swiftly as possible. But at the time, he had hope. He believed it meant Emmy was going to be all right.

Levchenko stood up.

'Thank you. Thank you. Make sure she is safe.'

And he had gone home that night – on the same old bicycle he is riding now – with a sense that it would be okay. Hicks would talk to John Doherty, to Emmy. He would recognise Doherty for the evil man he was, and he would arrest him and put him somewhere he could never hurt Emmy again. Because that was what was supposed to happen, wasn't it? That was what the authorities were there for – to protect the beauty from the overwhelming presence of the ugly. Back then, he still believed that.

And yet, two days later, Emmy was dead.

I'm sorry.

Levchenko's eyes blur slightly, and he thinks he should probably pull over for safety. The bicycle is going very fast now. For the moment, though, he blinks the tears away and continues on his way home, cutting quickly down the otherwise silent and empty country lanes. He wants to get home to Jasmina. He needs to hold her.

I'm sorry.

He is not even sure to whom he is addressing the apology. To God? To Emmy? Perhaps even, in some odd way, to the policeman himself?

For a moment, he nearly loses control of the handlebars, and he slows slightly, blinking at the tears blurring the road ahead. Regaining control of himself.

He needs to stop before he has an accident.

He needs to—

As he clenches the brakes, Levchenko focuses on the road for long enough to see that it is no longer empty. There is someone dressed in black at the tree line, just ahead on the left, running out of the woodland, as though coming to meet him.

What is— He barely has time to attempt a swerve—

And the world explodes.

Everything. Bright red.

Part Three

And then what happened?

To begin with, the boy tells the policeman, it is much the same as other nights. The brothers sit in their small, dark room, listening to the sounds from the far end of the house, while at the same time trying not to hear. At some point, the boy falls asleep without realising it, because he feels the jolt as his brother gets up.

The house is silent now.

He's gone to sleep, John whispers.

The boy nods miserably and lies down sideways on his bunk, drawing his knees up to his chest. He expects his brother to tap back up the creaking ladder to the top bunk, so they can both snatch sleep, but instead John remains standing in the dark bedroom. He is very still, but the boy can hear him breathing. There is something a little like electricity in the air.

John? he says.

Shhhh.

The boy sits up again, frowning. *John?*

His brother reaches down and touches his cheek. It feels like his hand is trembling slightly. *It's okay.* His voice is strained, thin. *I won't be long.*

Where are you going?

I've got his key.

It takes the boy a moment to work out what he means. By

then, his brother has moved away, over to the bedroom door, and is opening it slowly, carefully, so as not to make any sound.

The boy stands up.

John?

Shhh. Stay here.

His brother steps out into the hallway – dark now – and closes the door behind him, leaving the boy alone in the pitch-black bedroom. His heart is hammering, and he can hardly breathe. All over his body, the skin is tingling.

He is terribly afraid.

He does not want his brother to do this – wants to call out instead. But he is scared for John. Whatever he does, he is scared. Their father is insurmountable; they both know this. They do not confront him. They do not intervene. Even that does not guarantee their safety, but the opposite removes it entirely. They have to keep quiet. They have to hide and remain unnoticed for as long as possible.

Not do this.

'The key,' the policeman says. 'What did John mean by that? The key to what?'

The boy looks at him. Looks him right in the eye.

What the policeman sees there is, surely, not derision. Because that would be impossible. There is no way this child is old and wise enough to be mocking him. Perhaps he is lying – that much is possible – but a little boy would be keen to hide his lies, anxious that someone might see through them, rather than revelling in the fact that someone has and they both know it.

The policeman realises he is touching the cross on his necklace – that it has come out from beneath his uniform and he is rubbing it anxiously between his fingers. He forces himself to tuck it away. This child is not evil. He isn't. He has simply been through so much.

And yet . . .

'The key to what, Andy?' Sergeant Franklin says. 'The key to what?'

And with that same expression on his face, the eight-year-old boy says, 'The key to my father's gun cabinet.'

DAY TEN

Forty-Two

'Have we met before?'

I looked up from the coffee machine. I was in the lounge down the corridor from the operations room. It was a small room, with space for a sink unit and cabinets, the drinks dispenser I was standing by, and a couple of threadbare armchairs nobody ever had time to sit down in.

Franklin was standing in the doorway.

'I don't think so,' I said.

He took a step into the room. 'I'm sure we have. I've been thinking about it since I arrived, but haven't had the chance to ask. And I'm *sure*. Where do I know you from?'

'I guess I've got one of those faces.'

I did my best to shrug, half smile, and then, with my heart thudding hard in my chest, I turned back to the dispenser. Watched the hot water spitting and rasping into the thin plastic cup.

'You've never worked in Buxton?'

'Nope. Only ever here.'

Never worked in Buxton.

I grew up there though. My brother and me.

And yes, we have met before.

The coffee finally finished, I picked the cup out carefully, blowing the steam from the rim. Franklin was still standing there, still looking at me curiously, inquisitively. There was something about his body language that I didn't like. It wasn't cop-to-cop; it was more interrogatory than that, as though he'd decided that if he hadn't encountered me as a colleague, then at some point he must have encountered me in a very different capacity.

Which of course he had.

The key to what, Andy?

The key to what?

I had changed, though. That was something to cling to. My surname was different now; my face and body had grown and altered. Only the thinnest ghost remained of the little boy he'd interrogated all those years ago – at least on the outside. And I remembered him so clearly because of the circumstances, and the impact he'd had on me, whereas his life since must have been littered with other similar incidents, his encounter with me lost and only half recalled amongst them.

I looked at him.

He hadn't changed all that much from the policeman he'd been when he interviewed me all those years ago – back when I was eight years old. The brown hair might have silvered, but the face remained relatively unlined. The same bright blue eyes. I could see a thin chain around his neck, which I was willing to bet ended in the exact same crucifix I'd seen him touching as a young officer.

Faced with me.

This man, and the attitude he'd had towards me as a child, was responsible for so much of who I was. *Evil*. He'd thought I was evil. He hadn't even made an attempt to hide it. I'd spent so much time denying that to myself – I wasn't a bad person; there wasn't anything instrinsically wrong with me; there was no *evil* – that the denial ran through me as deep as blood, and just as important.

But now, finally faced with him again, all that psychological armour was crumbling. I felt cold and small: powerless before the intimidating authority figure staring at me, accusing me with his eyes of being something monstrous. *Do I know you? Yes, I know you. I know what you are.* The time that had passed didn't seem to matter any more. As I stood staring back at him, barely able to blink, I felt all the years I'd travelled, all the conviction I'd gathered, collapsing behind me like a bridge falling, the break rumbling towards me.

I opened my mouth to say . . . something. But nothing came out.

Then Franklin smiled at me. Shook his head.

'Oh, I'm getting old.'

'Sorry?'

'I mean I'm not thinking straight.' He half laughed, his manner changing instantly. 'I've just realised – it will be from the television, won't it? The press conferences. I remember seeing one of them. It must be from there.'

'Yes,' I said. 'It's probably that.'

He leaned against the wall, visibly relaxing. My gaze followed him. The rest of my body didn't move, aside from my heart, knocking hard against my lungs.

'To be honest,' he was saying, 'I don't know where I am at the moment. It's this case, I think. It's the worst one I've ever seen. And I've seen a lot.' He looked at me. 'How old are you?'

'Thirty-five.'

'Really? You look younger. Well, trust me, Andy – by the time you get to my age, you'll have seen far too much.' His hand went to his chest, to the crucifix I imagined nestling beneath his shirt. My gaze followed it. 'Far too much. And this . . . this is just evil, isn't it. Pure evil.'

It wasn't a question.

I said, 'I don't know if I believe in evil.'

'Really? Wait a while.' He lowered his hand and gave that half-laugh again. 'Wait a while.'

I should have been prepared to argue; in my head, I'd been doing so ever since. But I found myself nodding slightly, entirely unequipped for this moment that had arrived. Franklin's arrival had whipped off the flimsy film of self-deception, and now I just wanted away from this, not to engage in it, not to try to stand up to him.

'It's just this case, anyway.' Franklin moved away from the wall again. 'That's what's throwing me. Can't think straight in the face of it.'

'I get you. Believe me.'

He shook his head. 'Just don't tell anyone, will you?'

'Don't worry.' I did my best to smile back. 'I won't.'

I needed some fresh air.

Taking my coffee with me, ignoring the way it scorched my fingertips, I headed for the lift and pressed the button for the ground floor. As it descended, I told myself:

He doesn't recognise me.

As much as my defences had crumbled in the moment, I was already spinning the encounter. But still – it was true. The confrontation that had made such an impression on me, that had affected my whole life . . . *he didn't fucking remember it*. He hadn't looked at me and seen the evil little boy he had at the time, and he hadn't recognised something wrong with me now. So regardless of anything else, I was not that child any more. I was no longer what Franklin had thought I was all those years ago. If I ever had been at all.

That was what I'd been afraid of all these years. That was what I'd expected to face when Franklin joined the investigation. And it hadn't happened. What I felt now was almost relief, except that word wasn't strong enough. It was *euphoria*. I was still trembling slightly, but now there was so much energy coursing through me it felt like I could bounce on the spot. It felt like I could do anything at all.

Catch this fucker.

Yes, that was what remained. Catch him. End this. And we would. As the lift hit the ground floor, I smiled to myself, and took a sip of the coffee without thinking. The heat sang in my upper lip, but I barely even noticed.

Ting.

I stepped out and headed through the foyer, past the reception, towards the sliding glass doors that led outside. It was sunny out there today. No storm clouds gathering; even the ones in my head were clearing. Free, free, free. There was a woman at the reception desk, but I was so distracted that I barely caught what she was saying as I walked behind her.

'My *husband*.' She was clearly frustrated, obviously repeating what she had already told the duty officer. The doors slid open in front of me just as she said, 'Gregor *Levchenko*.'

A moment later, as I was still frozen in place, the glass doors slid closed again in front of me.

And then I turned slowly back.

Forty-Three

It is time, the General thinks, to end this.

Standing in his office, wearing his uniform, he keeps his back to the dreaded thing in the corner and focuses on the computer screen in front of him. He watches the videos, one by one, moving only to change CDs as each clip comes to an end. One by one, he places the discs in a growing pile on the desk.

The murder of Vicki Gibson: haphazard and hand-held, camera held so close that blood spatters the lens. He was still learning at that point.

Derek Evans. Murdered the same night, but far more carefully. The camera is balanced on a wall before the homeless man is approached and beaten.

Sandra Peacock, John Kramer and Marion Collins. All die in much the same way: the only thing that changes in the footage is the addition of one and then two bodies beside the dying victim.

Kate Barrett. This one is more hurried – a mistake. Her husband is audible in the background, shouting in distress, and the clip ends raggedly, the road juddering as he runs.

Paul Thatcher. The video begins with him already lying on the woodland floor, mouth gaping, one half of his head bright red. Even with the interruption halfway through, the torture shown is prolonged, and Thatcher takes an age to die. Again, he is learning.

Marie Wilkinson. The clip begins with the pregnant woman

already subdued, this time on her kitchen floor. She is struck several times in the face. There are inaudible words from outside of the frame. The camera remains focused on the dying woman on the floor as the intruding old man is beaten to death out of shot.

Seven more victims killed in the same woodland location in similarly abhorrent ways. None of them have been identified in the media yet, so he has no way of knowing their names. Not that it matters to him.

Sixteen murders, including the old man, and the code is unbroken.

It is enough. So, yes. It is time to stop this.

The General walks into the bathroom and takes one last look at himself in the mirror, wearing his father's army uniform. He never earned one of his own, much as he tried, but he has done his best since to honour his father's memory and make him proud. To become the kind of man he would have wanted as a son. He remembers the sequences he used to create as a child, all of which the old man broke. And so yes, in some sense, there is that too. Honour, become . . . and beat.

As he looks at himself, another memory of his father surfaces. Not telling stories at the dinner table, but at a later date: the man hopelessly drunk, lost, his wife – the General's mother – long gone. In the memory, the old man is wearing this same uniform, and he has a pistol in his hand.

I'm a soldier, his father says. Although the General is standing directly behind him, talking to him, he knows the old man is speaking to himself. His father looks down at the weapon in his hand with something close to bewilderment. As though the weight is a surprise to him. The gun weighs more than the buttons pressed and stories told; it has a tangible real-life heft. It demands to be held and carried.

I'm a soldier, his father repeats, slurring the words.

So I should be able to do this.

The General shakes his head, chasing the memory away – and the memory of what came later.

Dear Sir,
We reject your application on the basis . . .
No. He won't think about that.

Instead, he changes his clothes and gathers together the items he needs, trying to concentrate on the positives. *The code was not broken!* The other things that have gone wrong are not his fault – just dumb luck and misfortune, which can happen to anyone. Any soldier can stumble, especially in an operation as complex as this one. But the police never came close to breaking his code and catching him. And that is something. His father would surely be proud of that much.

The General shrugs on a coat, ignoring the horrific *thing* in the corner of the room behind him, and tries to tell himself all of this.

When he is ready to leave, he slips a rubber band carefully around the pile of CDs and places the bundle in his jacket pocket. Outside the house, he steers his car into the morning traffic and joins the loop road, heading towards the town centre, trying to keep the anger he feels under control.

Time to end this.

He heads for the train station.

Forty-Four

Back upstairs in the operations room, I phoned the warehouse to verify that Levchenko had indeed got that far and collected his order, then spent a few minutes studying my road map.

The place was north-east of the city, out in the sticks. His house was in the countryside too, but closer in. The area between was within our potential search area and had, according, to the reports already been visited. That didn't mean something hadn't been missed.

Okay. Making the assumption that Levchenko wouldn't have taken some crazy route, I drew a vertical eye shape on the map, with his house and the warehouse at the corners. Looking at the space in between, I could see two likely networks of roads he might have cycled along.

'What are you doing?' Laura said, putting a coffee down.

'I'm thinking.'

She peered at the map.

'What's going on?'

'Missing-persons report. This is where he was last seen; this is where he was going.'

I rubbed my jaw. It would take me half an hour each way, starting from his house and heading to the warehouse along one set of roads, then back again down the other. Levchenko hadn't been missing that long in the grand scheme of things, and I wasn't convinced anything had happened to him. But it was too . . . coincidental.

The birthday puzzle came back to me. Just because I had a connection to the guy didn't mean anything. Sooner or later, by the law of averages, those kinds of connection would arise. It probably didn't mean anything at all. Like Franklin's involvement, it was just the past intruding by chance.

'Andy?'

'We've already searched most of this area,' I said. 'It's probably nothing.'

'Right. So . . . what?'

I didn't say anything. I could still picture him. Levchenko. From memory, he was a good man – not the sort to stay out and worry his wife. And then, of course, I remembered Emmeline. A black-and-white image. A face with one eye bruised shut.

I stood up. 'I'll go.'

'You sure?' Laura shook her head. 'Hang on. What's going on, Hicks?'

'The woman,' I said. 'We've met before. Or rather, I've met her husband before. Look, it doesn't really matter. But I'll just check it out. It's probably nothing, but I'll check it out anyway, just to be sure.'

'O-kay.' Laura spread the word out, looking at me.

You're being weird here, Hicks.

'Because I owe it to them,' I said.

I owe it to them.

Eight years ago, Gregor Levchenko had come to me asking for help, and I'd failed him. Failed him and his wife and – most of all – his daughter, Emmeline.

At the time, she was living with a man called John Doherty, who had attacked her. I'd told her father the truth: that if she wasn't prepared to co-operate with us, there wasn't a whole lot we'd be able to do. Two days later, Doherty had beaten Emmeline Levchenko to death.

Because of me.

Because I failed to do my job and protect her.

On the way to the long, winding Hawthorne Road on the

outskirts of town, I drove past Gregor Levchenko's house and found myself stopping outside.

It was two up, two down, with windows like black eyes. Little more than a shack: a patched-together cube of brickwork and corrugated iron. The land around it was hard-scrabble: dust and dirt and miserable clutches of yellowing grass. Chickens from the property next door pecked at the gravel.

It looked like a place where nobody lived any more, but they did, the pair of them. And this was where Emmeline had grown up. They had been a decent, hard-working family who had never expected anything more from life than that the people who were supposed to look after and protect them would do so. It wasn't so much to ask. It shouldn't have been.

I owed them, all right.

And there was that sense again – stronger than ever – of being entangled. Of chains of cause and effect I could only glimpse brief links in, but which held taut out of sight. The sense that what was happening now was, at least in part, the present unable to keep the secrets of the past.

Everything unfolds.

Forty-Five

I drove north-east, unsure what I was looking for. The roads were quiet out here: a fringe hemming the top corner of the city, spreading out towards occasional factories and isolated properties but little else.

The land was half wild. For much of my journey, the road cut through woodland: walls of trees on either side, the branches sometimes meeting overhead, so that I passed through natural, leaf-lit tunnels filled with midges. The morning sun mottled everything. Where the trees cleared, it created bright expanses of shimmering tarmac. More than once, I saw deer darting between the trees parallel to the road, little more than shadows that resolved into animal shapes in my mind only after they had vanished.

I kept the window rolled down, my elbow on the sill, listening to the clicks of the undergrowth and the trill of birdsong.

For long stretches, I was totally alone. The few vehicles I met coming the other way were mostly rusted pickups, scooters, an occasional cyclist angling past. I drove slowly, the tarmac passing smoothly beneath my wheels, keeping my senses tuned for a sign. I didn't know what. What could there be that would be obvious?

But still . . .

And then I braked – a little quicker than I intended.

Something had caught my attention. For a moment I wasn't sure what it was. But as the car slowed to a halt, I heard a slight crackle and realised it had been that. Just a sound. The slightest variation in the texture of the road beneath the tyres.

I glanced in the rear-view mirror and saw nothing. So I cranked on the handbrake and got out of the car.

Outside, the smell of the countryside hit me properly. The area felt fresh and full and alive; a slight breeze wafting through the woodland brought out the rich scent of the undergrowth. The trees to either side were packed tight. The grass at their bases was swirled and messy, but had grown high enough in places to wrap around the lowest branches, forming green curtains.

I listened. At first, everything was silent, but then the world resolved itself into tiny clicks and buzzes. Not human noises. Looking all around me, I might as well have been the only person in the world.

I walked a little way back down the road, kicking at the tarmac, looking for whatever had made the noise. It didn't take long to find it – to find them. Hundreds of tiny white pellets of wax, scattered over the surface of the road.

I crouched down. The car tyres had smeared a lot of the wax into streaks, while the morning sun had already begun to melt other bits. It looked like glue on the tarmac.

He waits by the roadside, I remembered.

Maybe flags down cars for help.

Maybe knocks cyclists over.

I stood up quickly again. The world remained quiet and still.

It took a minute or two to establish the range the wax had spilled over and work out where the accident must have happened. Levchenko would have been riding from the opposite direction, back from the warehouse, and come off his bicycle a little past where I'd pulled up. At which point, the bike would have skidded along, the wax spilling across the road. I imagined the sound of rice pouring into a metal pan.

There was no sign of the bicycle itself, but that could easily have been hidden in the undergrowth somewhere along the road. The killer could have dealt with that. But not the wax.

There was nothing he could have done about that; there was too much of it. Maybe he'd figured it would disappear soon enough, as it was already beginning to.

Or maybe he hadn't noticed it at all.

I walked back to the car, feeling nervous but excited. I kept an eye and ear on the woodland to either side of me. It appeared deserted. *Dead.* Even so, I reached under my jacket and unclipped my gun holster. In all my years of active duty, I'd never had to use my firearm. Not once. And I didn't take it out now. Not yet.

Okay.

Now what?

My radio was on the passenger seat of the car. I picked it out, clipped it on to my belt, then locked the vehicle. The sensible thing to do – the right thing – was to call the scene in. SOCO wouldn't be pleased to have me trampling all over it any more than I already had.

I listened again. Nothing. No human sounds. It was deceptively tranquil here.

Let's just see first.

I walked up and down the road, looking for a likely entrance into the woodland. There was nothing obvious at first glance on either side, so I picked the beginning of the wax as my starting point. It must have been more or less where Levchenko had been struck, and it stood to reason that the killer wouldn't have wanted to drag a semi-conscious man too far up the road. He'd have wanted to get him out of sight as quickly as possible.

The undergrowth crunched beneath my shoes as I stepped through, using my shoulders rather than hands to support me against the trees. A little way in, the grass was more pressed down, and I spotted blood on a fanned blade of leaves. My stomach dropped, but my heartbeat picked up, my skin tingling. I could picture it in my head. This was where the killer had left Levchenko before returning to the road for the bicycle.

There was still no sign of that. Presumably he'd dragged it deeper into the forest, along with his victim.

I edged sideways between the trees, avoiding the blood, then crept softly through the foliage, moving branches aside as quietly as possible.

A short distance ahead of me, the trees opened out into a clearing of sorts. The ground was uneven, as though mounds of something had been dumped in piles and had then grown over. Here and there, recognisable debris poked out of the mulch. The rusted corner of a washing machine, rubber hanging from the rim of its huge, half-submerged eye. A scatter of empty CD cases. The twisted handlebars of a child's tricycle.

An old rubbish tip, I realised. Long forgotten now.

By most people.

I stood listening for a few seconds. Everything seemed quieter than back on the road. There was a hush to the place, as though the world was holding its breath. As though something invisible was standing nearby, keeping still and silent. Waiting.

Nobody here, though. Not right now . . .

And then, scanning the clearing, I saw it. There was a higher ridge of earth over to the left; it looked like the lip of a crater beyond. On the top, lying on its side, there was a bicycle. It was old and worn, but it clearly hadn't been here as long as the other rubbish. The handlebars were wrenched to one side. It looked like its neck had been broken.

Levchenko, I thought.

But he had to be here, of course. Didn't he?

I moved around the perimeter of the clearing until I reached the bottom of the ridge. The earth there was a mess of leaves and soil and litter. It compressed under my feet as I walked up, then lifted itself again behind me. I reached the top of the ridge and stared over. Down the slope, there was another clearing, and . . .

It was the place.

I fell still.

They were all here. Furthest away, two bodies were like husks, little more than piles of old clothes. What skin was visible was so discoloured that it barely stood out against the ground. I spotted a third corpse half in the trees on the far right-hand side: a man lying on his back, with his shirt wrenched up around his armpits, black holes spiderwebbing a pale, distended stomach. A fourth victim was lying on his front with his bottom in the air, like a baby sleeping. Another was seated against a tree.

The sixth was curled into a foetal position in the centre of the clearing. This was the man I'd watched being murdered in the video – and the sight of him made me shudder, because that hadn't been how he'd been when the camera turned off. He must somehow have still been alive when the killer left – just barely. Some meagre scrap of life had caused his body to move, searching out that first and final position of comfort.

And Levchenko . . .

He was lying on his back at the bottom of the ridge, just below me, his head tilted back as if to stare up at me. But he had nothing to see with any more. The killer had obliterated every feature below his hairline. His forearms poked up in the air, fingers splayed, as though frozen in the act of playing a piano. The slight breeze ruffled his hair softly.

This was the place. The killing ground.

I stared down at Levchenko, holding myself as still as the victims before me—

Squawwwk!

I spun around, my foot skidding on the mulch slightly, sinking in, sending a scattering of it down the ridge. It was the radio at my hip. Birds scattered in the trees above, but the first clearing, behind me, remained empty.

I unclipped the radio.

'Hicks,' I said.

'What's going on?' Laura's voice sounded loud and harsh in the silence of the woodland. 'Where are you?'

'I don't know exactly. An old rubbish tip just off the Hawthorne Road. Not sure where – a couple of miles up from the Newark end. It's . . . I found it.'

'The dump site?'

I glanced behind me at the bodies, then started back down into the first clearing. 'Yes. I'm going to head back to the road. I need support out here asap. This is . . . it's going to take a while.'

'Do we want . . . ?'

'To stake it out?' Did we want to draw attention to the scene, she was asking, or could we observe it from a distance – wait to see if 'Jimmy' returned. 'I don't know. He's taking them from the road, so if there's another way into the site, we could maybe access it from there, keep surveillance on the road itself.'

'I'm on it. Dialling IT with my free hand.'

'Good. I need people out here, Laura. I really need them. I'll keep it secure in the meantime.'

'Soon as.' She hesitated. 'Take care, Hicks.'

'I will.'

I shut down the connection, clipped the radio back on to my belt and walked back across the clearing, towards the road. Just as I reached it, something *clicked* in the undergrowth to the right, and I froze.

Listened carefully as I peered between the trees.

Nothing. Just the sounds of a forest growing.

Out on the road, the sun dappled the tarmac, the light trembling as the breeze gently shifted the boughs above. The back window of my car glinted, the roof steaming slightly in the heat.

It was so peaceful here. If you didn't know, it would be unbelievable to think that seven people had met horrific deaths only metres away, but the scene was burned into my mind. As I stood there, I felt it throbbing behind me. A pocket of darkness, hidden away amongst the trees.

What had driven someone to do this? The letters alleged that there was a reason – a pattern to be found – but the reality was entirely at odds with that. So the letters had to be a lie. Apart from anything else, the scene behind me wasn't the product of a rational mind. That wasn't someone sane at work back there:

dragging victim after victim to a stinking pit and filming their slow, tortuous deaths. Not the actions of someone creating a code, to whom the murders meant nothing. No, it was the work of a man who enjoyed suffering for its own sake, and for the power it gave him. Someone not indifferent to death but who revelled in it.

Which didn't fit.

I had a flash memory of Levchenko's missing face. I'd failed him again, hadn't I? That was how it felt. There was more to it than that, though. It was a coincidence that he was a victim here, and yet . . . it didn't feel like one. Once again, I had that familiar sense of gears grinding out of sight: cogs below the surface of the world, rolling and locking into place. As though everything that had happened had done so for a reason I couldn't see, and perhaps never would . . .

And then I heard it.

In the distance. The sound of a scooter.

I stepped back into the tree line and listened. My heartbeat was loud in my ears. The scooter was approaching from the direction of the city, and sounded some way off yet. I reached under my jacket towards my gun, but didn't take it out yet.

My hand hovered there.

Not necessarily anything.

Keeping in the undergrowth, I moved a little way in the direction the vehicle was coming from, and found a tree at the edge of the road to prop myself behind. The noise was louder.

I peered out.

The scooter was probably a hundred metres away now, leaning slightly to one side as the rider corrected from the meander of road that had brought it into sight. It was coming quickly too: an angry mosquito buzz to the engine. The rider was a man, dressed in black, with shoulder-length brown hair that was swept back by the speed he was driving at. I couldn't make out much of his face, but the scooter itself was bright crimson.

Kate Barrett's?

What had the registration been? I couldn't recall it – and then suddenly I could, at least a little. F765 something. I remembered that much. The numbers counted down.

I stepped out into the road.

Saw: F765 . . .

One hand still in my jacket, I held my other palm out.

'Stop! Police!'

He spotted me, of course – twenty metres away at most now – and I saw him stare in shock: raise himself back from the handlebars slightly, as though someone had clicked their fingers in front of his face. He was only young, I realised. Perhaps this was a mistake – but then he lowered his body again, expression grim, and accelerated straight at me.

Shit.

I pulled the gun out as quickly and smoothly as I could, but there was no time for a two-handed grip: I just fired three shots one-handed towards the scooter itself, heard the bang of the front tyre exploding, the *ching* of bullet on metal, and then leapt to one side. Too late, though. I had a momentary image of the bike suddenly on its side, coming at me like a scythe, and then my legs were flung sideways and I landed face first in the undergrowth.

Behind me on the road, there was a tortured scrape of metal as the downed scooter spun away along the tarmac.

And then nothing.

You're okay.

There was no pain. Then suddenly, a silent, dipping heartbeat later, there was more pain than I'd ever had in my life. My left leg felt like it had burst into flame: the burning unbearable. I rolled on to my back, mouth gaping open, but hurting too much to make a sound, and reached down out of instinct to grasp my thigh. Through the fog of pain, it made me realise that my hands were empty.

Where was the gun?

I shifted slightly, scanning the undergrowth around me, finding nothing, then glanced up the road. The rider was lying on his side a short distance from me. As I watched, he too rolled on to his back and then slowly lifted a hand to the side of his head.

Get up, Andy.

Get up!

I reached for the nearest tree and used a low branch to pull myself up slightly, then a higher one to get to my feet and support myself. There was no strength in my injured leg at all. My thigh muscle felt like it had been destroyed. When I tried putting my weight on it, pain flared and the leg buckled. I gripped the branch harder.

On the road, the man lowered his hand and rolled back on to his side, then over on to his front, pushing himself up on to his knees. Making an effort to stand. His hair trailed on the tarmac, and I could see him gritting his teeth. Then he let out an awful howl – pain at first, then rage – and pushed himself to his feet.

Where's the gun?

I looked desperately at the ground by my feet. Nothing.

When I glanced back up, he was standing in the road, swaying slightly, staring at me. There was blood down one side of his face. It didn't conceal the expression of absolute hatred.

'Jimmy,' I said. 'It's over.'

He stared at me for a moment longer – long enough for me to think again: *Christ, he's just a kid* – then he walked slowly and awkwardly up the road. Limping slightly, but not as injured as I was. My gaze followed him to the downed scooter, which had spun all the way to the opposite tree line. He couldn't think it would be of any use to him, surely? But he crouched down at the back, and I heard clattering, and when he stood up again, I saw he was holding a claw hammer.

Panic took me.

Not trying to get away at all, then. And as he turned and walked back towards me, I had an image of the bodies in the woods, only a short distance away. What had been done to them. What was about to be done to me.

'Jimmy.'

He continued walking towards me, carefully, as though he wasn't sure of his step. His fingers kept curling and uncurling around the handle of the weapon. Eyes fixed on me. Grim determination on his face.

'Jimmy, it's over.'

He ignored me. I tried to move back into the woods, where I would have a better chance against him, where it would be harder for him to swing that fucking hammer – but my leg gave out and I fell backwards into the undergrowth, then sat up again quickly.

He was still coming. This was going to be how I died, then. As badly as anyone had ever died.

It was Rachel I thought of, and the son I would never meet.

'Jimmy—'

But then I saw the gun. It was just a little way in front of me, lying in the grass close to the edge of the road. Pretty much where I'd fallen, and yet somehow I'd missed it. Now, it was as obvious as a stone. The panic inside burst and filled me.

Everything that happened next was a blur.

I launched myself forward, using my good leg, and ended up kneeling beside the gun – just as Jimmy saw it too. He came at me faster. I scrambled in the grass and found it. Jimmy shouted in anger, raised the hammer just as I raised the gun. But he wasn't close enough, and I was faster. I got there first. He didn't have time to swing.

My heartbeat in my ears.

We were both frozen in place for a time: me kneeling, pointing the gun at his face; him standing two metres away, hammer held up behind his head. Eyes locked on each other. I don't know how long it lasted. In the corner of my eye, I saw a droplet of blood fall from his ear. I heard the trill of birdsong and the click of the woodland behind me, impossibly tranquil.

Then:

'Jimmy,' I said quietly, 'it's over.'

He stared at me for a few seconds longer, and I think he wanted to do it – was weighing it up to see if he had the courage to die. But then his expression slackened and he took a slow, awkward step back.

'Drop the hammer.'

It clattered on the tarmac.

'Face down on the ground.'

He did what he was told. He kneeled down carefully, then lay on his front and knitted his hands behind his head. I lowered the gun as he went, keeping it aimed on him. Then he lifted his head to rest his chin on the tarmac. Eyes bright against the dark red blood beside them.

It took Laura another ten minutes to arrive. The whole time we waited, we didn't take our eyes off each other, and we didn't say a word.

Forty-Six

'Taken aback?' Laura said.

'A little.'

It was early afternoon, and we were walking – limping in my case – up the front path of a two-storey house on a quiet suburban road. The neighbouring houses were all the same – wide and low and white-faced – and the gardens were well tended. A few houses up, a sprinkler was pulsing out of sight behind a flat hedge. Driving up the road, I'd seen an old man pushing a buzzing mower back and forth. It was a good area, this one. Neat and upper-middle-class and expensive.

'I don't know what I was expecting, but not this.'

This was where twenty-two-year-old James Miller lived with his parents, and it was a world away from the home I would have pictured him growing up in. It was difficult, look-ing around the sunlit street, to imagine this was a place dark enough to have produced such a monster – but of course, I was only seeing the exteriors. And what does opulence mean, anyway? The bad things that go on behind closed doors require only closed doors.

We approached it now.

'How's your leg, Hicks?'

'I'm good,' I said. 'Don't worry about me.'

'Calm down then.'

'I'm calm too.' I reached out and knocked. 'I'm good and I'm calm.'

But I wasn't.

The injury to my leg wasn't too severe. I was going to have a hell of a bruise, but the muscle had been stunned more than anything else, and I could walk okay. But it was inside where I was most bruised. I still remembered the panic, the fear – the feeling that I was going to die. If anything, it was stronger now, almost shameful. And I still remembered the sight of the killing ground in the woods. What James Miller had done to those people.

Between the two, I was angry as all fucking hell.

Not good. Not calm.

From inside his home, I heard a chain being hooked on. A moment later, the front door opened a fraction and a woman peered out. She was in her fifties, small and wary, with a sun-browned face and wiry grey hair. His mother, I guessed.

'Janine Miller?' I held up my ID. 'I'm Detective Andrew Hicks. This is Detective Laura Fellowes. Unlock the chain, please.'

Her gaze darted between us, nervous.

'What – what's this about?'

'We have a warrant to search the premises. In connection with the arrest of your son, James. Here.'

I passed it through the gap in the door. She made no move to take it from me.

'James? Where is he? What's going on?'

'He's at the police station.'

He had yet to be formally interviewed. Since his arrest, he had stared blankly and without emotion – the anger and hate apparently gone from him now – and spoken only to confirm his name and place of residence, and to say he understood the charges against him.

In addition to the hammer, we'd found, in the holding compartment of the stolen scooter, a balaclava, screwdriver, hunting knife, several plastic bags, his video camera and a spray bottle of cleaning product. His torture kit.

'Open the door for us, Mrs Miller.'

'I don't understand,' she said.

And yet something told me she did. The nervousness, maybe – as though she'd been expecting a knock on the door like this for a long time. As though she knew something, but had been keeping her mind closed to it, refusing to look.

'Open the door.'

She said, 'But Charles isn't here. My husband. I can't – he should be here.'

'He doesn't need to be here. This isn't about him. We have legal right of access. You need to open this door for us right now.'

I was seconds away from kicking the door off its fucking hinges. Even if she didn't bear some responsibility for what her son had become, we couldn't afford to wait any longer. For all we knew, her husband might be inside right now disposing of evidence.

I took a slight step back. Laura, sensing what I was about to do, moved forward quickly.

'You can call him,' she said. 'And we'll wait for him to arrive before we do anything. Okay? But let us in. We don't want this to be difficult.'

Janine Miller hesitated for a moment longer, then nodded. The door closed, there was a click, and this time it opened wide.

'Thank you,' Laura said.

We stepped inside into a plush little hallway. The carpet was beige and clean; the walls were painted bright white. There was a small polished table by the base of the stairs with a vase of blue flowers on it. Up ahead, a gleaming state-of-the-art kitchen. It looked like a show home.

'Mr Miller?' I called out.

There was no answer from the house.

'I already told you—'

'Where is James's room?' I said. 'Is it upstairs?'

It would be. I didn't even bother waiting for an answer; I was already starting up them. Behind me, I heard Laura reassuring Janine Miller.

'Come into the lounge. You can call your husband.'

'But you said—'

'Come through here and sit down.'

Upstairs, there was a landing with four doors leading off it. Three were open: a bathroom, a main bedroom, and a spare room that looked as though it was being used as a study. I glanced into each, made sure they were empty, then approached the final door, which must have been James's bedroom, and turned the handle.

Locked.

It would be, of course.

I took a step back and kicked it hard on the centre bar of the frame, close to the handle. It jarred my bad leg, but the flaring pain felt good for some reason. The door splintered a little but didn't give entirely, so I kicked it again, ignoring the shouts of protest coming from the lounge downstairs.

This time it banged open.

I stepped into Jimmy Miller's bedroom.

The carpet in here was older and more threadbare than in the rest of the house. Sunlight leached through the closed red curtains, painting everything a dull crimson colour. The place stank: warm and meaty. The single bed in the centre was unmade, the covers left in a tangle that lay half on the floor. On the nearest side, there was a toilet roll and bunches of tissues, and a stained pint glass half full of misty water. Piles of clothes were strewn around. There was a rickety plywood bookcase filled with magazines, knick-knacks, a filthy ashtray, an empty brandy bottle . . .

I stepped over to the bed, looking around, and spotted the desk in the far corner, beyond the bookcase. On it, a closed laptop was humming gently. The laptop was key, obviously, but it was what I saw on the wall above that made me pause.

Holy shit.

Several A4 sheets had been tacked up. They appeared to

be printouts from photographs or single frames from video footage. Most showed dead animals, similar to what Renton had shown me in the dark room. There was a dog hanging from a tree branch, tongue lolling, belly slit open and emptied. In another, he'd crucified a white cat and filled its mouth and eyes with what looked like glue.

But there were others. There was a photograph of Derek Evans's grave and the excrement that had been left on it. A blurred image intruded from the side and it took a moment to work out what it was. As Miller had taken the photograph, he'd used his free hand to give the dead man's grave the middle finger.

The people who have died mean nothing to me.

I looked down to the laptop, and then around at the mess of the room. The rest of the house was so pristine. I found it hard to imagine that Miller had been allowed to keep his room like this, lock or no lock.

I realised I was heading down the stairs, my feet thumping hard on the steps, and then into the living room.

Laura looked at me. 'Andy?'

'*Did you know?*'

I shouted it in his mother's face. She was sitting on the settee, knees pressed tightly around her hands, not looking up. At the sound of my voice, she shrank down even further.

'Did you? Did you fucking well know?'

'Andy—'

I grabbed hold of Janine Miller's shoulders and started shaking her.

'Did you fucking *know* what a monster you raised?'

The woman began sobbing, and I felt Laura drag me away from her. I didn't resist, but I kept staring down at her. She was shaking her head. I had no idea what she meant by it: I didn't know; forgive me; I can't take this any more.

'Andy. Mr Miller is on his way. Let's just keep this calm for now.'

'You've not seen upstairs.'

'Andy,' Laura said, a little helplessly, but then I turned around and she saw the look on my face. She stared into my eyes for a moment, then sighed. 'All right. All right.'

Forty-Seven

'James can't have done the things you're accusing him of,' Charles Miller said.

It was an hour later, and Laura and I were sitting across from him in the interview room. He was a short, wide man, dressed in beige chinos and a white shirt open enough to reveal whorls of grey hair at the top of his barrel chest. Almost bald – just patches of silver above his ears.

A former military man. We'd waited patiently for him to arrive home, and then brought him and his wife in under caution. Neither had been arrested, and Charles had blustered more than a little about accompanying us. I'd made it clear that if they didn't, they'd both be arrested for obstruction of justice and I'd deal with the consequences of that later.

'He can't have done it.'

From Charles Miller's tone of voice, the matter was already settled. He was hard-faced, and he kept my gaze the whole time, practically daring me to look away. Right now, I had no problem staring right back.

I said, 'I can assure you that he did.'

'But that's not for you to decide. Is it, *Officer*? We both know that. Your job is to gather evidence.' He leaned forward and tapped the desk. 'It's for the *courts* to establish guilt. Not people like you. Thank God.'

Laura, ever polite, said, 'What's that supposed to mean, Mr Miller?'

'It doesn't mean anything.' He leaned back. 'Forget I spoke.'

'We'll try,' I said.

By now I'd learned enough about his record – the medals and decorations – to know he was a man used to getting his own way: to being listened to and respected. Society had granted him a position of authority on its behalf, and he'd bought the hype. He believed it was something about him that demanded respect, rather than the position he'd once occupied. Well, *I* wasn't buying it.

'What makes you so sure James couldn't have done these things?'

'Because he doesn't have it in him,' Miller said. 'He's *a pastry chef*, for God's sake. Or he was. He couldn't even do that right. The boy's scared of his own shadow.'

A pastry chef – he said it with derision, as though he could hardly imagine an occupation less befitting a grown man. And he couldn't even do *that* right.

As the afternoon had worn on, the team had begun to assemble a history of James Miller. He'd done adequately at school, but was a withdrawn, apathetic student, and had left at the first opportunity. Few teachers recalled him; he had no real friends. Those that did remember him spoke of him being timid and invisible, a flinch of a child.

After leaving school, he'd spent a lot of time unemployed. Pastry chef, whatever his father thought of the job, was probably the highlight of his CV. For a brief time, two years ago, he'd worked as a taxi driver, but he'd been let go by the company for reasons as yet unknown. Since last year, he'd been unemployed.

I said, 'I'm not at liberty to discuss the evidence we have against James, but I can assure you it's substantial. And, with the greatest respect, James being a pastry chef is not going to balance it out.'

Miller stared at me. The contempt he felt for me and my fake authority was fairly clear.

Laura coughed, leaned forward.

'We're going to need your recollections of James's movements over the past few weeks.'

'I'll do my best.'

I said, 'Did you ever go in his room?'

'No.'

'You sure about that?'

'Absolutely. Not in years.'

'I wonder why you're so adamant about that. It's not like you know what we found in there or anything, is it?' I didn't give him a chance to respond. 'You look like a man whose home is his castle, Mr Miller. Why didn't you ever go in?'

'Because he was old enough to keep his own counsel. Be responsible for himself. He's a grown man, as much as he ever will be. I'd done all I could.'

'So you're not aware of what was taped on the wall above his desk?'

Miller shook his head, keeping my gaze. There was something in his eyes, and it made me think of his timid wife. It was hard to believe that, even without going into that room, neither of them had sensed something rotten under their roof.

But I changed tack.

'So. What did you mean when you said that he was scared of his own shadow?'

'I meant that he was a coward.'

'In what way?'

'He was always a weak child. Always scared.'

'Strange that, with you as a father.'

Miller shook his head, misunderstanding me. 'I did my best to help him.'

'You did your best to "help" him?'

'I wouldn't expect you to understand.'

For a moment, looking at Charles Miller, it wasn't him I saw, but another man. One who had taken me outside on to the lawn, in front of all the neighbours, and tried to teach me how to be a man by slapping me.

I leaned forward slowly.

'Try me.'

'He's scared of heights.'

'What the hell has that got to do with anything?'

'Scared of blood, too. Can you imagine that? When he was growing up, we had a dog. He was scared to give it a bath in case he scalded it.'

'And what did you do to teach him about that?'

Miller said nothing.

'Did you ever go into his room?'

'I already said. No.'

'Did you ever go into his room?'

Miller looked at me.

'Did. You. Ever. Go. Into. His. Room?'

'I told you. No. And I want a lawyer.'

I stood up slowly, took a deep breath, and leaned forward on the desk. Moved my face as close to his as I could get. Once again, I wasn't quite sure who I was looking at, but I recognised something in him and I wasn't afraid. Laura said, 'Andy.'

I ignored her.

'Mr Miller,' I said. 'The whole time, you've been looking at me like you wish this desk wasn't between us. That it wasn't in the way.'

He kept my gaze, his jaw rolling slightly. He didn't deny it, but he didn't make a move either. I waited, giving him a chance, but he just stared.

'Do you know what?'

I leaned away again, not breaking eye contact.

'I wish that too.'

Forty-Eight

And finally, James Miller himself.

At a little before five o'clock, Laura and I stepped into the interview suite. Two constables were waiting silently on either side of the room. We nodded to them and they left, then Laura shut the door as I took a seat across from Miller. She joined me a moment later, the metal chair scraping against the floor.

Miller didn't look up at us. He was slumped in the chair, and seemed much smaller than I'd been anticipating. Over the past week, because of what he'd done, he'd assumed a monstrous stature in my head. The truth – as always – was far more prosaic. However inhuman the actions, they're always perpetrated by human beings, and if you're expecting some kind of demon, the reality inevitably disappoints.

Not evil, I told myself.

In fact, sitting in the chair, cuffed, James Miller looked like nothing much at all. Not any more. He was dressed in a black T-shirt, sleeves cut high to reveal normal arms, not much hint of muscle to them. His hands were below the table, out of sight. He had an average build: mostly slim, but carrying slight weight around the chest and stomach. If you'd seen him slouching down the road towards you, with his carrier bag, you wouldn't have worried about him at all.

Vicki Gibson, struck as she walked home and pushed through that hedge. She wouldn't have looked twice at him.

And that was how he'd done it, wasn't it? His sheer innocuousness was how he'd got away with so much.

I pressed the button on the recorder.

'Detective Andrew Hicks. Conducting interview of James Miller, resident at 18 Tavistock Place. Also attending is Detective Laura Fellowes. Interview commencing at 16:56, twenty-third of May, in connection with charges relating to the murders of Vicki Gibson, Derek Evans, John Kramer . . .'

I read the names from the sheet in front of me. As I did so, the room seemed to grow quieter around me. There were twelve names, and another four victims as yet unidentified. By the time I'd finished – 'Unidentified victim 4, male' – my skin felt cold.

I glanced at the video camera mounted in the corner of the interview suite. In the operations room upstairs, nearly a hundred people would be crowded around the monitors right now. Normal business had been postponed throughout the department. So many people had worked on this case, and each and every one of them had been touched by it in some way.

'All right, James. Do you understand the nature of these charges and why you're here today?'

He nodded.

'That was a yes,' I said. 'Is there anything you'd like to tell us, James? Before we begin. Do you wish to make a statement with regard to your involvement in these deaths?'

He didn't move.

'The interviewee declines to respond,' I said. 'James, at the time of your arrest, you were in possession of a motor scooter licensed to Kate Barrett, which was stolen at the time of her murder. Can you explain how that vehicle came to be in your possession?'

Nothing.

'No response.' I slid photos across the table towards him. 'I am now showing the interviewee several photographs of the items found in his possession. Specifically, a hammer, screwdriver and hunting knife that are believed to have been used in the murders so listed. James, do you recognise these items?'

I gave him time.

'Interviewee refuses to look at the photographs.'

I leaned forward, trying to peer up and catch his eye, but he lowered his head even further to avoid my gaze.

'James,' I said. 'We have more than enough evidence to proceed with charges. And I think we both know you committed these murders. It's over now. You've caused people untold suffering, but it's done. The best thing now is to co-operate with us. That way we can bring some peace to the people you've hurt and begin to draw a line under this for everyone. Including you.'

No response.

I leaned back, folding my arms, thinking.

'We've spoken to your father.'

That got the slightest of responses.

'He told us you were afraid of heights. He said you couldn't have done it because you're scared of blood. Is that true? Are you—'

'I'm not scared of anything.'

His voice was confident: proud, even. And finally, he looked up at me.

'Your father told us you were.'

'No.' Miller shook his head calmly. 'I used to be, but not any more.'

'What about the animals, James?'

'What about them?'

'You were scared of blood, weren't you? That's what your father said. What did he do about that?'

Miller just looked at me. He had the same piercing eyes as his father; I remembered them from the road, waiting for Laura. He had the same hard face too. I wondered if that had always been the case. But of course, it hadn't. He wasn't born this way.

I said, 'When I was a kid, my father was a lot like yours. Worse, maybe. You want to know what he did?'

He didn't reply, but I carried on anyway.

'I was only six years old. A small kid back then. Weak – I got bullied a lot. When my father heard about that, he tried to teach me to fight. Took me outside, in front of all the neighbours, and showed me how to box. But he wasn't really doing that. He just kept slapping at me, telling me to keep my hands up. Because he wasn't really teaching me, you see?'

Miller nodded. 'Yes.'

'Exactly. It was about him. He was bullying me too. Making himself feel strong against someone weaker than him. Sounds to me like your father was kind of similar.'

'Maybe.'

'What did he make you do to the dog, James? You had a puppy, right? What did he make you do? Drown it?'

Miller nodded again. But he still had that proud look, as though, once upon a time, the memory would have upset him, but not any more.

Of course, after everything else he'd done and seen, that memory was probably nothing. But it tied in with Carl Johnson's testimony of what had happened on Killer Hill – about Miller poking the cat in the cage, burning it alive, looking around like he'd done something that other people should be impressed by. Not doing it to shock – or not entirely – but to prove to them that he could.

'So the animals were to impress your father.'

'No. Never him. I did it all for myself.'

'But he knew?'

I wanted him to say yes, for what it was worth, but he just shrugged.

'I don't know. I keep my room locked. I told them both to keep out. They're scared of me.'

'I have a hard time imagining your dad is scared of you.'

'My room is mine.'

'Not any more,' I said. 'It's ours now.'

That got me a glare.

'Yeah,' I said. 'We've been in there. We've seen that lovely little photo display you've put up. Why did you do that to his grave, James? Did these people really mean *nothing* to you?'

'Nothing at all.'

'We're going through your computer right now, along with your video camera. You know what we'll find, don't you?'

'Yes.'

'So why the murders?' I said. 'Why the games? Did they make you feel powerful?'

'They were something to do.'

I let the answer hang for a moment, unsure what to say, and felt Laura shift slightly beside me too. *Something to do.* We were both used to the banality of murder, but this was something else altogether. In the silence, I saw Miller notice the discomfort his words had caused, and a slight smile curled at the side of his mouth.

It was gone almost as quickly as it had appeared, but for that moment he looked far older than he really was. The sullen man in his twenties disappeared, and I had the strange impression I was looking at someone or something else altogether.

I shook my head.

'Something to do?'

'That's right. And a way out of that fucking place.'

'What? That stinking bedroom?'

'That's right.'

'How does that work? Go on – you might as well explain. You've already admitted it. But actually, you've succeeded, haven't you? Because you'll be spending the rest of your life in prison.'

'I'll be famous, won't I? Everyone will remember me.'

He looked so proud it disgusted me.

'Maybe,' I said. 'But not the way you think. And trust me, people will forget soon enough.'

'No, they won't. Because it's out there and you can't stop it. I might not have got rich, but people will remember me. They'll still be afraid of me.'

'What do you mean – out there?' I shook my head. 'And how were you ever going to get rich? You didn't rob any of them – we know that and you know that. What are you talking about?'

He looked at me. And again the smile came. But this time it stayed in place.

'You'll never catch him,' he said.

I stared back, allowing the silence to pan out.

'Who?'

'The General.' His smile broadened. 'You'll never catch him. Nobody will.'

Beside me, Laura leaned forward. I remembered what I'd thought back at the woods – that the scene there was totally at odds with the calm, rational tone of the letters we'd received. That everything about the murders always had been.

I've spent a lot of time thinking about the problem: how to generate a code even you won't be able to crack.

And there was something else, too. That name . . .

'The General?' Laura said. 'Is he the one who sent us the letters, Jimmy? And the video?'

'What?'

The General. I remembered it now. It was a username from the website Renton had shown me – the one with the video of the cat being beaten to death.

Miller's smile had vanished now, but he was still too confused to be angry.

'What *letters*? What did you get sent?'

The_General. That was the username on the comment directly below the video.

Great work! Can't wait to see more!

Forty-Nine

DS Renton was waiting in the dark room for us.

'It's going to be a long night,' I told him as Laura and I entered, closing the door behind us.

'I gathered,' he said. 'What do we have?'

'The General.'

We took our seats beside him at the computer, and I explained what James Miller had told us in the interview, after he'd calmed down. When he learned about how he'd been betrayed – about the letters and the video clip – he proved suddenly far more eager to talk.

'Miller says he was contacted by the user The_General after he posted the animal video on the shock site. This guy apparently said he was a great admirer of his work and wanted to see more. And he had a proposition for him.'

'A proposition?'

'Twenty snuff movies,' I said. 'That was what he wanted. The plan was for Miller to film the murders. The General would pay him a thousand pounds for each clip.'

'What for?'

'To sell them.'

Renton shook his head. 'There's no such thing.'

'No,' I said. 'But it seems that the General wanted to change that situation, or that's what he told Miller. He said he was based overseas – a big name in the pornography world who wanted to remain anonymous. Said he already had a string of buyers lined up for the films.'

'I doubt that's true.'

'Me too.'

I didn't believe it for one second, in fact. Whatever the General's real motivation, I was certain the story he'd given James Miller was just a bluff: a cover to convince the boy. There was never going to be any distribution of snuff movies. And I was equally sure the General wouldn't turn out to be based overseas. No – he lived here, in our city. That was where the letters had been sent from, after all.

A code even you won't be able to crack.

His communications to us were personal; they didn't involve James Miller. The boy was just a tool he'd been using to create his pattern. All along, the 'code', whatever that meant, had been unknown even to him. How did that satisfy his stated aims, assuming they were genuine? I didn't know. Clearly, though in *some* way it did.

'Is there any way of listing all the General's postings on the website?'

'Shouldn't be a problem.' Renton set the site loading. 'A hell of a risk, isn't it? From Miller's perspective, I mean. Someone contacts him out of the blue with a suggestion like that, and he just takes them at their word?'

'He says the General paid him five thousand in advance, no strings attached. The idea was to show goodwill, but it was carefully worded. Miller could take the money and walk away, no questions asked, no laws broken. But if he *did* kill someone, the police would be in serious trouble. The General was proving it wasn't entrapment.'

Renton tapped on the keyboard. 'This was by email?'

'No, on here,' I said. 'By private message. We've got Miller's password. Only problem is, he says he deleted all their communication at The General's request.'

'Oh, brilliant.'

'Won't it be recoverable?'

Renton shook his head. 'Probably not. You delete a file from a laptop, most times we can recover that. But these messages are stored online, not locally. They're part of the site. Once they're gone, they're gone.'

'Right. Shit.'

'Exactly. Here we are anyway. The General.'

The screen was filled with the results of the username search he'd performed: all the posts made by The_General. There weren't many. And they all read more or less the same. Variations on: *Great work! Looking forward to more!*

'Looks like he's never posted any footage himself,' Renton said. 'All he's ever done is express his appreciation for other people's pictures and videos.'

'Fishing.'

That fitted with what I was thinking. Miller was probably one of many users the General had initially targeted. He'd probably figured this site was a good place to find the kind of man he needed, and he'd been right.

'Where is he from?' I said. 'Any way of telling?'

Renton pulled up the General's profile.

'Not really. He hasn't filled any information in. No personal details, no country of origin. It wouldn't help us much anyway.'

'Why not?'

'People can put whatever they want. The site doesn't base the location directly on IP addresses or anything. If it did, none of these people would be able to say that they came from "The Depths of Hell", which half of them do.'

I peered at the screen.

'Any way to access his account?'

I already knew the answer.

'Not his, no.' Renton shook his head. 'No way. For the same reason we couldn't access Miller's: the site owners would never co-operate, even if we could pin them down. What's Miller's password?'

I gave it to him, and he logged in as Jimmy82. Miller had

been telling the truth about that much, at least. Renton clicked a few links and pulled up his message history.

'Empty.'

So maybe he was telling the truth about that too.

Renton leaned back in his chair. 'I've never heard of anything like this before.'

'No.'

'Have you considered the possibility that he's lying through his teeth? Making all this up?'

'Yes.'

Miller was caught, and he knew there was no way out. As proud as he seemed of the killings, it would make sense to try to lay the blame at the feet of someone else – psychologically, if nothing else. Or perhaps he was playing with us in some way I couldn't guess right now.

'But it feels too elaborate,' I said. 'It's not the kind of story he'd just make up on the spot, and it would take too much effort for him to have set it up in advance.'

And there was, again, the matter of the letters. Miller's reaction to them had seemed genuine. He'd been shocked, and, as dangerous and vicious as he came across, I didn't think he was that good an actor. I was willing to bet he hadn't known about them: that someone else had written and sent them, without his knowledge, and that person had to have got hold of the video somehow.

Plus, the story fitted with the *contents* of the letters too. The details in the first, for example, had been noticeably scant – back when the General wouldn't have known anything specific. It was only after Miller started supplying him with the videos that he'd been able to include more detail, and even send us a copy of one of the clips and pass it off as his own.

But why?

That was the question.

'How did Miller send the clips?' Renton said. 'We might be able to track that. Did he email them?'

'No. Too risky, apparently. This guy arranged for a locker in a storage unit in the centre of the city, near the railway station. They both had keys. A local courier for the General – supposedly – would deposit the money there and pick up the CDs Miller left.'

'How did Miller get the key?'

'By post. He burned the envelope, so once again, we can't prove it for sure. But we found the key in his bedroom, along with a good chunk of money.'

And that was our one glimmer of hope.

Miller had said he'd deposited a bundle of CDs last night. News of his arrest was being kept strictly under wraps, and plain-clothes officers were en route to the storage unit right now. We would join them shortly. The plan was to keep the area under discreet surveillance and see who, if anybody, came to the locker. There was a chance – just a small chance – that the General, whoever he was, might show up. 'That's good,' Renton said, 'because as things stand, you won't get him this way.'

'No.'

I thought of the locker at the train station. Was that our only hope?

'No,' I said again. 'But we will get him.'

Fifty

'He won't show up,' Laura said.

'Probably not.'

Trestle Storage was a seedy twenty-four-hour locker unit situated down an alley behind the station. It was basically just a long room with a single entrance – a glass door at one end – and one wall taken up entirely by the battered metal lockers. Laura and I were sitting opposite those, sipping coffee in a slight alcove behind the counter.

We'd relieved the receptionist of his duties for the night, and ten additional officers were stationed discreetly in the streets surrounding the unit. Between us, we had Trestle Storage totally contained: nobody could get in without us seeing, and nobody could get out once they'd arrived. So far, nobody had tried to do either. Aside from the buzzing strip lights overhead, the unit was eerily silent.

The General had chosen this location well, I thought. There were several premises like this in the city centre, and their principal appeal was that questions weren't asked. The main customers were homeless people looking for a safe place to store whatever valuables they didn't want to cart around with them, and low-level drug-dealers. A locker cost two pounds a day to hire. About a quarter of the two hundred in here were in use right now. The money was barely enough to cover the rent, but the owners of these dives were generally mid-level criminals who got their cuts elsewhere.

As such, security was minimal. The CCTV was cursory at best. It covered the main entrance, and was wiped at midday. We had a little under eight hours of footage to check through, but all it would show was people coming and going, not which locker they visited. Similarly, a name was required upon rental, but no ID. If you didn't come back, you just lost the contents.

We'd already checked the 'database' – a clipboard of curling A4 sheets covered with scribbled biro – and the locker we were interested in had been rented to James Miller for the last three weeks. That didn't prove anything one way or the other, of course. The General could have given whatever name he wanted, and both keys were missing from the pegboard of clips behind us.

'Quiet in here,' I said.

'You think the receptionist put the word out?'

'Probably.' Bad for business to have known clients turn up and find police behind the desk. 'To some people anyway. Maybe not to the General.'

'I'm starting to think "the General" doesn't exist.'

'He exists. His name's right there on the website.'

'Yeah, but we've only got Miller's word for it that they ever talked to each other. And the rest of it. He could even have written those posts himself – set up the username.'

It now seemed even less likely to me that Miller would have gone to such lengths. For what? He committed the murders; he wasn't denying that. This bit of subterfuge wouldn't achieve anything. But he might have his reasons, and for me, there was something even more conclusive.

'What about the letters?'

'I don't know.'

'Did he strike you as being that articulate?'

'Not really.' Laura sipped her coffee and grimaced at the taste. 'Jesus. But the only way we'll know for sure is if he walks through that door. Without that, this could all be a figment of Miller's imagination. And there's another thing too.'

'Go on.'

'Let's say the General exists, and that it all played out exactly as Miller described it. And let's imagine he walks in here and opens that locker in the next few minutes.'

I glanced at the smeared glass of the entrance. Nothing but night out there for the moment.

'I'm imagining that.'

'Okay. The question is: can we prove any of it anyway?'

She was right. If the man turned up, the only evidence we had for his involvement in the killings was Miller's word. The online messages inciting the crimes had been deleted, and the letters we'd received had been impossible to trace. If we caught the General right here and now, then unless we found further evidence – at his home, say – it would ultimately come down to his word against Miller's. And unlike Miller, the General was smart enough to have thought ahead. He could come up with a million explanations for having the key in his possession.

'You remember what Miller's father said, though?' I sipped my drink; Laura was right about the coffee too. 'It's not our job to prove any of it. It's just our job to catch him and gather whatever evidence we can.'

'Yeah, like that's ever been enough for you.'

'No,' I said. 'I guess not.'

'At least we can be sure of one thing – regardless of whether Miller turns out to be a lone gunman on this, we've got him. He's our murderer. If the General really exists, then we need to catch him, sure, but at least we've got Miller.'

I nodded. Even if the General existed and was guilty of instigating the crimes, Miller was the one who'd carried them out – and he was behind bars now, going nowhere. Which meant that nobody else was going to die. And that *was* something.

At the same time, it wasn't enough: not for me, anyway. Miller was responsible for his own actions, of course, but the General had helped to cause them.

And aside from catching the bastard, I wanted to know *why*. What was the code? Why the letters? Why do such a monstrous thing in the first place? With Miller, it felt like I could understand a little. He was a young man who'd grown up twisted and bullied, learning the lesson well that inflicting fear and violence on the world was a way to make yourself bigger. His motivations – money and self-empowerment – were twisted but logical.

For the General, I couldn't even attempt an answer.

Without catching him – without knowing for sure – the case would remain open in more ways than one.

'I'm tired,' Laura said. 'Tired of all this.'

'Me too.'

'I want to go home.'

'Me too.'

She put her cup down.

'How are things?' she said. 'At home, I mean. Better or worse?'

I thought about it, remembering the way it had felt to embrace Rachel the other night: the sense that the distance between us had closed slightly. And in the woods today, when I'd been sure I was about to die, it had been her I'd thought about. Her and our child.

'Better, I think.'

'Really? That's good.'

'We've still got a long way to go.'

But for the first time in months, it did feel like we might be able to get there. And for once, I had an idea of how to help that happen. Talking, yes, but before I could do that, there was something else I needed to do. Something I should probably have done a long time ago.

Laura said, 'What do you think—'

My radio squawked. I grabbed it up off the counter almost before the sound registered. One of the officers stationed outside.

'Here,' I said.

'Hicks.'

My heart sank. It was Young, back at the department.

'Sir?'

'We've got a *problem*.'

I listened as he explained, slowly and quietly, what had happened. And although he kept his voice even and his tone calm, I could sense the anger. If he'd been talking to me in person, I imagined he wouldn't have blinked the whole time. Someone was about to get obliterated over there, and I took no pleasure right now from knowing who.

I put the radio down and turned to Laura.

'It's over.'

'Why? What's happened?'

'Charles fucking Miller has happened. He's given a statement to the press, right outside the department. In full military regalia, too. Can you believe that? He told them he's convinced his son is innocent and that we're fitting him up to save our skins.'

'Shit.'

'Yep.'

Shit didn't even cover it. If the General was anywhere near a television set, he would now know that Miller had been arrested and the storage unit was compromised. Which meant that our only way of catching him had just disappeared.

We gave it another hour, just on the off chance. The unit received three customers in that time, two women and one man; they were all obviously homeless, but we had them detained anyway. Aside from that, the radio remained silent.

'All right,' I said eventually. 'Let's do it.'

We walked across to the lockers and located the number Miller had given us. I used the key from his room to unlock it. The door screeched slightly as it opened.

Laura peered in at the contents.

'Where does that leave us?'

It's over.

I stared at the neat pile of CD cases, secured with a red rubber band. Sixteen in all.

'Nowhere,' I said. 'Nowhere at all.'

Part Four

Franklin leans forwards.

'The key to your father's gun cabinet?'

The boy – Andrew – nods.

'And then what happened?'

Andrew looks like he's about to cry. Once again, Franklin tries to summon up some sympathy from inside him. He has been through a lot, after all, this boy. Whatever happened in the house, he must remember that. Andrew is eight years old but looks younger. Whatever happened, it must have been awful and traumatic. It is understandable. There is nothing to gain from pressing him, not really.

'Andrew? Can you tell me what happened?'

The boy shakes his head, unable to meet his eye. But again, he thinks, that doesn't mean anything. He is only eight years old.

'You can't?'

'I don't know.'

'You don't know what happened next?'

'I stayed in the bedroom, like John told me.'

Despite himself, as Franklin looks at the boy, he absently touches the cross he wears around his neck.

You're lying, he thinks. Andrew, you are lying to me.

Fifty-One

The morning after the failed stake-out, I drove out to Buxton.
There was something I needed to do.

The road was wide and flat. On my way, I passed a few
cars, but mostly just speed-limit signs and the lines of indistin-
guishable houses: dull wooden faces with shadowed windows,
set back behind their fences. When the breeze picked up, dust
billowed across the tarmac. The sky ahead was featureless: a
single, implacable shade of grey.

When I reached the house – one I hadn't returned to for over
twenty years, or at least not physically – it was obvious. Not
only from the indistinct but shivery familiarity I felt at the sight
of it, but because it stood out from all the others I'd passed. As
ramshackle as its neighbours might have been, at least those
buildings were habitable, even if only barely, but this house
was clearly derelict.

I parked up outside. When I killed the engine, there was no
sound at all, not even birdsong.

I stared at the worn façade of the house. The red paint had
long since flecked away. The windows had no glass, giving
oblique views of the peeling wallpaper in the dank rooms
within.

A family had lived here once.

There was a man and his wife and their two sons. By all
accounts, they were innocuous. Nobody who knew them had
anything bad to say about them; nobody would have marked

this particular family down as having something wrong with it. They wouldn't have suspected there was a seed of violence nestled at its heart, waiting for the right time to bloom.

The man was former military, retired through injury, and clearly a little rough and bitter. He drank. The woman was cowed and nervous in a fidgety kind of way. None of that was enough to differentiate them from other families in these parts.

The two boys, though . . .

With hindsight, some people did say they'd appeared haunted: too quiet, both of them. It was as though they were making an effort to keep silent about something. As though there was something they wanted to say but wouldn't, or couldn't. When they looked at people, they didn't seem to see them.

And with hindsight, those same people probably wondered if they should have recognised that something was wrong with that family. If they might have done a little more, even though doing something is not what people do, and especially not back then.

But that was all a long time ago.

As far as I knew, nobody had lived here since what happened. Not in the ordinary sense, anyway.

Finally, I got out of the car.

My brother was two years older than me, but he was always smaller and weaker. It really was as though we had different fathers, although I don't believe for one second that's true. It was just that John took after him, while I carried more of my mother's genes. Although perhaps that's just wishful thinking on my part.

Regardless, my brother always felt the need to protect me, because he was older. Even though he wasn't physically capable of doing so, somewhere deep inside him he felt like he should, and his failure to do so ate at him. The more he hated our father, the more he also hated himself for being unable to stand up to him. When our father mocked him for being weak and ineffectual, it stung, because he believed it was true.

And yet, despite his hatred, John had still taken on board our father's ideas about what it meant to be a man. He'd absorbed the idea that one way to deal with the frustrations of your life is by using violence against others to make yourself feel bigger. That wasn't the whole story of why he did what he did that night, but it was a part of it.

On the night my father died, I told the policeman who interviewed me – Franklin – that I'd stayed in our bedroom: that John had gone downstairs and unlocked the gun cabinet by himself, dragged the shotgun upstairs alone, and that I hadn't seen what happened in my parents' bedroom shortly afterwards.

Of course, that was a lie.

The gun cabinet was gone now – everything was. The downstairs room, like the rest of the house, had been stripped bare. The floorboards were exposed, broken in one corner, and the walls were pale, with permanent shadows of mould cast on the plaster. The remains of the fireplace formed a broken black mouth in the pale wall, the floor in front speckled with flecks of wallpaper and wood, as though the house had begun eating and spitting itself out.

But standing in the doorway and looking through the lounge doorway, I could still remember where everything had been. Memory added fixtures and fittings to this empty space; it superimposed furniture, and leached colours on to the grey shell. A ghost of an old life, flitting – briefly – across the world. A room seen through a window, passed by at speed.

I shook my head and moved back into the hall. It smelled of mildew and earth. Bubbles of moisture had formed on the walls and hardened like pearls. An empty doorway revealed the corpse of a kitchen, recognisable as such only from the square stains where cupboards had once clung to the walls. Behind me, daylight leaned in through the open front door, but didn't reach the staircase I was looking up. The landing above was dark, and somehow both empty and full; the wooden stairs themselves looked precarious and soft.

I tested each step, all the way to the first floor.

With the far window exposed, the corridor up here was like a dark, weathered tunnel. Doorways led off at various points down the hallway, the first to what had once been a bathroom, the second to the bedroom I had shared with John, the third to what had been my parents' bedroom.

There was no heartbeat here, not like in my dream, but the air had a pressure that might have been mainly inside my head. I hesitated. Then I walked all the way along to the last doorway.

Just as I had that night, all those years ago.

I'd gone downstairs with my brother.

I'd been there with him when he lifted the shotgun from the rack. He'd carried it himself – that much was true – because he didn't want my fingerprints on it. He kept telling me to go back into our dark bedroom, but I wouldn't, and it annoyed him. Perhaps he thought I was undermining him – that this was his action, one he should be doing alone, and there was me, trailing him like an equal partner. Saying nothing, because I hated our father and I wanted him to do it.

And yes, I followed him into our parents' bedroom.

The door creaked slightly, but neither of them woke. Our father was snoring softly, lying on his back with one beefy arm thrown above his head. Even in the gloom, I could tell his mouth was wide open, slack. Our mother was curled up on her side of the bed, her back to him and her legs drawn up, as though she was trying to get as far away from him as possible.

It happened quickly. I think John was scared that he wouldn't be able to go through with it if he faltered, or perhaps that our father might sense us there and wake up. If he had, I doubt John would have done it. Our father would have taken the gun off him, and God only knew what would have happened next.

John lofted the shotgun awkwardly, and somehow got it pointing at an angle down into our father's face. He paused, suddenly unsure of himself.

Do it, I whispered.

Do it, John.

And then he pulled the trigger. The room immediately transformed into a judder of noise and smoke and vibration. The impact lifted the barrel vertical and knocked my brother backwards with the force. Below us, my father's face and head had been replaced with nothing. The rest of him didn't even move; he died instantly where he lay, his arm remaining where it was. Our mother jerked awake with a screech and nearly fell out of bed, blood spattered all over her bare back.

That's all I really remember. I was back in my bedroom, sitting alone, when the police arrived.

Looking back, I suspect Franklin had known I was present at the murder, but both John and I stuck to our stories closely enough for him never to be able to prove it. Why did I lie? I'll never be sure, but I think I did it for him – for John – because he so desperately wanted to have done it by himself, without my help. He had wanted to protect me, and I, in turn, had played the role required of me. It wouldn't have mattered anyway. I was below the age of criminal responsibility. So John was charged and sent to a remand centre for eight years; I was fostered. Due to press interest at the time, both of us received new and separate identities.

Regardless, I've never forgotten that look on Franklin's face. An expression that said that when he looked at me, he saw it in me – something evil, malformed and wrong. Not just an abused, scared little boy, but something worse. Something of my father in me. And although I got away without any official sanction, I've lived with the implications of that look ever since.

I've lived with telling myself, over and over, that it couldn't be true. That I wasn't like my father. That everything has a human explanation. That there is no evil.

Standing in the doorway to my parents' bedroom now, I looked at the dim wine stain of blood that remained soaked into the back wall. And then I moved back down the hallway towards the second doorway along: to my old bedroom. I hesitated at the frame, a part of me not wanting to peer in, but then I did.

The first thing that struck me was how small it was.

Could two boys have ever slept comfortably in here? It seemed impossible to imagine now. Even without the furniture, it was little bigger than a cupboard: a dark, windowless cell. But we *had* slept in here, and it was in here that we had woken up that night, and the rest of my life had begun to unfold.

Despite my best efforts, a part of me had remained here ever since, and in that interview room with Franklin. I'd never quite believed the things I'd told myself; I'd protested too much. But now . . . that could change, couldn't it? Franklin hadn't recognised me as an adult. And this room, in reality, was empty. There were no ghosts here. No pale children huddled, shivering, where a bed used to stand. No sobbing black-and-white woman to come screeching at me for failing to save her.

It was a space to be filled, as and how I saw fit.

So I thought: *I'm not evil.*

I won't necessarily be a bad father.

I won't necessarily have a bad son.

I stood there for a few more moments, filling that nothing, and then I left.

As I walked the rest of the way back along the hall, carefully down the stairs and out into the dull grey daylight, I thought about Rachel – about the list of characteristics on her dating profile that had first attracted me, which I'd talked about in the therapy session. There had been something else on that list that I had not mentioned. Two details she'd given that at the time had been the most important ones of all.

Children, she'd written: no.

Want children: never.

I'd always had that safeguard in place. Until she changed her mind so vehemently last year, that is, and I'd been forced to make a choice: confronting my fears of becoming a father and what that might mean, or losing the woman I loved and needed more than I could ever explain. I hadn't been able to bear the thought of either thing, and balancing them had been pulling me apart ever since. Pulling us apart.

It's like there's something he wants to say and won't.

Yes. It had been like that.

But maybe, soon, that could change.

Fifty-Two

It happened in the middle of the night.

I don't know for sure what I was dreaming, only that it was something about James Miller. In part of it, he was coming slowly and steadily towards me at the side of the Hawthorne Road. Holding that hammer, with that look on his face. There was nobody else around, and this time, I couldn't find my gun.

'Andy, Andy, Andy.'

I woke up suddenly in the dark bedroom, struggling to make sense of what was happening. It was Rachel tapping me on the shoulder, frantically.

'What?'

'It's happening. Oh God.'

'I'm awake.'

I was – instantly. I sat bolt upright in bed. Rachel was sitting on the edge, her eyes wide and bright even in the darkness.

'How far apart?' I said.

'I don't know. I've been awake for a while. Four or five minutes?'

'Okay.' I reached out and touched her face, did my best to smile. 'It'll be okay. I'm here and I'll look after you. It'll be okay.'

'All right.'

I swung out of bed, found my trousers on the floor. We'd done the inventory already, but I did it again in my head, suddenly unable to find everything. The suitcase was packed, waiting in the spare room. There were two other bags we needed. Nothing else. I grabbed a shirt from the wardrobe and flung it on.

'Oh God.'

Rachel knelt down and leaned over the bed. I massaged her back as best I could the whole time. I felt about as redundant and powerless as I ever had in my entire life.

'It'll be all right,' I said.

'I can't do this.'

'You can.'

'*I fucking can't.*'

'I'm going to phone the hospital.' My mobile? On the floor next to the bed. I grabbed it, then put my hand back on her shoulder. 'You *can*. You're the strongest person I know.'

The whole way to the hospital, that was what I kept telling her and what I kept thinking. Everything about her was strong and tough – she was so single-minded, so determined. Stuff that would faze a normal person, I told her, one hand on the wheel, the other on her thigh, it was nothing to her. She was going to be fine. Other people did this every day, and she was stronger than them, so she'd do it too.

'I love you,' I told her.

'I love you too.'

'Really love you.'

She looked at me, crying. 'Really love you too. Watch the road.'

'Don't worry.'

It was a half-hour drive, but I did it in twenty. By that time, the contractions seemed to be at four-minute intervals. I parked up as neatly as I could, and helped Rachel inside the hospital and up the stairs to the fifth floor, to the maternity ward we'd been shown in the pre-natal classes.

'Rachel Hicks,' I told the receptionist. 'I phoned ahead.'

Beside me, Rachel started screaming.

'It'll be okay,' I told her. 'I promise.'

But I think even then I knew it wouldn't.

Everything else is a blur of memory.

I can hardly bear to think back on it, and I rarely try. Better, I think, that most of what happened is simply lost. There is nothing important there: nothing worth remembering. But some things remain – just glimpses.

The birth suite resembled an elongated bathroom, lined with sinks and mirrored cabinets. My wife lay on an elaborate bed, surrounded by machinery and cables, her brow damp with sweat and her hair plastered to her head. A hatstand contraption beside the bed had bags of misty fluid hanging from it. A midwife monitored our baby's heartbeat on a green monitor, as a machine skittered and stitched the contractions across an unfolding roll of gridded paper.

The contractions wouldn't stabilise. They would come at minute intervals, each lasting a minute, and then there would be nothing for five minutes. Every time they upped the chemical to help stabilise them, the baby's – our son's – heartbeat thinned and became erratic. In the same way that – once – I hadn't wanted him to be, it seemed that he did not want to be born.

Rachel kept apologising to the midwives and doctors. I remember that. Even with everything that was happening, she kept saying sorry, as though it was her fault. It wasn't, and it wasn't mine either, but it was all I could think. It was going bad, and it was because of me.

'It'll be okay,' I kept saying.

He did not want to be born.

I want you to be born, I kept thinking.

I do now.

You have to be okay.

Both of you.

The midwife called it: the contractions weren't right, but it had been going on for too long. It was time for Rachel to push. And she did, for an hour, squeezing my hand so tightly each time, her face red as a clenched fist.

But he didn't want to be born.

The surgeon used a suction cup on his head, pulling so hard it was like he was doing a tug of war. People had to brace him. I couldn't watch. And still my son wouldn't be born. The whole time, his heartbeat was fluttering. They tried with forceps, the ugliest pieces of metal I'd ever seen, as huge and brutal as swords.

I don't remember what happened next.

All I know is there was blood in the air: I have a vague impression of that. The room was suddenly full of people. I had time to realise they must have been gathered in the corridor out of sight, ready and waiting, and that there were more of them than I could count. I was shoved back against a wall as they moved around Rachel, talking to her, shouting instructions to each other, disconnecting her from everything.

This can't be happening.

This doesn't happen.

My wife's face. Rachel. Looking at me with the purest expression of terror I'd ever seen. I did my best to smile at her, try to be reassuring, but I was too shocked, too scared.

And then they were rushing her – both of them – down towards emergency surgery. I'd never seen anything move so quickly. I chased the bed down the hallway, telling Rachel I loved her, over and over again, holding her hand for as long as I could, But then they disappeared through green plastic curtains and I was left standing there.

I needed some fresh air, which meant I needed my jacket. But that was in the birth suite, and for some reason the nurses wouldn't let me go back in for it. It was only afterwards that I realised they were scared of what I would see, and what my reaction would be. In the meantime, one of the midwives had to get it for me.

Outside, it was night again.

It was cold, and that was probably just what I needed. My skin was shivery, but my insides were hot; it was like there was a furnace burning in my chest and head. There were benches dotted around the car park; even at this time, residents wrapped in dressing gowns smoking near the entrance. I didn't know what to do with myself. I'd been sitting all day, so I paced a little way out into the car park, then back again.

I'd lost them both.

I knew it.

After a while, I took my mobile out and turned it back on. Not that I was going to phone anyone, but it was something to do – check for messages, stop myself imagining what might be happening with Rachel back inside. Immediately, I got a text from Laura.

Hope all well? Assume you'll call when news. Fingers crossed! Call me asap tho.

It was from an hour ago. I called her.

'Hicks,' she said. 'What's going on? How is she?'

I started to answer. Couldn't.

'Hicks?'

I've lost them both.

'Hicks?'

'I don't know,' I said. 'Rachel's had to go into surgery. It doesn't look good.'

She was silent for a moment.

'It'll be okay,' she said.

I said nothing, because I knew it wouldn't be.

'It happens all the time.'

'What's happening there?'

'Here? No news. Nothing that can't wait, anyway. Miller's still sticking to his story. Nothing useful from the CCTV at Trestle. Still no evidence that the General exists outside of Miller's head.'

'Laura, I—'

But just then, one of the nurses I recognised burst out of the entrance. She scanned the car park, saw me, then beckoned me across.

'Andrew?'

I felt sick.

'I've got to go.'

I hung up on Laura and ran back across the car park to meet her. I was dreading what she was going to tell me, but then I realised from the expression on her face that it couldn't be bad news. It couldn't be.

The baby's heartbeat had stabilised, she said. That meant Rachel could have the emergency Caesarean under local anaesthetic rather than general.

Which meant – if I was quick – I could be with her.

Again, I don't remember much.

I know I left my clothes in a locker room and changed into green scrubs and cheap slippers. They let me sit up on one side of Rachel, by her head, and talk to her. The doctors had erected a sheet from just under her breasts to keep the operation out of sight. I told Rachel I loved her, and that everything was going to be okay.

I remember this.

Sitting on the other side of the bed, the man in charge of the anaesthetic spoke to her reassuringly. Rachel was terrified, trying not to cry, and he kept talking to her very calmly, the way you imagined he would to a friend. There was no way, he said, that he would let anyone in the room hurt her. He wouldn't allow it. As he altered dials on the machine by the side of him, he kept asking what she could feel. Was it pain or pressure? Not to worry, he said. Stay calm. Nobody will do anything until I say they can.

'I'm so scared,' she whispered.

'It's nearly over,' I said. Then: 'Look!'

From the far end of the bed, someone lifted a baby high enough over the screen for us both to see. It was a tiny, fragile thing, slathered in purple light, and only there for a few seconds before they lowered it again.

Our son.

I didn't feel any huge burst of love; it was too stressful for the moment to feel profound. But I do remember the relief. That was the first moment when I thought it was going to be okay. That I hadn't lost them both at all, although I might have come close. Closer than I ever had before.

Thank you, I thought.

I remember that. I don't know who I was directing it to, but I thought it anyway, over and over again.

The rest is a fracture. I remember them calling me over to cut the cord, and then being handed him wrapped in a dark towel – and panicking because I didn't know how to hold him. But I managed. And I sat with him cradled against me, a knot that seemed to want to untie itself, by Rachel's side. She was bleary with the drugs, but she turned her head and could see him, could smile at him.

'Our son,' I kept saying. 'You did so well. So well.'

There was far more, but none of it really matters.

Thank you, though.

I remember that.

Fifty-Three

They moved Rachel and the baby to a bed in the maternity ward, and because it was night-time, I wasn't allowed to stay. They told me to go home and get some sleep, come back in the morning. Visiting hours began at eight. Right then, sleep seemed impossible, but I went home anyway.

I texted Laura to let her know that everything was okay and immediately got a reply. It made me smile. Despite everything that had happened, and the late hour, she had been waiting to hear from me.

At home, I lay down on the bed, and without much hope of success I closed my eyes. It was pointless – but the next thing I knew there was sunlight streaming through the curtains, and it was coming up on nine o'clock in the morning.

As I parked up back at the hospital, my mobile rang. I was expecting it to be Laura, but it wasn't – the number was unknown.

'Yes?'

'Detective Hicks?'

'This is me.' I recognised the voice. 'Professor Joyce?'

'It is indeed. I've had a chance to look over the documents and information you gave me. Assuming you're still interested, of course?'

'You've seen the news, obviously.'

'Yes. But only what's been reported. So I don't know if my services are still required.'

'I don't think so.' I got out of the car and locked it. I didn't really want to talk to her right now; I just wanted to get in and see Rachel and our son. 'We know more or less what happened. We don't think there ever was an actual pattern or code. It was all just a piece of misdirection.'

'I suppose that's good, in a sense.'

'Why good?'

'Because it's the conclusion my team and I reached after analysing the data. We couldn't find any indication of a sequence.'

I nodded to myself.

Just misdirection.

Over the last few days, I'd had time to ponder the case. Each time, I'd come up empty-handed. If we believed Miller, he'd been paid to create and deliver snuff movies – as diverse a collection as possible – but the General had no other connection to him. He couldn't have influenced the victims Miller targeted, or where or when those murders took place. So if the General existed, there couldn't be a pattern. If he didn't, Miller was still denying sending the letters or any knowledge of a code, which didn't make sense.

And yet my mind still kept turning it all over.

I said, 'You found nothing at all?'

'Nothing useful. Given any large enough pool of data and variables, it's possible to find patterns, but we didn't come up with anything conclusive. For what it's worth, we've made a note of what we did find, along with the clusters and anomalies.'

'Thanks.' I paused a second. 'Anomalies?'

'Oh, nothing to get excited about. Just instances where the data points were unique. For example, the third item, "SP", had a unique variable for ethnicity. The eighth, "MW", was the only interior location. And so on. I'm looking through the documents now . . . well, there are a handful of others, but not many.'

I nodded to myself, understanding what she was getting

at. Sandra Peacock, the only black woman murdered; Marie Wilkinson, the only person killed inside a building. And so on. The kind of apparent anomalies any random data set invariably throws up, just as it does coincidences.

She said, 'The clusters were much as we discussed. They're obvious – you'll have already seen them. To be on the safe side, we removed different combinations in case there was a pattern hidden in between them.'

I remembered the term she'd used. 'Static.'

'That's right. And there was nothing.'

'No.'

And of course – once again – there couldn't be. So why was something *still* nagging at me? Someone had sent the letters. To that someone, it had been clear that the code was important. Beating us with it had mattered to him. My gut was telling me there *was* something there, something that—

'Shall I send my report by email or . . . ?'

'Email is fine,' I said. 'Along with your expenses, of course.'

'There won't be any expenses.'

I started to reply, but she didn't let me.

'Normally there would be. But given the circumstances – and the fact that I've been of so little help to you – I wouldn't consider it ethical.'

'You have been helpful, I promise.'

'Well . . . still.'

'Thank you, Professor Joyce.'

After she hung up, I phoned Laura back at the department and related what Joyce had told me.

'Report should be on its way,' I said.

'Already here.'

'She's very efficient.'

'Like me, then. Whereabouts are you?'

'I'm only just arriving at the hospital now. Because I'm not very efficient.'

I started to walk across the car park towards the reception. Clusters of patients were standing smoking underneath the

324

balcony by the entrance. One man was propped on a pair of crutches, a bandaged foot held off the ground, while a friend held the cigarette for him.

'So no other news yet?' Laura said.

'No. But everything was okay when I left. And he's beautiful, Laura. He really is.'

'Takes after Rachel, then.'

'Ah ha ha. Nobody's ever used that joke before.'

Laura laughed softly in return, and I was about to say something else when, up ahead of me, the doors to the hospital reception slid silently open and a man stepped out from the bright light into the morning gloom, pack of cigarettes in hand.

And I stopped, halfway across the car park.

Laura said, 'Give her my love, won't you?'

But I didn't reply. I stood still, watching the man tap a cigarette from the pack and raise it to his mouth. He cupped his hands round the lighter, and I heard the distant *click-click-click* as he tried to get a flame.

'Hicks?' Laura said.

The man lit the cigarette, and a plume of smoke appeared in front of his face. Then he looked up, slipping the lighter back into his pocket.

Tony Wilkinson.

Of course, it was no real surprise he was at the hospital. His own son remained critically ill in the special care baby unit, so of *course* he was here. The only reason I'd hesitated was the conversation I'd just had with Professor Joyce – because his wife had been mentioned a few moments ago, and then suddenly here he was, right in front of me. Just a coincidence. It was odd, but it meant nothing.

And yet the back of my neck was tingling.

An anomaly, I thought.

The only victim murdered inside.

'Hicks?'

'Just a second, Laura.'

I started moving then, heading towards Tony Wilkinson,

keeping my eyes on him. I had no idea what I was going to say. But a second later, he turned his head slightly and saw me walking purposefully towards him. Phone still held to my ear. With God only knew what expression on my face.

Our eyes met.

He had been in the process of raising the cigarette to his lips, but it faltered, and then he slowly lowered his arm again.

'Mr Wilkinson?' I called over. 'Detective Hicks. You remember me?'

Wilkinson dropped the cigarette, turned around and walked quickly back into the reception.

I started running.

Fifty-Four

By the time I got inside, into the sickly yellow light, Wilkinson had vanished from sight – he must have started running himself after he got through the doors. He'd been on the right-hand side of the area, though, so I banked on him taking the corridor that led off that way. I jogged quickly past the humming vending machines, glanced left to be sure – saw nothing – and took the right-hand corridor.

I knew this route well already. It was the quickest direction to take for the maternity ward on the fifth floor – which was close, I presumed, to the special care baby unit where Wilkinson's son was being cared for.

The lifts . . .

I ran harder, but got there as the doors slid shut – just too late to jam my fingers between them. I punched the 'call' button over and over, but it was no use. The lift was starting on its way up. I hammered on the closed doors anyway, and shouted—

'Tony!'

—then remembered the stairs, two doors further down the corridor, and set off again, reaching them a few seconds later. I slammed through into the echoing stairwell and headed up, skipping steps, using the banisters to swing myself round at each small landing. Counting off the floors, trying to imagine myself keeping pace with the lift, even though I couldn't possibly be.

Still not sure what was happening here.

At the fourth floor, I half collided with an orderly trotting down, footfalls echoing.

'Hey!'

I was already past him, plunging upwards.

'Police.'

I hit the fifth floor and pulled open the door, realising as I did that I'd slipped my phone in my pocket without disconnecting the call. As I moved in the direction of the lift, I picked it out.

'Laura, I'm still here. Are you—'

'What the fuck's going on?'

'Don't know yet. Get backup to the hospital. Wilkinson's here, and something's not right. He saw me and started running.'

I reached the lift: the doors were open. Empty. Wilkinson hadn't passed me, so he'd probably gone further on. Down towards the maternity wards.

'What? You mean *Tony* Wilkinson?'

'Yes.' I started off. 'I don't know what's going on. But Professor Joyce said Marie Wilkinson was an anomaly. She was the only person killed inside. Not sure why Wilkinson's run, but there's something going on with him. And he's in here somewhere.'

I didn't wait for a reply – just pushed the phone back into my pocket and concentrated on where I was going. The maternity ward: that was where Rachel was. The door was magnetically sealed. You needed to push a button and give your details over the intercom to get in. Wilkinson had no business going in there. He wouldn't even be allowed in.

But I had to check she was okay.

That *they* were.

I buzzed the intercom for the maternity ward. A second later, the door opened without check. *Christ.* There was no way Wilkinson could know about my wife and son, but perhaps he had panicked, tried to hide. I had to make sure.

I held up my badge at the first nurse I saw.

'Police. Nobody in or out now except me, understand?'

'What?'

I gestured behind me, angry. 'Lock that door. Keep it locked. Anybody entered in the last few minutes?'

'No . . .'

She wasn't sure.

'Keep it that way.'

I headed around the corner. There were various internal wards here, all open, and I'd left Rachel in the nearest one last night. There were six spaces, three to each side, all divided off from each other by green curtains. She was on the middle on the left, and the curtains were closed across the front. I found the join, moved it to one side and peered in.

Rachel was lying on her back, sleeping. Her head was tilted to one side, mouth slightly open, covers gently rising and falling. In the cot beside the bed, our son was sleeping too, almost mirroring her position. So small and vulnerable. But both of them were okay.

Relief – illogical but real – flooded through me.

'Stay safe,' I whispered.

Then I closed the curtains and ran back to the entrance, where the nurse I'd spoken to was standing guard.

'Nobody in,' I repeated. 'Nobody out.'

'I know.'

'The police are on their way.'

Back out in the corridor, I headed down to the special care baby unit – realising that *of course* Wilkinson wouldn't have gone after Rachel. That was the whole fucking point. He didn't know my wife had been pregnant, and that was why he'd reacted the way he had outside. I'd known he had a reason to be here, but he could only think of one possible explanation for my presence. He'd thought I must be here for him.

I still didn't understand why. Regardless, he'd run from me. He'd come back for . . .

The special care baby unit.

Obviously, this door was also sealed. I buzzed the intercom and waited. A moment later, the intercom crackled and – once again – the door simply opened. I pushed in quickly. As I entered, I reached under my jacket and unclipped the button on my gun holster. Not retrieving the weapon. Just being ready if I needed it.

You won't need it.

But I might.

The reception desk was a little way down, past a number of closed doors. Two nurses were stationed behind it, and I pulled out my badge as I reached them.

'Wilkinson,' I said. 'Where is he?'

The nurse nearest to me folded up her newspaper slowly, perhaps shocked by my sudden entrance.

'What . . . ?'

'*Tony Wilkinson.*' But she still looked blank. I struggled to remember what he'd said when we interviewed him. 'The baby's called Jake. Is he here? The father, I mean.'

'I don't know.'

'Has anyone come in over the last couple of minutes?'

'No, I don't think so.' Flustered, she checked a sheet she'd found, then gestured back the way I'd come. 'Jake Wilkinson is in five-two-oh-two. It's just back that way.'

'Keep the main door sealed. Nobody out.'

I moved to the room she'd indicated, stood to one side of the frame, then turned the handle and pushed the door open in one quick gesture.

'Wilkinson?'

He wasn't here.

I stepped inside. It wasn't a big room – little larger than the curtained-off bed space I'd left Rachel in down the corridor. Jake Wilkinson was lying in a Perspex crib at the far end, on his back, limbs splayed, sleeping peacefully. Around him, various pieces of machinery monitored the tubes and wires attached to his body. I was shocked by how tiny and weak he looked. My son, although born later, was technically the same age and yet twice the size.

Do you know what Marie used to tell me about Jake?

I remembered Wilkinson's tear-stained face when we'd talked to him in the suite.

She used to say that she couldn't wait to meet him.

What I'd thought at the time, but not said, was that at least he had his son. That as horrible as it was, it could have been worse.

And yet he hadn't come here.

I headed back out, closing the door gently behind me. A doctor was coming down the corridor from reception, a worried expression on his face.

'Let me out,' I told him, holding up my badge again. 'The police are on their way. Don't let anybody else in until they get here. *Nobody.*'

He buzzed the main door open for me, and I stepped out into the corridor, wondering what the fuck to do now. Wilkinson had to be here somewhere. We'd have to lock down and search the whole building. God only knew what he'd—

That was when I heard the screams.

They were coming from the direction of the lift. I reached it seconds later. Several people were bunched here: nurses and doctors, surrounding a figure lying on the floor, working urgently. Another woman was standing to one side, dressed in overalls, holding her mouth in shock.

'Police,' I said. 'What happened?'

The doctors working at the figure on the floor ignored me. The woman – a janitor, I realised – lowered her hands.

'The storeroom,' she said. 'He just . . . burst out.'

I looked towards where she was gesturing: a storeroom, full of mops and buckets and blankets, its door hanging open. Right opposite the lift.

The doors were closed. He was gone.

Fifty-Five

'Hicks?' Laura said. 'What's going on?'

'Wilkinson's assaulted somebody at the hospital. An orderly. Not sure how badly.'

'Officers arriving there now. Where is he?'

'I don't know. I think he's gone.'

'Where are *you*?'

Where was I? I was holding the mobile phone in one hand, the steering wheel with the other, powering the car quickly but carefully between the remaining strands of morning traffic. It was an unmarked vehicle, but I'd stuck the transit light on top and set it going. It wasn't doing me much good.

'I'm on my way to his house.'

'His house? Surely he wouldn't go there?'

'He might. I haven't got any better ideas.'

I'd picked a main road, busier but wider, with better scope to manoeuvre. The shops were flashing past. I blared my horn at a van in front that wasn't shifting out of my way, watched it lean slowly off into the pavement, then accelerated past.

I said, 'If he's planning to run, there might be stuff he needs to get first.'

Not his son, though.

That much was obvious. He was sharp: he'd figured there was no way past me out front of the hospital, so he'd led me back inside, made me think I knew where he was going. But it seemed that he'd never wanted Jake . . .

Jesus, was that the whole point?

'Did we check Wilkinson's alibi?' I said. 'Not for *all* the murders. Just for Marie Wilkinson. For that morning.'

'Hang on.'

I tried to remember the chronology – we'd made him go over it enough fucking times. Left for work at eight thirty, or thereabouts. Phone call logged from Marie Wilkinson's neighbour fifteen minutes later. Police on the scene by nine . . .

'Yes,' Laura said. 'But we couldn't confirm it for sure. He said he got there at nine, but nobody saw him. He had an alibi for some of the others. He – oh, Christ, Hicks.'

'What?'

'He works at the army base.'

I nodded to myself. 'The General.'

'He's a janitor,' Laura said. 'But why would he get Miller to—'

'Static.'

'What?'

'*Static.*'

I blared the horn again. *Get out of the fucking way.*

'You remember what Joyce said – that the pattern might be hidden amongst the clusters? Well, it was. Except it wasn't a pattern at all. It was just one murder. Everything else was the static to hide it from us.'

It was unimaginable, but it was the only explanation I could think of. Wilkinson had paid Miller to provide us with so many killings that it became impossible to keep track of every detail, every alibi. *The people who have died mean nothing to me.* And of course they hadn't. Only one person had, but by the time he'd killed her – him, not James Miller – that victim appeared to us to be just another part of the series. His uncrackable code.

'That's why he got Miller to videotape the killings,' I said. 'Nothing to do with wanting to sell them. He just wanted to see them. Study them. So he could make the one he carried out look identical. Or as close as possible.'

The only indoor murder.

I wanted to punch the steering wheel in frustration at having missed it.

The truth is, I still don't know quite when it will begin myself. That is why it's going to work.

That is why you'll never catch me.

'But Hicks, this is . . .'

'I know. Incomprehensible.'

Evil.

And although I didn't believe in that, I didn't know another word to describe what Wilkinson had done. It didn't fit anywhere in my architecture of crime. It wasn't from any kind of room at all, no matter how dark. It was something from the outside.

'I know,' I said again. 'I need backup, just in case.'

'They're on their way. I'm heading out too.'

'Good.'

I knew I would get there first.

But I sped up anyway.

Five minutes later, I arrived at the semi-detached house where, until last week, Tony and Marie Wilkinson had lived. That whole time, she must have believed they were in a happy, loving relationship, expecting their first child together, when the opposite was true. The whole time he'd been planning, ever so carefully, to get rid of her. To get rid of his son.

And it had all been for nothing. His plan hadn't worked, because he'd been disturbed before he could finish the only murder he'd intended to start. Jake had survived.

His car was outside the house – or at least, a car was: a silver hatchback parked across the driveway. It looked abandoned. I pulled close in alongside it, blocking it in as best I could, then got out and crouched down, surveying the house. I was vaguely familiar with its internal layout from my last visit, but the exterior was a different matter. How many exits did I need to take into account?

There was a driveway to the left, ending in a garage, with a wooden door beside it that appeared to lead off behind the house, presumably into the back garden. The house itself was two storeys. The front door was shut. There was a living room to the right of it, I remembered, and a small kitchen to the left, where we'd found Marie Wilkinson, and where the desperate paramedics had been forced to deliver Jake Wilkinson. I hadn't been upstairs. Looking up to the first floor now, there were two windows of equal size. Both sets of curtains were closed.

He won't be here.

Because, as Laura had said, why *would* he be?

And yet, the thought that he might be escaping out of the back of the house even now was too much for me. He couldn't be allowed to get away, not after what he'd done.

I wasn't going to let him. And so, for the second time in my career – and the second time in a week – I took my gun out of its holster and started forward.

Making my way around the car, I kept my gaze focused on the front door but took in the areas around it too, trying to catch any movement in the windows or the driveway, and then headed up the path as quickly as possible, crouching low, gun held double-handed, pointed at forty-five degrees, ready to raise it.

My heart was thumping, and I tried to breathe slowly to keep myself calm. But when the front door opened without a sound, my heartbeat went up again.

Someone's here.

Unless he'd just left it unlocked.

Peering inside, the house felt silent and empty. There was nobody in the hallway. Nobody visible at the top of the stairs.

I stepped in, immediately covering the open kitchen on the left. The last time I'd been here, bloodstains had been swirled and crusting on the floor. In the intervening time, someone had cleaned the blood away, but the air still smelled faintly of it. A couple of flies had settled on the tiles and were turning slowly, as though pinned in place.

No sign of Wilkinson.

I cleared the rest of the ground floor quickly, sweeping the living room and then the kitchen at the rear of the house. The window there gave a smudged view of the back garden, enough to tell it was fenced off on all sides. Nobody in sight. I tried the back door anyway, but it was locked.

I moved back to the staircase and scanned the first-floor landing again. Nobody to see. I listened carefully, and heard nothing.

He wasn't here.

Sometimes you just know. The silence has a different quality when a place is empty. He had probably been back here, because the front door was open, but I'd missed him.

In the distance, I could hear sirens.

I raised my gun anyway and started up the stairs, which creaked softly under my feet. I slowly lowered it to horizontal as I reached the landing, turning to face the small hallway. There were three doors up here: two open, one closed. The open ones revealed a bathroom and the main bedroom, both empty. I approached the closed one more cautiously, keeping to one side of it as best I could. Just in case. Took one hand off the gun to turn the handle and push—

Wilkinson was here.

He was standing with his back to me, head bowed so far that I could only see his neck and the bottom of his crew cut, gelled black by sweat.

He was dressed in full military regalia – a starched-straight dark-green suit with red tassels circling the shoulders. *The General*. He looked impossibly broad. His arms were at his sides, slightly away from his hips. In his right hand, he was holding a gun.

I stepped away to one side of the door frame and pointed my own gun at the centre of his back.

'Tony.'

I said it softly, not wanting to startle him, but he showed no signs of hearing me. Didn't move the single muscle it would

336

probably have taken for me to open fire on him right there and then.

I looked around the room.

It was a nursery – or the makings of one, anyway. The walls were painted a childish sky-blue, but needed a second coat, and there was a half-constructed crib resting in one corner. Opposite, against the wall, there was a desk with a computer monitor on it. At the far end, beyond Wilkinson himself, the cream curtains were closed, catching the morning sun and filling the room with soft light. To him, if he had his eyes open, it probably felt like facing heaven.

'Tony. Put the gun down.'

Again, no response. I edged even further to the side of the door frame, as far as I could get while still maintaining my aim. Despite his stillness, or maybe because of it, there was a tension to the air. The feeling that something might explode at any moment.

I forced myself to ignore the sensation. It was the kind that can hypnotise you if you let it. It can get you killed.

'What are you doing, Tony?'

No reply – but the answer was obvious enough. He knew we'd discovered the truth, and that sooner or later we'd catch him, so, rather than running, he'd returned here to get changed into this uniform and wait. He could have ambushed me if he'd wanted – or tried to, at least – but he hadn't. Which meant that, despite the gun, he wasn't planning to take anyone else down with him. But he hadn't surrendered either.

Suicide by cop.

'Tony . . .'

'He would have been proud of me, you know.'

He sounded almost wistful.

'Who would?'

'My father.'

'I doubt that somehow.'

'Oh, but you didn't know him.'

337

Outside, the sirens were louder now. Almost here, perhaps. Not that it would solve anything.

I said, 'Is that his uniform?'

'Yes. He was a good man. A military man. A soldier.'

'Right.'

'He was a code-breaker. A hero.'

'I believe you.'

'And this is his weapon. That's what you call it. That's what he told me: always a *weapon*, never a *gun*. Because you never know for sure what your enemy is holding, only that he's armed.' Wilkinson paused. 'And you're armed, of course.'

The tension in the air went up.

'Yes.' I checked my grip on the gun. 'But I don't want to shoot you, Tony. What I want is for you to kneel down very slowly and place the gun on the floor.'

'You mean the weapon.'

'Yes.'

'And if I don't, then you'll shoot me?'

I didn't reply. Behind me, from downstairs, I heard footfalls. The backup had arrived and was inside. Laura called my name, but I ignored her. Wilkinson did too. He seemed oblivious to the officers storming the house below us.

'Why did you do it, Tony?'

It was his turn now to remain silent.

'Was it that bad for you, the prospect of becoming a father?' No reply, so I fought for something else to say. Some other desperate insight. All I had was close to home: 'Were you worried your son might turn out like him?'

'No.' His voice flushed with sudden anger. 'He was a good man. He never laid a hand on us. Raised me well. Or tried to, anyway. I never made it easy for him. But he'd be proud of me now. Finally.'

'Not if he was such a good man, he wouldn't. Not after what you've done.'

People on the stairs behind me: feet clattering on the wood.

I didn't turn around, but I took a one-handed grip on the gun and waved behind me urgently—

Stay back.

—then got a better grip on the gun again.

I said, 'You think he would have been proud of you killing your wife?'

'He would have understood my reasons.'

'Which are?' He didn't reply. 'What about all those other people, Tony? None of those people deserved to die.'

'He wouldn't have minded about them.'

'No?'

'He would have called them collateral damage.' Wilkinson's voice sounded smaller now. Was he starting to cry? 'They would have meant nothing to him.'

Christ.

'Why the hell did you do it, Tony? What were you trying to prove? If you didn't want a child that badly, you could have just walked away.'

'You wouldn't understand.'

'I want to.' *Needed* to, even. 'Try me.'

'I would no longer have been able to serve.'

The answer pulled me up short. *To serve?* What – as a fucking janitor at the army base? But then, like his father before him, he worked for the military, didn't he? Albeit in a far more limited way . . . perhaps one that wouldn't pay enough to support a child.

Was that really what it came down to? All of this so he could continue to work at the base. *He'd be proud of me now.* But it couldn't just be that. If that was all he'd wanted, then he wouldn't have sent the letters, because they were the only evidence we had that Miller hadn't acted alone. To risk that, the challenge in them must have been necessary to him too. A code we wouldn't be able to crack. Except that both the job and the code were broken now. Whatever he'd hoped to achieve and prove by his actions, he'd failed.

'Tony,' I started – but he shook his head. He was talking very quietly, almost a whisper. I couldn't make out the words.

His hand, holding the gun, twitched slightly.

'Tony,' I said. 'Don't.'

'You're a soldier. So you should be able to do this.'

And now that I could hear him, it sounded like he was talking to someone else. His hand twitched again.

'Tony,' I said. 'Don't make me.'

'You should be able to do this.'

And before I could react, he lifted the gun in one swift, furious movement to the side of his head, and pulled the trigger.

Part Five

'Andy.'

Franklin leans forward. The little boy has finished his story, and he is not satisfied with the ending – the way the boy stays in his dark bedroom. Does nothing. Sees nothing.

'Andy. Did you shoot him?'

'No.'

The boy shakes his head vehemently. For the first time in this interview, he looks properly distressed. Shaken.

'You're sure?' Franklin says. 'It was John?'

'Yes. I mean, it must have been.'

'But you saw it, didn't you?'

'No.'

'You were there and you saw what happened.'

'*No.*'

And at that, Andrew begins to cry. For the briefest of moments, Franklin feels a flash of anger. The boy is lying – about part of it, at least. But at the same time, the tears are real. The distress is real. There is no longer a trace of the older, wiser, slyer boy he suspected of sitting in front of him before. Now, he is simply faced with an eight-year-old boy, sobbing his heart out, far smaller – once again – than his years.

Franklin touches the cross inside his shirt.

And he thinks: *what of it?* What does it really matter whether Andrew was there or what he saw? The facts remain, and they are obvious. This little boy has been through so much. He is not evil. Evil is what was done to him. Evil is to neglect and beat a human being who is at your mercy and should be able to rely on you. Evil – he realises with another flash, and this time not of anger but shame – is to make a child cry, without reason, without justification.

'Okay, Andy. Okay.'

He leans back and lowers his voice, tries to sound sympathetic.

'It's all right. It's nearly over now.'

The boy is still distraught and sobbing. But then, his words are meaningless, aren't they? It isn't nearly over. It never will be. In one way or another, this child will be haunted by what he's experienced and what he's seen for the rest of his life.

'I want to see my brother. I want to see John.'

And Franklin, thinking of the scene at the house and what was done there, has no choice but to shake his head.

'I'm sorry, Andy. That's not going to be possible.'

'When can I? When can I see him?'

'I don't know,' Franklin says. 'I don't know.'

Fifty-Six

There has always been a part of her that knew it would come to this. Burying her husband.

They had never discussed it over the years, but the knowledge was there regardless: that Gregor would be the one to die first – to die first *again* – and that Jasmina would live long enough to live without him. It was not a feeling based on health or risk, but on fate. There had always been a sense that her husband was living on borrowed time. They had both known it.

In some ways, it had helped. It had made every day precious, and cast even the quietest of loving moments into gold. But it leaves her worse than empty now. It is as though, having known this was to come, even more should have been made of the time they'd had together. Even though that makes no sense, because you can never love anybody enough to make up for their sudden absence.

You must think of the good memories.

That was what her sister Corinna told her this morning, in the car on the way to the chapel. She meant think not of the manner of his death but the manner of his life, and the life they had lived together. Jasmina has been doing that, of course, but it does not help in any way. Thinking of that life only reminds her it is over, just as happy memories of her daughter's life inevitably bring her to the vast hole of that absence. What good does it do to recall happy memories from the past when the future is empty? Better to think of nothing at all.

Already, she has cleaned the house from top to bottom. Already, her beautiful husband's shop is immaculate, as though at any moment he might return and place a pan of rattling wax on the cooker.

You must think of the good memories.

In the car, she had squeezed her sister's hand, pressing her own against its good intentions.

Just as she does now, seated at the front of the chapel.

The coffin is larger than she has been expecting. It would have to be, of course, to hold him.

The casket is closed, but a photograph of him rests on top. In the picture, he has a full head of black hair and a thick moustache, and although it is a photograph primarily of him, you can make out – if you know – the faces of his wife and daughter squeezing in from the sides to touch their cheeks to his. He is smiling. However haunted he might have been – whatever omens hung above him – at that moment he was happy.

Behind them, there is the hush of movement – of bodies gathering – the sound of suits brushing suits, of throats cleared politely, of quiet, understated talk that forms a soft sea in the air.

Jasmina turns to watch the rows filling. So much black. There is love in this room too, but it has nowhere to go any more, like a lost animal.

Death is disgusting, she thinks, turning back. Despite their inevitability, there are too many funerals in this world, because even one is too many. Their inevitability is the tightest knot of life.

Corinna leans in and asks quietly:

'Are you all right?'

She nods once. 'Yes.'

It is true in the sense that it matters – she will survive this. She has survived a great deal, and this will be no different.

At the front of the chapel, the priest is waiting patiently; he catches her eye and smiles gently. She does her best to return it. It is different for him, perhaps, being a man of confident faith. Jasmina is not sure what she believes any more, although she has always tried to respect her husband's world view. He believed, as much as he could – though again, perhaps it was easier for him, given his second life. Regardless, it is not too much to hope that he is in heaven now, beginning a third, and that whatever impenetrable purpose God kept him alive for is over now.

Even if nobody can ever know it.

Even if they would never be able to understand it if they did.

Fifty-Seven

Eight years ago, Gregor Levchenko came to see me because his daughter, Emmeline, was living with a man who had seriously assaulted her. The reality, as I'd told him, was that if she wasn't prepared to co-operate with us, there wasn't a whole lot we'd be able to do about the situation.

I knew that.

And yet the afternoon after talking to him, the memory of Emmeline Levchenko's pale face, framed by dark hair, with one eye swollen shut, had remained with me. I'd decided I was going to do something about it anyway.

When John Doherty opened his front door, I towered over him. He was short – five foot five at most – and what little there was of him looked pudgy. His hair was brown and wispy, receding, and as soft as his body. His eyes were bleary, as though he was either drunk, had just woken up, or else had been crying. As I held up my warrant card, I wondered if it was all three. It wouldn't have surprised me.

'Mr Doherty?' I did my best to hide the disgust I felt for him. Ever since my childhood, I've always despised violent men. 'Constable Hicks. Can I come in, please?'

He nodded, looking predictably sorry for himself. Even this early in my career, I'd seen the reaction countless times before. Sometimes when you were dealing with domestic abuse, the perpetrators toughed it out, but often it was the opposite, mostly it was like this – the men apparently contrite, ashamed, disgusted with themselves. Afterwards, it was all too easy for the victims to believe the apologies, the promises that it would never, ever happen again, because often the men really meant them. On the surface. Until the next time.

'Where's the front room?'

'Just there on the right.'

His voice was as weak and flimsy as the rest of him, but . . . something about it struck me. Not a straightforward recognition, but familiarity of some kind. Instead of heading to the front room, I turned around and looked at him, closing the door behind us.

Do I know you?

'Just there on the right,' he repeated.

I frowned to myself and went through to the living room. It was cluttered with random belongings, as though he just accumulated things without having proper places to put them. There was no settee, just four armchairs, backs pressed against the walls as though space had been cleared in the centre of the room for a party or a fight. The television was on a coffee table above a swarm of cables, and there were feathered piles of magazines by the chairs. An ashtray was balanced on top of one; a coffee mug, half full, on another. Tangled bunches of clothes were scattered around.

I wrinkled my nose at the musty smell of it all. It had been a long time since anyone had opened a window in here, never mind tidied up.

'I'm sorry about the mess.'

That *voice*.

I turned around slowly, looking at John Doherty again. *Do I know you?* He was clearing a pile of papers from one of the chairs, his back to me, a roll of belly fat appling out at his hips. His arms were hairless.

Where do I know you from?

'Look,' he said, 'I know why you're here, okay.'

And I would have replied, but that was when I realised. That was when I recognised my brother.

It was obvious as soon as it clicked. There was no mistaking him. In the twenty years since we'd last seen each other, he'd barely changed at all. The height, the weight, the soft hair: all the same. Maybe it was the fact he *hadn't* changed that had obscured his identity, simply because you expect people to. I certainly had, and he showed no sign of recognising me in return. We looked nothing alike, if we ever had. Seeing us together now, it would be easy to imagine we'd had different fathers. But of course, that wasn't the case.

'I know why you're here.' He placed the papers he'd cleared on the floor and ran one hand through what remained of his hair. 'Christ. Don't I just know. I can't tell you how sorry I am.'

John Doherty.

After we'd been separated, we'd both been given new identities. He'd disappeared into the system, and I'd been fostered. I was born Andy Reardon; my brother had been John Reardon. I'd kept my first name and changed my surname. Apparently John had done the same.

I cleared my throat.

'Mr Doherty. Would you calm down, please?'

'Yes, yes, of course.'

'I'm here because of Emmeline.'

'Yes.' He gestured at the chair he'd cleared. 'Sit down, please.'

I wanted to – I felt strange, shaky. The room itself seemed odd and off kilter, as though this might be a dream. I knew how I *should* be acting, and I knew how I'd *wanted* to act before arriving here, but the encounter had undermined me: regressed me slightly. I needed to re-establish myself.

'I'll stand. You sit.'

Doherty hesitated, then took the seat.

'Is Emmeline here?' I said.

'No. No, she's gone out. You don't need—'

'Yes. I will need to talk to her.'

'*Christ*.' He shook his head, looking down at the faded carpet. And was there a flash of anger there? My brother had never been an angry boy. Not on the outside, anyway. 'She doesn't need it. She has enough to deal with. We're working it all through.'

'I've received a complaint.'

'From her parents.'

He shook his head again. *From her interfering parents.* Almost as though Gregor Levchenko had wronged him some- how by reporting what had been done to his daughter. Once again, this was common behaviour – a glimpse of the reality that existed just below that contrite exterior, the everyday 'nice' guy. In his head, in spite of what he'd done, he was also the victim here, and he was annoyed because the world was forcing him to confront that awkward truth, piling on the pressure, giving him even more to cope with.

Common behaviour. I'd seen it all before.

But this was . . . this was John.

'I'll be talking to Emmeline to see if she wishes to press charges against you. In the—'

'She won't. She doesn't. I told you. We're dealing with it together.'

In the meantime, I'd been about to say, *I'm arresting you on suspicion of assault*. But something stopped me. I didn't know quite what. Maybe I wanted to hear what he had to say. Maybe it was something else.

'Look. I *know* what I did.'

He held his hands palms up, trying to emphasise how honest and straightforward he was being. The anger was better hidden now. If anything, he seemed to be on the verge of tears.

'I *know* what I did. And I know it was wrong. You don't understand. I came from a . . . violent home. I can't believe that I did what I did. I . . . I mean, I *abhor* it. It sickens me. *I* sicken me.'

I didn't say anything, realising that John's prior conviction could be used to supplement this offence; I didn't know for sure, but it was more than possible that he was on a life licence of some kind. But instead of thinking about that, his words were reverberating in my head. Because I knew exactly what a *violent home* meant. I'd lived there too; I'd lived it with him. Right up to the point where he took our father's life, and sent both of our own lives on their different courses. We had come from the same place, he and I.

'I'm going to anger management.' John was crying now. 'I've promised to go. We're going to go to therapy too. I mean, you can't imagine how disgusted I am with myself; I'd sooner hurt myself than her – I really would. I love her so much.'

'If that's true, then you shouldn't be together.'

He shook his head.

'Because you *will* do it again, John.'

'No. No. I'm not a . . . *bad* person. I'm not that kind of person at all. I know how it looks, but you have to believe me.'

I just looked at him. It was ridiculous, of course: I'd heard the same thing a hundred times before; it's what everybody says. I'm not a bad person. So no, I didn't *have* to believe him, and I knew that I *shouldn't*. But this was John. We'd grown from the same place. And if he was a bad person, then what was I?

You already know the answer to that question.

No.

Yes, you do.

'I'm not a bad person. It will never, ever happen again. You can't . . . you can't imagine.'

My brother shook his head.

'You have to believe me.'

Have to?

No. I didn't have to. So why did I? I've gone over it a million times since. There are days when it's all I think about. I've told myself it was down to the shock of seeing him again after all those years, and a misplaced sense of loyalty to him over what he'd done as a child to protect me. And perhaps it was partly that.

But it was also who he was, what he was. My flesh, my blood. Our father had been a disgusting, violent man. I didn't want to believe that my brother had grown up into a similar monster, and that – just maybe – those seeds had been with him from the beginning. Because if my father was abusive, and my brother was too . . . what did that say for me? I wasn't prepared to accept the possibility. I'd spent my life denying it.

Whatever the reason, I didn't take him in and I never did get to talk to Emmeline. I slipped that day, and the result was that somebody else fell in my place and broke instead. Two days later, Emmeline was dead at my brother's hands, and John had taken his own life.

A senior detective handled the murder inquiry; all I did was pass on the details of my visit and tell parts of the truth – that I hadn't thought there was enough evidence to pursue the matter without talking to Emmeline, and I'd never had the chance to do so.

In our country, two women die every week from domestic violence. It's horrible, but not inexplicable. I cling to that belief, still, that there are always reasons. And for Emmeline, I was one.

Fifty-Eight

Outside the chapel, the assembled crowds have dispelled slightly throughout the sunlit grounds – dark suits standing out like shadows on the areas of bright, neatly tended grass.

Jasmina drifts between them, shaking hands and accepting condolences, until, after a while, she spots the two police officers standing to one side. She presumes they are both officers, anyway. It is the detective she reported her husband missing to, and he is standing with a woman who looks very much like him. They are talking quietly between themselves.

She touches her sister's arm. 'Excuse me for a moment.'

'Do you want me to . . . ?'

'No, no. I shall be fine.'

She approaches the officers, remembering the man's name just as she reaches them.

'Detective . . . Hicks?' she says.

He looks up. He looks haunted.

'Yes. This is my partner, Detective Fellowes.'

'Thank you both for coming.'

'Not at all,' he says. 'I'm sorry for your loss. We both are. I'm so sorry that it didn't turn out differently.'

'It is not your fault.'

Hicks appears awkward at that; he looks down at the ground for a moment. She has no idea why, when he did everything he could, but some people are like that. They take on too much weight. They take on all the weight they can see, even when it does not belong to them.

'What about the man?' she asks. 'The man who did this?'

'James Miller.' He looks up. 'The man who did this is in prison. The man who planned it was called Tony Wilkinson. He took his own life during his arrest.'

Again, that awkwardness – but of a different kind this time. She understands instinctively that Hicks saw Tony Wilkinson die, and that the sight weighs heavily on him. She feels sorry for him, although in many ways it is the best possible outcome. She does not mourn Wilkinson; he deserved to die. But that does not mean someone else deserves to have killed him.

'I am sorry,' she says. 'Was there a . . . reason? Some explanation for why he did what he did?'

'We're not sure.' Hicks shakes his head. 'We think his motivation was to murder his wife. To hide that crime amongst others so we didn't realise he was responsible. She was pregnant, you see . . . we think he didn't want the child.'

Jasmina frowns. It makes no sense to her that someone might not want their child. She has spent years doing nothing but.

'But why . . . ?'

Hicks misunderstands the question. 'Why not just leave? Again, we're not sure. He worked in the military as a janitor. He wouldn't have been able to keep the job; it wouldn't have paid enough to support a child, whether he was with the mother or not. He would have had to find something else. And we think working in the military meant a lot to him.'

'Why?'

'His father was in the army, you see. He was a code-breaker in the war. But Wilkinson failed the entrance exams on medical grounds. He had several early episodes of self-harm on file. And he saw his father die and was hospitalised with an overdose just afterwards. When he applied, he was judged psychologically unfit to serve. But it seems that he was trying to, in his own way.'

He goes on, painting an incomplete picture of the man

ultimately responsible for Gregor's murder. A man wanting to be like his father, but also perhaps competing with him. A man wrestling incompatible memories, desires and needs. A man who, ultimately, could not be fully understood from the outside.

Jasmina understands that much. Wilkinson's motivations and reasons will remain sealed in a room to which they have no access; they can only guess and suppose. Even if those reasons were laid out, plain to see, what would it really matter? They would still not be enough. The effect remains the same.

In the end, the effect is all that matters.

'We don't know.' Hicks looks pained. 'I realise it doesn't make much sense. I wish it did. I wish we could explain it all.'

'It does not always make sense,' she says.

Hicks looks even more troubled at that. He seems to consider something. Then he gathers himself together. 'I also wanted to tell you that I'm sorry about what happened to your daughter.'

Emmeline. The mention stings a little more than usual today. But still – it is an old wound, and he means well. She nods once.

'Thank you.'

'It wasn't right what happened. I'm sorry.'

'It is not your fault. What is right is rarely the same as what happens. All we can do is try to live with it.'

Emmeline's face is in her mind.

'Do you have children, Detective?'

'Yes,' he says immediately.

'Well, you must look after them, as best you can. It is all you can do.'

He looks at her, then nods.

'Yes,' he says. 'I will.'

That night, Jasmina lies alone in the huge, empty bed. Her sister offered to share it, but she refused, so Corinna is now sleeping downstairs on the settee. Jasmina left her slumbering, gently placing a blanket over her before retiring upstairs. And although they are both old, she remembers how young her sister looked in repose. Sleep erases lines, restores the peace of childhood. It soothes troubles, however transiently.

If only she could have that. But sleep escapes her.

A lamp glows softly on the bedside table. Beside that is the photograph of her daughter, now joined by the framed image of her husband she chose for the funeral. They are together now, in whatever way they can be – even if that is simply here, on her table and in her thoughts.

And before the photographs, the candle.

Jasmina lies staring at it for a long time. And then, because she cannot sleep right now, she slides out of bed and searches the drawers for the box of matches she knows is there.

The match makes a crisp, fluttering noise as it strikes and flares, the flame confused and frantic for a second – then suddenly shy and vulnerable. She cups it gently, protectively, as she lowers it to the wick. There is a tiny crackle as it takes. The flame grows, while a single spot of dust lights on the wick, glowing bright yellow before winking out seconds later.

Jasmina shakes the match out, then licks her fingers and cools the tip.

She lies back down on the bed and watches the candle burn. As it begins to melt, she smells the honey her husband infused into the wax. It was cast at a single moment, this candle – the night of their daughter's murder – but it seems now to enfold an even deeper history: a string of cause and effect that stretches beyond that day. It begins many years ago, with the paramedic who saved her husband's life; it passes through the horrific, endless evening when they learned Emmeline was dead; and it ends today, here, in the combination of circumstances that have led to its lighting.

Jasmina watches the smoke drifting up from the flame, history unravelling in spirals in the air. It is impenetrable to her – but then, perhaps that is how it works. One moment leads inexorably to another, and everything is built on what precedes it, but there is no obvious reason or purpose behind it. A pattern will never be discernible to the human eye, and none of it will make sense in a way that matters to us. But that does not mean there is no pattern. It does not mean that, in some unfathomable way, there is no sense. All it means is that from the inside, we cannot see it.

Jasmina closes her eyes, surrounded by honey and history.

Yes, she thinks. That is how is.

Perhaps that is how it works.